HIGH SCHOOL

ROCKET SCIENCE

(FOR EXTRATERRESTRIAL USE ONLY)

STANLEY B. TRICE

Place of Publication: New Bern, NC

Formatting, interior design, and cover by Woven Red Author Services

Stock images for cover from DepositPhotos.com under Standard Licence
Image of Mercury-Redstone 3 (Freedom 7) launch on May 5, 1961 courtesy of NASA under Creative Commons CC0 License

Library of Congress Control Number: 2020904287

ISBN for Print: 978-0-9909265-0-4
ISBN for Ebook: 978-0-9909265-1-1

Chapter 1

Timothy was sure his dad was an extraterrestrial. Otherwise, he would have to explain to people at his high school that his dad was a drunk. Timothy liked telling his classmates and teachers that his dad pretended to be a drunk so no one would suspect he was an alien from another planet. Timothy liked believing this story. It kept people from visiting his house.

He had no use for friends, anyway. He told the story last year when he was a sophomore in the county's only high school. This year as a junior, his classmates and teachers still laugh at him about his dad story. Timothy was all right with this because it gave him an excuse to be alone. Otherwise, people might ask about his mom and Timothy had no good explanation for her death.

He never fully understood how she died that summer before he started high school. It was during the county fourth of July fireworks with different colors and noises streaming across the night sky. He came home with his dad, who said his mom would not be there when they arrived.

Timothy wanted to think she was on a long trip and would come back soon. He got this from his dad who thought that way, too. Except, Timothy remembered how his mom had been sick a lot and relatives he had never seen before attended the closed casket funeral with them.

They held the funeral in a house no one had lived in for over a year. His dad said it was okay that no one in the community came. Timothy didn't know why and did not care. Timothy figured the only way his mom would come home again would be as a ghost.

The thing that helped Timothy about his mom being gone was that he and his dad didn't talk about any of it. Timothy had nothing to say to him after he took up drinking. Maybe his dad picked up the alcohol to avoid any ghosts showing up.

Instead of talking to his dad, Timothy got a picture of his mom for his bedroom dresser. It was just as good as talking, he figured. If he wanted to say something, and he sometimes did, he explained to the photograph of his smiling mom how much he missed her.

His dad didn't start drinking right away. As Timothy disappeared into his freshman year of high school trying to understand the down east North Carolina talk, his dad claimed to be building rocket engines for a special rocket fuel.

Timothy rode the bus home each day to find his dad cannibalizing the house and appliances when the hardware store didn't have what he needed. His dad worked like someone in a panic, leaving the house a questionable dwelling. Timothy took art then and the teacher was into abstract paintings. "Abstract" was the right word for the engines.

It didn't take his dad long to finish them. One afternoon, Timothy came home from school and found that his dad had hidden the engines somewhere on the premises. He was worried that spies would find them. Timothy thought this was paranoia since his dad had found his liquor by then. Timothy was just glad there was enough of the house left to live in.

After the engines were built and hidden, Timothy came home from school each afternoon to attempt supper. As he did so, his dad would sit at the kitchen table, that now had three legs instead of four, drinking and explaining about how the rocket formula went with the engines.

Like his mom, his dad was no rocket scientist. Both his parents were just two people who used to work for NASA in support of rocket launches, mostly helping to launch the Space Shuttle in Florida. Timothy listened to his dad because a lot of times he ended up talking about his mom.

His dad would not talk about why they moved to down east North Carolina. When asked, his dad would say the formula and engines were Timothy's destiny. Timothy didn't like destinies, particularly when he would inherit them.

Eventually, Timothy concentrated more on being the parent by fixing meals and attempting to keep the house from collapsing and animals moving in. At school, he got used to not making friends so he didn't have to talk about either parent. The story about his dad being an extraterrestrial helped keep people away.

He was also aware that his head was like a triangle with arms too long and a pencil-like nose. Now, as a high school junior, he knew his looks hadn't improved.

Timothy wondered about his dark skin and light tan hair. Kids last year said how he could be descended from southern Europe, north Africa, or Scandinavia. He was not sure what they meant, but it was as if they were calling him a miscolored. This made him connect even less with anyone in school.

Yeah, he heard how weird he was and how he never talked to anyone. But they never talked to me, Timothy thought. And I'm not interested in being social, anyway. There's enough to deal with taking care of his dad.

It was late August when Timothy started his junior year. The engines were still hidden and he had no desire to find them. His dad had gotten into a habit of repeating what he knew about the rocket formula, much like a chant, and Timothy always made sure he said good morning and good night to his mother's picture. In September, a few weeks after starting school, he got off the school bus as usual and went to the tool shed to check on his dad.

The weather was colder than normal when Timothy found him very dead in his beach chair. His dad looked like an alien clutching a fat manila folder across his chest. Timothy just knew the rocket formula was inside.

The first thing he did was hide the manila folder in his bedroom behind the dresser with his mom's picture on it. He wasn't sure he wanted the rocket formula, but he didn't want anyone else to get it. At least not right away.

When he got back to the shed to call 911, since that area had the best reception, men and women in purple uniforms pulled into the driveway in vans and long, dark cars. Timothy was too upset to consider how they knew to come. They carried his dad away as more people came in and out of the house.

They claimed to be distant relatives from a place called Tyche. Timothy wondered if they were from Greece since Tyche was a Greek goddess. At least that's what he remembered from English class. He believed them because he had seen some of these same people years before when his mother died.

His dad's funeral was on a Tuesday at a place a few miles away down an old logging road. The building looked like a flying saucer. Someone decided on a closed casket. The only people at the funeral were Timothy's strange relatives because the newspaper notice came out on Wednesday when his relatives left.

Maybe these strange people thought someone else was staying. Timothy encouraged this assumption since he wanted to be alone. That Thursday after his dad's funeral, Timothy briefly answered the emails and phone calls from people at his school who he barely knew. At least no one came by, mostly because he kept up the false assumption some of his relatives had stayed.

He would have invited a classmate over if he knew any of them good enough to invite. After eating too much buttered pasta, he fell asleep on the worn couch trying not to think about what to do next.

Friday morning, he walked around the house he would be living in as an orphan. It needed more repair than he realized. There was no heat since the gas bill had not been paid. It was even colder with the front and back windows opened since they wouldn't close all the way.

At dawn on the Saturday after his father's death and with all the pasta gone, Timothy looked at the contents of his dad's manila envelope. He struggled to read the messy handwriting explaining where to go with the formula. He thought about how there would be no more talk with his dad about flying a rocket into space.

Timothy went to the shed and peered into the doorway left opened by the men and women who had carried his father's body out. He hesitated before tiptoeing inside, careful to stay away from the beach chair and an empty vodka bottle. He avoided various tools scattered around and the narrow metal sheets of no specific size with some type of design on them like hieroglyphics. He hit his head once on a low beam.

Hurrying through the clutter, he jabbed his knee, bumped his thigh, and scraped his shin before reaching the aluminum briefcase his dad had hidden in the back. Where to find the briefcase was explained in the notes from the manila envelope.

Inside the briefcase were more documents and small bottles carefully wrapped in bubble wrap to protect something special. Timothy left the shed door open on his way out, taking the briefcase and manila envelope with him.

Back at the worn house, he stuffed a backpack with whatever clothes he could jam into the bag. He took his mom's picture and carefully wrapped it in his best shirt since it was not as thin and worn as the rest of his clothes.

It was a little warmer that Saturday morning when he walked east along the back road that led from his home. The road was flat and mostly straight, like all roads in down east North Carolina.

A mile later, he followed the directions written by his dad and headed into the pine forest, trying to avoid the marshes.

Timothy walked past fields of cotton, tobacco, corn, and soybeans. He saw a lot of singlewide trailers, a few looking better than where he had been living. In front of several houses were small boats sitting on trailers ready for the Pamlico River or the Sound where it met the Neuse River not far away.

He stopped a few times to eat a snack and eventually found his way onto a narrow back road with no traffic. Timothy wondered if he was the only one left in the world. This road led to a long dirt driveway pointing at a two-story house.

On both sides of the driveway was an impoverished lawn with more bare spots than grass. Both sides from the driveway led to a thin list of pine trees bordering the far edges of the property. Timothy noticed that the house needed painting and could have been built a hundred years ago. Or, at least before he was born. He headed toward the house wishing he had some place else to go.

He checked the address with the note, but his dad hadn't written down who lived there. Timothy decided to find out since he had come this far. He went up a set of stone steps, across a broad porch that creaked, and to a wooden front door almost big enough for two people to walk through side by side. He pounded his fist on the door until he heard footsteps.

The high school janitor Eddie opened the door.

Chapter 2

"What are you trying to tell me, knocking on my door?" Eddie had a head of curly white hair, blue eyes, a stooped-over nature to his body, and a cracked voice. He was half a foot shorter than Timothy.

Timothy wasn't sure how to answer the odd question.

"My dad left a note with this address." He held it up for the janitor to see.

Eddie leaned in to see the note better. "Where's your father?"

"Dead. He left me his formula for rocket fuel and this note to come here."

The elder man straightened up and moved as if he would shut the door. "I don't believe you. This some kinda of game?"

"Hey, I don't know why I bothered coming. According to these papers, you have a rocket, but you're just the janitor."

"Yeah, that's me. Just the janitor. I was expecting your father." Eddie paused before adding, "I'm sorry he's dead. Really sorry."

"Yeah, well I'm sorry I'm here."

Eddie opened the door wide. "I haven't always been 'just the janitor.' Besides, how do you know I have a rocket? And, does the formula work?"

Timothy had no idea whether the formula would work or not. "My dad's notes said to come here for a rocket. You get me the materials on this list and we'll test the formula out to see if it works." He reached out his hand, holding other slips of paper with his dad's writing scrawled on them.

"Sounds too simple, but all right. I have a model rocket we can use." Eddie took the paper and studied it for a few seconds before disappearing into the house. He left the door opened.

Timothy looked behind him and didn't see anywhere else to go. Also, he was tired from walking. He went looking for Eddie who called back somewhere inside, "I was getting ready to eat lunch. I'll fix you something. We'll talk after."

Timothy found Eddie in a long hallway that ran the length of the house. The elderly man ducked into the second door on the left. Timothy followed and banged his knee into a table near the doorway. Wincing from the pain, he watched Eddie shuffle down the length of a kitchen that spread out back toward the front of the house.

He exited the kitchen through the first door they passed muttering about teenagers leaving front doors opened. Timothy wondered why they didn't enter the kitchen there. He could have avoided the table.

Sitting at the table, Timothy surveyed the kitchen's cracked tiled counters, knotty pine cabinets, and old kitchen appliances. On the right over the kitchen sink was a pane glass window. Beside the sink was an electric stove and across from that a simple refrigerator.

Eddie came back and poured what he claimed was homemade tomato soup into a pot. The soup was made without onions, he explained. In the pot, he also dumped previously soaked and cooked kidney, black, navy, and pinto beans. In the oven, he heated thick slices of sourdough bread that he had drizzled with olive oil and sprinkled with peppercorns, vanilla beans, and cooked black eyed peas.

On the counter in a glass bowl, he mixed canned tuna, yellow mustard, raspberry jam, smashed blueberries, chopped walnuts, and a large crumbled chocolate bar. He spread the mixture on the bread he pulled out of the oven. It was all served with a glass of iced cold water, butter pickles, and a wedge of cheddar cheese.

Neither spoke as they ate their sandwiches. Timothy ate slowly and Eddie fast. Soon, the elderly man got up to wash the dishes, storing them in his dishwasher instead of the cabinets.

That reminded Timothy of when he washed dishes after his dad cannibalized the dishwasher. He wondered if the janitor had done some cannibalizing to build a rocket. As Eddie washed, he explained his house as multidimensional.

"There's a second floor and a half basement. I have a front and back entrance at both ends of the hallway and the only room that has two doors is the kitchen. The other doors lead into single rooms. When you first come in the house, you should use the second door into the kitchen."

"Why?"

"It's bad luck using the first door when first entering the house."

"You're superstitious." Timothy wanted to say "crazy" but he thought that would irritate the janitor.

Eddie gave out a snort and found some more dishes to wash.

Timothy saw the house as nothing like where he had lived before. He wondered where he would be living next.

When he finally finished, Eddie said, "Let's go down in the basement and see what I have that fits your list." He rushed past Timothy, into the hallway, and through a nearby door. Timothy banged his other knee on the table rushing to go after Eddie.

In the basement, Timothy expected to find mummies or some other dead things. It was basically a large dirt hole without enough hanging light bulbs to illuminate the corners. He imagined small animals or large insects lurking around.

The basement was cluttered with wooden tables, lopsided cabinets, and sagging cardboard boxes stacked on pallets to keep them off the dirt. Timothy wished there was more light so he wouldn't trip over anything—like a rat.

At the back of the basement where the light was dimmest, Eddie found the latch to a metal door. Metal scraping on metal echoed like a scream. Timothy wanted to run, except Eddie had already disappeared into a small, brightly lit room. Timothy felt he had to find what was in that room.

Excessive neon lighting reflected off thin metal shelves and mason jars glowing with various colors. Timothy hesitated. Labels on the jars explained that the chemicals inside were highly combustible in enclosed spaces.

"I got most of these when the owner of a local hardware store died and his kids sold everything at auction," Eddie said. "No one wanted the chemicals since they looked toxic."

Timothy examined the labels more closely. "I think they are toxic."

"Only if you touch them too much."

Eddie pulled out a small tin box with several glass tubes. He studied Timothy's list, used eyedroppers to siphon chemicals into the tubes, and hung each tube on a wire mesh attached to the inside of the tin box. When finished, Timothy pulled three small glass vials out of his pocket. They were from his dad's briefcase.

"These need to be added with the rest. All of them have to be mixed in the sequence that's in my dad's instructions."

Eddie studied the vials in Timothy's hands without touching them. "Is something moving in there?"

"Maybe."

Eddie shrugged and hung the vials in the box with the glass tubes. After they were all secured, he stuffed old newspapers and pieces of wrapping paper around everything to hold them still. Since he struggled to close the lid, Timothy hoped nothing would get crushed or the house would become the rocket.

Eddie looked at Timothy. "And you need these other things on the list, too?"

"Yeah, I need all of it." Timothy didn't know what he needed of anything. He certainly didn't know what he was doing in a basement with the high school janitor and surrounded by explosive chemicals.

"Okay. To put all of these in a sequence I can rig up a dispenser with two D batteries and some timers." Carrying the tin box, Eddie led the way out of the room. Timothy quickly joined him, wanting to get far away from the chemicals and whatever was living down there in the semi-darkness.

Upstairs, they went out the front door and to the left of the house toward a cinderblock shed. Not wanting to go into any more enclosed spaces with Eddie, Timothy stayed outside. While waiting, he peered around the back of the house.

In the distance he saw an abandoned field. What grew from the ground could have been crops in years past, but were now weeds. At the end of the field rose a lone silo that was fatter than newer ones Timothy saw recently. This old, fat silo also had about ten rows of concrete blocks added to make it taller. An aluminum dome covered the top.

Eddie popped out of the cinderblock shed dragging a toolbox stained with old grease and plastered with stickers that once said something when they were unstained. Timothy hoped the stickers weren't warnings about what was inside.

"Here, you can carry this to the jeep," Eddie said as he walked toward the back of the house.

Timothy hurried to catch up and found Eddie standing next to a dented, doorless, and roofless jeep. Someone had used a brush to paint it yellow. Timothy heaved the metal box into the back and Eddie used some heavy straps to ratchet it securely against the side.

As he jumped in, Eddie pumped the gas pedal twice before starting the jeep. The engine sputtered to life and Eddie shifted gears like he had been doing that all his life.

They were parked at the start of a second dirt driveway that ran in a loop around the abandoned field and back toward the silo. Instead of taking this level, smooth road, Eddie shot across the field toward the silo.

The seats were cracked and lacked padding to the point of not even being seats. Eddie drove like someone with little time left in his life and a lot of padding on his butt. Seeing no seatbelts, Timothy held on to the sides to keep from being catapulted out. The box was more secure than he was.

"In case you're wondering, this is a '73 CJ5 four-speed with a 258 straight-six engine and the original one-barrel carburetor. It still puts out 110 horsepower," Eddie shouted over the rattling and banging.

"I have no clue what you're saying." Timothy wanted Eddie not to worry about explanations and instead try to avoid some of the ruts in the field.

The old man used one hand to shift gears and the other to grip the steering wheel, which Timothy thought should be held with two hands and maybe a foot. Just before he braced for them to crash into the silo, Eddie slammed on the brakes sending up a cloud of weeds and dirt.

Timothy caught some of the debris in his mouth and, by the time he had stopped spitting and coughing, Eddie was headed toward the silo. Timothy jumped out, caught his foot on the rim, and fell face down on the ground.

"Stop horsing around and get that box out. We need to get things set up before it gets too late in the day."

From a small metal shed near the silo, Eddie dragged a model rocket to the jeep. He opened it down the center so both halves sat apart.

"There's a junction box at the nozzle here." Eddie pointed at the bottom of the rocket. "We'll fasten the glass tubes and vials around the inside of the rocket at different heights with hoses to the junction box. There'll be a clamp at the end of each hose with a wire going to the timer and batteries in the cone section. Based on your instructions, each of the contents will be mixed separately in a timed sequence."

"They're not my instructions. They're my dad's."

"Does it matter that much? Because, I really don't care."

Timothy kept quiet because it cared to him.

An hour later, they finished putting everything inside the small rocket. Eddie and Timothy fastened the two halves together and lifted the rocket onto a metal stand. Once it was upright, Eddie got a step-ladder that was too short to reach the top. He climbed to the highest step to set the timer in the cone.

"Come up here and help me close the connections or we'll be fertilizing this field with our body parts."

Timothy thought the ladder didn't look sturdy enough with one person on it. Yet, Eddie stood at the top wiggling his fingers impatiently for Timothy to join him. Inching up the ladder, he tried to avoid Eddie's butt.

They wired a timer to a lever and to the batteries. "When the timer goes off in ten minutes, the clamps will open allowing the fuel to mix in sequence. Ten minutes should be enough for us to get away from the rocket," Eddie said.

He came down the ladder so fast that Timothy landed on his butt in the weedy grass to keep from being stepped on. They then ran to the jeep, which refused to start. Timothy smelled gasoline.

"The engine's flooded. Let's get behind the jeep," Eddie said. "Hurry."

"Shouldn't we just run? You said we had ten minutes."

"I think my timer might be off. It's ticking kinda fast."

Timothy hid behind the jeep with Eddie. A few feet away, the rocket hummed slightly.

"There's nowhere for the blast to go," said Timothy.

"Oh, yeah. I forgot about that. Maybe it won't be that bad."

Timothy wondered what else the old man forgot when they heard a loud pop making Timothy's ears hurt. He looked over the jeep and saw a plume of white smoke and dust running toward him.

"All I'm looking for here is some serious altitude, kid," Eddie shouted over a rapid series of successive pops.

They crouched behind the bumper as plumes of dirt-filled smoke forced them to get down even lower. Popping sounds raced over them as a white cloud threw itself over their heads. When the cloud cleared enough, Timothy peered over the jeep to see the model rocket accelerate into the clear blue sky. He watched a thin white flame follow the model rocket up.

They stood beside each other, watching the flame push the rocket higher and higher into the sky until all they could see was a tinge of bright white. A single, much louder pop echoed down on them as a puff of pale yellow smoke indicated the model rocket was no more.

As if saying goodbye, the last of the rocket's structure let out a screech like it was excited to be free.

Eddie grinned. "Wow, your fuel almost didn't tear the rocket apart."

"It wasn't that much fuel," Timothy said shocked they weren't killed.

They both stood watching small clouds of smoke float away in the wind and pieces of the rocket dive toward the distant Sound. It had gotten that high.

"I hope NORAD and STRATCOM didn't notice," Eddie said.

"Who are they?"

"North American Aerospace Defense Command and the U.S. Strategic Command. Both are military organizations that watch what goes up, flies over, and comes down. We need to start working on launching our bigger rocket before we get a visit from them."

"I think we need to do more testing before we go bigger," said Timothy brushing off the dirt and dust from his clothes and hair.

Eddie got into the jeep. "We are more than ready to go big."

"You mean launch a rocket into space?"

"Yeah, one that can carry a satellite into outer space."

Timothy looked at the sky where nothing of the model rocket remained but a few puffs of smoke. He thought about his parents and wished they were here to deal with this high school janitor who somehow knew far too much about rockets and the special fuel.

Chapter 3

Eddie took the smoother dirt road back. As he pulled up to the back of the house, Timothy asked, "What's in the silo?"

Eddie avoided the question and stepped out of the jeep while it was still moving. Timothy started to jump away before the vehicle hit the back of the house, except the jeep sputtered and jolted to a stop. He caught his foot somewhere. After he got through rolling around on the ground, he ran to catch up with Eddie.

Three concrete steps led to the back porch—a shaky wooden platform with rotting wooden banisters that had long since fallen off and lay on the ground. Eddie rushed through a wooden door in need of paint with Timothy close behind trying not to touch anything for fear of getting a splinter.

The back door opened into a mudroom large enough for coats to be hung, boots to be kicked off, and a washer and dryer. To Timothy, it was a mudroom because it smelled of old mud. Nothing hung on the coat racks, no shoes sat on the floor, and rust spots peppered the washer and dryer.

Eddie went through another door that opened to the long hallway stretching the length of the house. A good skateboard kinda hallway, Timothy thought. With closed doors on both sides, Eddie stepped into the first one on the left.

Timothy went into the room, too, before realizing he was standing in the round, tower section at the back of the house. The part of the house he thought would probably fall first if the place collapsed.

Timothy's mouth fell open. "Wow. Where did you get all this stuff?" With the electronic equipment surrounding them, he thought the room looked like a small, NASA Mission Control center.

"I got a lot of this on the Internet."

"What Internet? The one everyone else uses or some secret one the government runs?"

"I bought a lot of this as excess equipment during the last two years of the shuttle program," Eddie said. "The Russian equipment I got from some Asian websites. Most of the equipment still works. There's even some European and Chinese stuff here."

Timothy walked over to a long table with monitors, cables, and tall metal boxes with small video screens and dark buttons on the front. "Where'd you get the money to buy all this? I didn't think janitors got paid that much."

"I'm retired from NASA. I needed a job which is why I got into the janitor business."

"They gave you this stuff when you retired?" Timothy thought that would be some retirement party.

"No, I used my retirement savings. And some inheritance when my parents died."

Timothy read some of the labels. "This equipment looks very official."

Eddie pushed cardboard boxes together to create more floor space. "I worked for the shuttle program from the start in 1981 until the last flight of Atlantis in 2011."

"Were you a rocket scientist?"

Eddie chuckled. "No, I helped do a lot of things to get the shuttles ready for launch."

"Did you go to college to learn how to use this stuff?"

Eddied shook his head. "While I cared for my dying parents, I took engineering classes, but never graduated. When my parents died, I got a job at NASA's Langley Research Center in Hampton, Virginia. I taught myself about rockets, physics, and communications. I impressed enough people that they kept me on to work as an engineering assistant. Yet, I knew more than most of the engineers."

Timothy scanned a nearby long, aluminum lab bench that held three flat screens with keyboards in front of them. Cables of various colors ran behind the bench. Some went up the wall, some into the wall, and some Timothy had no clue where they went. Landline phones sat at both ends of the room.

"I got two generators out back. One for power and a backup, if necessary," Eddie said moving boxes around.

Timothy helped him restack and sort through the electronics equipment. Eddie explained the functions of the equipment, but Timothy couldn't keep up with the technical terms. Eventually, they cleared a long table.

"When we do the launch, this will be your station," Eddie said. "You'll be able to control the rocket once I have the equipment set up."

Timothy shot Eddie a wary look. "What do you mean? I don't know how to fly a rocket. Certainly not one big enough to carry a satellite into space."

"You'll get to know the formula better after we do some more testing. The most important part of the rocket is controlling the thrust, not actually flying the rocket."

"I didn't come here to fly a rocket into space. I only came because my dad left those notes. I brought you the formula because... I don't know why. He died and said I should."

"I know you can fly this rocket."

Timothy shook his head. "I can't fly any rocket. I'm only a junior in high school and now an orphan. This whole mystery about the formula and you and whatever rocket you have in that silo is stupid. What we just did was use a piece of the formula. It wasn't the whole thing and didn't include the special engines, which are hidden back at dad's house. This is a lot more complicated than you think."

"Stop it." Eddie raised a hand. "You know more about the formula than you think. Stop denying your destiny."

"Stop saying it's my destiny. That's what my dad called it," Timothy cringed. "This is real life. I'm a homeless orphan talking to some eccentric janitor and I don't want to be responsible for any of this. I'll give you the formula and you can do whatever you want with it."

"I need you for this. I can't do this alone. You've got to stay here and help me launch my rocket."

"You've got a big rocket in that silo, don't you?" Timothy glared at Eddie while pointing out the room's bay window with a view of the silo. "If it's as big as that, that's too big for me. I'll probably blow it up and this house. You'll have to find someone else to fly your rocket."

Eddie sighed. "You misunderstand. Most of the launch is automated. All you have to do is make sure the fuel is synced up with the launch and there's enough thrust to reach orbit without the rocket exploding or falling out of the sky."

"That's a lot to do!" Timothy waved his hands across the room in frustration. "This is too much to take in. Besides, you need more people than just you and me."

Eddie paused and faced Timothy. "Yeah, you might have something there."

Timothy looked at the door wanting to run away. Yet, it was too late to walk back to his house, which was unlivable anyway. "I'll tell you what. I'll stay here for a while and at least help you straighten things up."

Eddie scratched his chin and pulled on his left ear. His hands ended up resting on top of his head. "You gotta keep going to school. I'll keep pretending to be a janitor cleaning the bathrooms and you pretend to learn something useful."

"I am learning something and you are cleaning bathrooms."

"Also, we won't mention this to anyone. At least for now."

"Why do we need to keep this a secret?" Timothy asked. "How much of this is legal? I'm not doing any illegal stuff."

Eddie laughed slightly. "Launching the rocket isn't too illegal as long as we don't hit anything already flying. We'll launch it over the Atlantic and all we'll be doing is irritating those government agencies

I mentioned. We just need to be careful to keep quiet about this and not attract any spies."

"What do you mean spies?" Timothy narrowed his eyes at Eddie. "Is the government spying on us?" He remembered his dad being suspicious like this, too. "All you old people who grew up in the Cold War believe too much in spies."

"The day before you showed up, I saw two men walk around the edge of the woods taking pictures. They looked professional."

"Professional what?" Timothy looked at Eddie not sure what to say next. "Okay, let's assume there are strangers walking around spying on this place? What'd we do about it?"

"Keep doing what we're doing and see if they show up again."

"If they're spies, of course they'll be back."

Timothy eyed the equipment surrounding him, looked at Eddie once, and nearly tripped on a mess of metal cables as he stepped back to see it all more clearly. He caught himself in the doorway and wondered if those spy men, if they existed, were outside right then taking pictures of him stumbling around.

"Let's not worry about other people," said Eddie. "Right now, you need to get to know all about your dad's formula before we launch."

Timothy wasn't sure what his dad's formula was about, let alone how to use it to launch a big, big rocket. Timothy decided not to tell this to Eddie. There were too many things to think about.

"Where will I sleep?"

"Where's your suitcase?"

"I got a backpack with some clothes. It's in the kitchen."

Timothy followed Eddie out of the tower and down the long hallway back to the kitchen at the front of the house. He avoided the table this time as Eddie pulled out some pots and pans from the knotty pine cabinets.

"There're several rooms you can use as a bedroom. Right now, I'm hungry. I'll make us something to eat," said Eddie.

"Isn't it a little early to eat dinner?" Timothy sat at the kitchen table.

"You want to eat or not?" Eddie started grabbing things out of a nearby pantry.

"Yeah, I'm always hungry. I guess you're in the habit of eating early 'cause you had no electricity when you were young. Did you go to bed at sunset?"

Eddie banged a pot down on the stove. "I'm not that old. You want to eat or not?"

"Yeah, sure."

In a pot, Eddie brought water to a boil before slipping in several long, thin noodles. On a sheet pan, he opened and drained a can of sardines and slathered peanut butter over the fish. The pan went under the broiler.

When done, he drained the noodles and mixed in previously cooked black eyed peas. He drenched the mixture with melted butter and mixed in the fish/peanut butter. Timothy liked this odd supper. No one was getting drunk.

After eating, he pulled his dad's folders out of his backpack. "He called the engines electrogravitic. You can look through these papers and drawings to see what I mean."

Eddie took the papers as though he were handling a fragile, rare gem. He sat at the kitchen table and read them at least twice. At some point, Timothy got bored thinking the tower section was a lot more interesting than a dull kitchen.

He went there, thumbed through the manuals that needed more pictures, and tried out the dials on some of the equipment. He couldn't get anything to light up. When he got back to the kitchen, Eddie was gone.

Eventually, he found him stretched out on the living room couch. It looked like a living room because it had a couch. But it had no TV. Eddie was slightly snoring and holding on his chest, like a blanket, the papers about the special engines. Timothy left everything as they were and covered Eddie with a nearby beach towel thick enough to work as a blanket. He left the old man and wandered through the house looking for a bedroom.

Next to the tower, he found another room with more old space equipment, tables and chairs, and several flat screens. Eddie must have gotten the flat screens in a clearance sale, Timothy thought.

He went to another room with a shower and a toilet that smelled as if they had been doused in a gallon of chlorine. At least they were clean—very clean. This bedroom had a dresser, nightstand, and a bed with new sheets. The two pillows were still in their store wrappers. Everything had a slight coating of dust as if Eddie's guest never made it or maybe I'm the guest, Timothy thought.

He walked around the house and found a lot of rooms. A few had equipment and boxes stacked in them, some were empty, others had an assortment of furniture as if Eddie couldn't make up his mind what to use the rooms for, and one he figured was Eddie's bedroom.

This room had a four-foot-tall model of a Saturn V rocket on a night table. One wall had pictures of the moon and planets taped to it. On the other wall was an oversized picture of the Milky Way. The bed was a stack of sheets, blankets, and pillows. In the corner of the room was a large closet.

Timothy went back to the very clean room and this time noticed a book of rocket propellants on the bedroom nightstand. Also, a flat-screen TV was hanging on the wall.

He watched a low-budget, science fiction movie about the U.S. military fighting interplanetary spacecraft. "This movie is stupid," he said to the off-color screen. He was still wide awake and started reading the rocket propellant book.

An hour later, Timothy thought he heard a noise outside. He walked out the back door and saw nothing. He walked around the side of the house to the front where he was just in time to see a dark sedan pull away from the driveway.

Chapter 4

Timothy waited to see if the car would come back. He listened to a loon call out, an owl hoot, and a whole bunch of tiny frogs making squeaky sounds all around him. After a few minutes, he was too bored to wait any longer and he walked behind the house.

With clear skies, the full moon cast eerie shadows onto the field of broken weeds and distant silo. Timothy decided he couldn't wait until morning to find out what was inside the concrete tower.

He started across the field and only fell twice on a hunk of soil and twisted weeds. When he finally got to the silo, he walked up to a metal door and grabbed the door handle. But, in the dim moonlight Timothy stumbled against the silo footing, missed catching himself, and bumped his head into the metal door.

Aggravated with himself, he rubbed his forehead and shoved down on the door's handle to force it open. It didn't budge, so he pushed down harder and the handle snapped off.

Timothy stood there in the moonlight staring at the bent handle in his bruised hand. He looked around wondering if there was another entrance when the metal door creaked opened toward him. As he pulled on the door, it swung easily except for lots of squeaking.

He groped around inside for a light switch. When he flipped it on, it took a moment for him to adjust his eyes and understand what was in front of him.

Before him rose a wall of white metal stretching to the top of the silo like a mountain. Timothy read the word REDSTONE stenciled in bold, black letters on the side of the metal structure.

The whole thing frightened him. The rocket was larger than he ever imagined and he had a hard time picturing it shooting out of the silo with his help. Timothy eyed the doorway and considered running away from this rocket, Eddie, and his dad's inheritance.

Yet, what if this rocket did fly into space, he wondered? That would be something, he thought with excitement. He looked up and managed to see something of a capsule sitting on top of the rocket. With building curiosity, Timothy wanted to see all of the rocket and he followed the path between the rocket and silo wall.

On his trip around, he scanned skinny benches set against the concrete walls and littered with small tools. In other places, he noticed metal shelves holding odd pieces of electronic equipment. Above him, taut cables hung between the rocket and silo wall. The cables created a look of stability and he hoped it was stability for the rocket and not the silo.

Timothy examined the rocket's four fins neatly folded against the rocket's base. A steel skirt of metal ran around the bottom of the rocket below the fins. Timothy figured the skirt helped hold the rocket off the ground. Inside was probably the rocket's exhaust nozzle.

Yet, the most interesting object he spied was a one-person elevator not far to the right of the metal door. It was a metal seat with handles on the side and cables to pull it up to the top of the silo. He didn't want to take time and figure out the controls since it looked like Eddie made the flimsy structure and Timothy wasn't sure it worked.

Just past the elevator was a square opening in the side of the silo about four by four feet wide. Enough for someone like him to scoot through. Poking his head through the opening, Timothy saw a string of small light bulbs illuminating a ladder that clung to the outside of the concrete. Except the ladder was not outside, but enclosed in a tube-like metal chute and leaving more than enough room for someone to climb up.

Inside the silo, he saw a series of closed doors. They were equal distance to the top of the silo. Looking back through the square opening, Timothy realized the doors had bars on the outside and these made up the ladder going to the top of the silo. He wanted to climb the ladder, but he also wanted to see the rest of the rocket, too.

Timothy followed the silo wall back to the metal door where he hesitated. Along his walk, he had avoided touching anything. Now, he stepped up to the white metal structure and rubbed his hand along the smooth metal surface that felt weak and strong at the same time. Like an electric shock, he jumped back and faced the rocket again.

"So, Eddie thinks I can fly this giant thing?" He heard his voice echo strongly against the rocket as if the structure was talking back to him that it was ready to go.

He snapped off the light, scrambled out of the silo, and pushed the metal door shut as best he could. Outside under the moonlight, Timothy walked as fast as he could, successfully avoiding the weeds this time while trying not to think too much. Almost at the house, he looked up and saw a light on in one of the upper floor windows.

Timothy went to the illuminated room and found it lined with bookcases. The shelves held binders filled with rocket manuals, picture books showing rockets throughout history, and more picture books of the capsules the rockets carried into orbit. Timothy figured the light meant he was to find this rocket room like a moth to a light.

Although he was tired, he pulled out a few binders and settled into a cushioned chair with a footstool. He opened the *Redstone* rocket binder first and read about the thin gauge, stainless steel skin that was the signature of the rocket design.

He scanned a few pages where he learned that single-one-stage rockets, like the *Redstone* were better. They had no stages to jettison or worry that the stage engines would not light up.

Another binder showed how the *Redstone's* propellant tanks used high pressure to keep the rocket structure from collapsing. If the tank pressurization failed, the rocket skin would crumble and the seventy-five by ten-foot rocket would collapse under its own weight. Obviously, the cables were keeping the rocket from falling over.

Timothy thought about all the things that could happen during the violent throws of flight that could make the rocket a pile of burned metal. He worried if his dad's engines with the special fuel would be enough to prevent this catastrophic failure from happening. Mostly, he worried that he could pilot that big rocket out of the silo and into orbit.

At some point, he fell asleep and dreamed about his dad.

Chapter 5

"Listen to me, Timothy. This is important," his dad had said a year before his death.

It was a temporary sober moment for the man and Timothy tried to understand what his dad was telling him. Spread out on the kitchen table were drawings of the engines his dad had said were stored in two sections ready for assembly. The assembling was what he was trying to explain to Timothy.

"They use an electrostatic charge to work. At an important junction of the flight, the charge runs along the metal frame of the rocket to help with thrust and into outer space. There's a lot going on here, I know. What with the fuel and the engines. I know you'll get it if you try."

His dad's voice and the dream faded as Timothy woke up to daylight coming from the only window. He rubbed his hands across his face to help him wake up. He smelled something cooking coming from the kitchen.

Eddie stood in front of the stove as tiny eruptions of grease sprang from a black skillet. On a nearby counter, the smell of coffee rose from a percolating urn that looked ancient. The dark liquid bounced every few seconds into a small glass bubble on top of the urn. Some of the grease splattered onto the urn's shiny aluminum.

"I don't like coffee," Timothy said, sitting down at the table.

"I'm making scrambled eggs with honey, yellow mustard, and pesto."

"What's in the oven?"

"Sourdough bread with mozzarella on them. There's a bowl of berries, bananas, and orange slices on the table. If you don't like coffee, drink it black."

Without anything else to drink but water, Timothy poured himself half a cup of coffee. After a few sips, he filled the cup and sat at the table, letting the caffeine rush through his head to keep him awake. At least through breakfast. He was hungry.

"I saw the rocket last night."

Eddie dished out the breakfast food. On top of his eggs, he plopped a dollop of chocolate ice cream.

"The original rocket had balloon tanks for fuel made of very thin stainless steel," Eddie explained. "The tank pressure provided the rigidity needed for flight. Right now, there are no tanks, just thin aluminum girders and cross beams on the inside to stabilize the rocket's structure. I'm assuming your dad's engines are not meant for internal support."

Timothy didn't want to talk about the engines that his dad built because it reminded him about being an orphan. So, he changed the subject. "Where'd you get the rocket?"

"I knew this NASA guy when I first started working for the shuttle program at Langley. But, first let me explain a short history of the rocket. NASA used the *Redstone* for the first two U.S. rocket launches of the manned *Mercury* capsule. In 1964, NASA started using Atlas rockets for the rest of the *Mercury* missions and the *Redstone* was retired. Except, not really. The Chrysler Corporation, who made the rocket, had a surplus that they used in a joint US/UK/Australian program until 1967."

"And this guy got part of that surplus?"

Eddie shook his head. "No. The *Redstone* was funded by the U.S. Army and they were told to get rid of it when the Government started using rockets from the Air Force, Navy, and NASA contractors. The Army wanted to keep their rocket, so they classified the *Redstone* as a black program, or super-classified. That way few people would not know they were giving money to Chrysler to continue building *Red-stones.* All the way into the early 2000s."

"What did the Army do with all those rockets?" Timothy imagined a desert filled with thousands of unused rockets pointing at the sky and never to be launched.

"They stored them in the desert never to be launched. When they ran out of desert, they dismantled the rockets and used the parts to build newer ones."

Timothy took another sip of coffee, the caffeine swirling in his brain. "If the program was classified, how'd this guy get one?"

"The only people who knew how to fly the *Redstone* were engineers from the original program. They eventually either died, lost their memory, or were too old to climb stairs. That NASA guy got one of the last ones before they were all destroyed. He put it in the silo. I think he wanted to use it for himself one day."

"Nothing about this sounds legal."

Eddie took another bite of food before continuing. "When a classified program shuts down in the Defense Department, no one cares what happens to the inventory. Everything becomes legal."

"How'd the NASA guy get the rocket here?"

The old man chomped down on a forkful of eggs as though it were his last meal. "It was a memorable event. This NASA guy got some friends of his to bring the rocket in a tractor-trailer. They invited everyone in this area to help. We had the greatest party here. So many people knew about the rocket that it was forgotten about a few months later. All anyone remembered was the party."

"What was the NASA guy's name?"

"I never knew. I always called him ET," said Eddie not looking at Timothy. "I never trusted him, but I let him put the rocket in the silo anyway.

Timothy scratched his head. "There's something missing with all of this. Why didn't someone launch the rocket already? My dad didn't live that far from here and he had the formula and engines."

What kind of crazy plot was he getting involved in, Timothy worried? He ate several forkfuls of food trying to think or maybe not.

Eddie stopped eating and said, "It all started with a woman."

"That's a cliché that doesn't work in this story." Timothy drank his coffee in several final gulps. "What was her name?"

"Reanette."

Timothy choked up his eggs and coffee onto the table after hearing his mother's name.

Chapter 6

"What about the woman?" Timothy wiped up his mess.

"I was in love with her."

Timothy tried not to choke again.

Eddie avoided looking at the teenager. He blurted out, "But she was married to your dad. That's how love goes sometimes."

Eddie continued to eat as if hoping that was the end of that. Timothy didn't think so.

He pulled Eddie's plate away from him. "What do you mean you were in love with my mom? This is bizarre. I want to know everything." Timothy glared at Eddie.

"Nothing happened between your mother and me," Eddie said leaning back from the table. He looked at the floor. "She never knew how I felt. We got to know each other while working together at Langley. Yet, she fell in love with your dad and I doubt she even remembered me after marrying him and moving away."

"Then how did you end up living a few miles from where my mom and dad lived?" Timothy was getting angry.

"I knew where she and Roy moved to and I followed them here." Figuring the meal over, Eddie gathered up the plates and utensils and took them to the sink before continuing.

"Before you say anything more, I know it wasn't the right thing to do. I realized that when I got here. You see, not long after the Shuttle program ended, NASA laid off a lot of us and I moved to Cape

Canaveral to try and relive my NASA days working on other projects. I ended up working in retail instead and I just got lonelier." At the sink, Eddie started scrubbing the plates hard.

"Yeah, I kept up with people from my NASA days through social media. It just wasn't the same. Believe me, your parents never knew I moved here. I kept away from her and your dad and spent my time collecting the rocket stuff you see around here."

Timothy pictured Eddie as a stalker, yet someone who also had morals. Someone who needed love, but missed the opportunity. At least he stayed away from my mom, Timothy thought. He had a sudden nightmare. How close had Eddie come to being his father?

"Why did you pick this place?"

"It has lots of room to store the rocket stuff I collected. And I took the janitor job because I needed something else to do before I went crazy."

"Did you go to my mom's funeral?"

"No, I saw the notice in the paper, though." Eddie stopped washing the dishes and looked like he was searching the suds for answers. "I can imagine how your dad felt." He turned toward Timothy. "Are we cool with this?" Tears glistened in Eddie's eyes.

Timothy came over to help Eddie dry the dishes. "Yeah, we're cool. I miss her too."

There was no need to get angry or upset, Timothy thought. He felt like he was a lot like Eddie. Someone lonely. Also, they were now two people who had a rocket to launch.

After a few moments, Eddie changed the subject abruptly as if distancing himself from memories. "The Army continued to use simple copper wiring and analog electronics throughout the *Redstone* program. As long as everything worked, they didn't change anything."

"So, your rocket is analog and not digital?" Timothy thought this could make it even harder to fly. Any current software programs wouldn't work with the analog systems.

"Yeah, which makes it easier to fly. It's good we're here in down east North Carolina. There's flat farmland and small towns with more abandoned buildings than people living here. Also, we're close to the Atlantic, but outside of shipping lanes because the rivers are shallow."

"I guess it's good in case the rocket crashes," said Timothy.

"I'm not worried about that. I don't want anyone to see it until it's in space."

"Were there other space programs with weird technology like my dad's?" Timothy had stopped drying and was looking out the window at some big birds soaring in the air. Their flying looked easy.

"At the beginning of the U.S. space program, there were lots of scientists looking for alternate fuel designs like your dad's. Your dad's fuel system and engines were made for a rocket like this."

Timothy remembered, "My dad talked about a place called the Naval Research Laboratory and an Air Force lab at Wright-Pat. He said they worked on a propulsion system that didn't use liquid and solid fuels."

"Yeah, in the early sixties the Navy stopped funding their program without knowing the Air Force had already flown a three-foot-diameter disk-shaped craft using electricity," Eddie said, pushing suds around with a fork. "Later the Air Force stopped their program and spent the money on building the next fighter. Neither the Navy nor Air Force knew about the other's program because everything was classified within that Service."

Timothy kept drying the same plate. "My dad said some foreign governments and large U.S. companies were working on an electro-gravitic engine." Even in his drunken state, Timothy's dad was very sober on these points. "He said everyone had some success, except they were all so secretive with their technology that no one shared anything."

"That's exactly what's wrong with classified programs. Everyone is in their own little bubble and no one knows what anyone else is doing." Eddie dried his hands on a towel.

He swung around and headed out of the kitchen toward the back door before Timothy could put down his plate. He raced after Eddie.

"Let's go look at the rocket in the daylight."

"Wait. Before I saw the rocket, I saw a car take off from the driveway."

Eddie stopped before reaching the back door. "Yeah, I suspected we were being watched. But I don't think they know what's in the silo."

"How do you know that?"

"If they knew about the rocket, they'd be snooping around the silo and not the house. I think they are after what you brought. Let's talk about it later and go see the rocket."

Chapter 7

Timothy hurried to catch up to Eddie. For an old man, he moved pretty fast, he thought. They stepped onto the back porch where Eddie continued out into the weedy grass and toward the silo.

"Why aren't we taking the jeep?" Timothy asked, avoiding a hunk of weeds.

"Whenever I feel up to it, I walk in the morning to the silo. I feel up to it today."

Without stumbling this time, Timothy came up behind Eddie and they quickly headed toward the concrete tower. Eddie had a lot of energy, maybe from the coffee or maybe from some of those pills he swallowed before eating breakfast.

Eddie kept walking as if the silo was some type of shrine. When they reached it, Eddie went around the side facing away from the house to show Timothy five ditches. Each ditch held long metal tubes extending out from the concrete wall and separated the farther they went. They ended about thirty feet away at a pile of stone three or five feet high that would meet anything coming out of the pipes.

"They're to deflect the rocket blast," Eddie explained. "If there is any."

Timothy looked beyond the ditches at another field with fewer weeds. At least there was nothing there that would catch fire from what came out of the pipes.

"I also have a generator in a shed on the other side," Eddie said. He led the way to the silo's metal door.

Timothy remembered the broken handle. "I couldn't get in last night and I accidentally broke the door."

Eddie surveyed the broken handle. "I haven't been able to move that handle since I've been here. All you had to do was pull the door open."

"You don't lock anything?"

"Out here it's too easy to break into anything. So, I keep everything unlocked. If anyone comes by, they figure there's nothing valuable inside. Even if they go in, it'd be hard to steal a rocket."

"That makes sense, I guess. What about the other stuff around here?"

"I feed a barn owl that hangs out nearby. If someone messes around here, the owl lets out a screech and swoops in to protect its food place. One night a year ago, two guys walked out of the silo with some tools. The owl did it's screeching and swooped on top of the crooks. They dropped what they had and now there's a rumor the silo and this place is haunted. Not by ghosts, but a demon." Eddie chuckled. "Great security. Ghosts attract people. Demons drive them away."

Timothy's brow furrowed. "I was in the silo last night and didn't hear any screeching."

Eddie pulled open the metal door. "That's because you didn't try to take anything. In that tree over there, I'm sure the owl was watching you."

"What's the owl's name?"

"Something free and wild can't be named." Eddie headed inside the silo.

Timothy followed him. He was taken aback thinking how the metal wall of the *Redstone* rose around them like a secret wanting to be exposed.

Eddie disappeared to the right, following the curvature of the silo walls. Overhead, daylight seeped in through the dome making Timothy think of the place as one of those ICBM missile sites. He decided if a missile could be launched from something that looked like a silo, maybe he and Eddie could launch this rocket out of a real silo.

Timothy walked up to the rocket's metal wall and once again ran his hand over the smooth surface. A real rocket, he thought. He let his hand follow the metal wall up until he could reach no further. He went after Eddie and found him digging in one of the narrow metal benches.

"What about these fins folded against the rocket?" Timothy pointed to the nearest one of the four.

"It's a special modification. When the rocket clears the silo, they'll pop out and give stability in flight."

"What about stability in the silo?"

"Not needed, I hope. The immediate thrust should launch the rocket straight up and out."

"I want to see it fly," Timothy said with confidence that surprised him.

"I want the same thing." Eddie sat on the bench and leaned against the wall. The rocket filled his entire view.

"This is a big thing. I'm not sure how much I can help," Timothy said.

"The formula is more than numbers and words on pieces of paper. It's also what your dad trusted to tell you. It's about what you learned from listening to him, even when you pretended not to."

Timothy felt like his dad haunting him with the formula. Like he had to accept this inheritance for the haunting to stop. "You don't know anything about me or my dad. I know what he told me and it didn't make sense."

"Yeah, it made sense because you were listening."

"Shut up," Timothy snapped. "I should just leave you with your stupid rocket. I know what I know about my dad and that's it."

"You might not like it," Eddie said sternly, "but the formula is your inheritance. You and the formula are one and the same."

Timothy wasn't sure what to do. This had all been a lot to think about in twenty-four hours since he knocked on Eddie's door.

"I wasn't thinking straight yesterday when I showed up at your house. I was still recovering from my dad's death. But I want to know something. You knew my parents and said you never contacted them; then how did my dad know your address?"

"There's an explanation for all of this. I promise. But I need you to have some patience with me. I'll explain everything soon." Eddie's pleading surprised Timothy.

He couldn't resist. He felt sorry for the old man, but he was getting impatient.

"My dad never mentioned you or this rocket. I found out only after he died and left me his notes. And you know what? Maybe this rocket isn't what I want to do with my life."

Timothy looked at the rocket trying to remember his dad sober. It was before his mom died and he barely remembered her. Timothy wanted to leave the silo and this crazy old man. Actually, he didn't know what he wanted to do. He worried what his destiny would become if he left or stayed. His life had changed so much and he wasn't even out of high school.

Chapter 8

Eddie strolled around the rocket. Timothy followed, not sure why. It was everything he saw before except the walk made him feel less frustrated and lonely. They arrived at the metal door where Eddie stepped out and headed for the house.

Timothy took one more look at the rocket before closing the metal door. He tried but couldn't ignore the immensity of the structure looming above him.

He chased after Eddie who finally slowed up when they got to the kitchen. "I need a little snack. How about cheddar cheese, mixed nuts, cinnamon, and ketchup? I usually sprinkle some nutmeg on everything. Just a little, it's a strong spice."

Timothy gathered some bowls and they sat at the table.

"The maximum speed of a rocket is limited by the amount of fuel it carries," Eddie said putting everything out on the table. "I'm assuming this formula will make a fuel that's different and changes the equation for rocket propulsion, making our situation unique."

"I'm not exactly sure what will happen with the fuel. It's not just some chemicals mixed together. I also have to add the right amount from those special vials that came from my dad."

"Your dad called the engines electrogravitic and wrote that they use the negative energy coming out of the Earth for propulsion," Eddie pushed cheese and nuts into a ball with nutmeg on the outside. "I couldn't find any scientific evidence of this energy except when connected with geopathic stress that can affect people's health."

"My dad said it's like measuring gravitational waves, negative energy from the earth has not been measured because no one is looking for it," said Timothy.

"I think the ancients had some sense of this energy. But we lost it long ago. These engines and fuel will help us rediscover it. Is the negative energy going to happen all the way into space?"

"In one of the upper levels, the mesosphere, the negative energy gets weak," Timothy explained. "There's something in the atmosphere at that level to add more energy. After that, the engines use negative energy leaking from outer space."

Eddie's eyes got wide. "Whoa. That's a lot to take in. You're talking about a new branch of science."

"I'm just repeating what my dad said." Timothy shrugged. "The Earth uses positive energy and sheds negative energy. The engines create something like a shield against negative energy riding it like a surfboard on a wave."

Eddie put ketchup on his cheese and nuts. He said, "Negative energy is used in physics to explain things like gravitational fields and travel that's faster than the speed of light."

Timothy laughed lightly. "My science teacher, Mr. Greg, said going faster than the speed of light is impossible." He never really liked science, except his teacher and his dad seemed excited about it.

"I have some books on how the Earth produces positive and negative energy in its core. Oddly the process is supposed to create a vacuum," said Eddie.

Timothy thought it would be more important to find out how the Earth used internal energy—just in case interfering with the negative might impact the positive and the world would stop working.

Eddie turned around and looked at Timothy. "Do you ever wonder how we all ended up here?"

"What are you talking about?" Timothy finished eating.

"I mean, according to your dad's notes, here in eastern North Carolina the Earth's gravity is strong meaning there's more negative energy being emitted. Okay, gravity strength also depends on the time of day, the phases of the moon, and low and high pressure in the atmosphere from solar storms. But I think we could be at one of the best places in the country to launch a rocket with your electrogravitic engines.”

“It’s my dad’s engines, not mine,” said Timothy wishing Eddie would get that straight.

“I haven’t read all your dad’s papers,” Eddie said, ignoring Timothy, “but what I have read somewhat describes a design the Air Force funded in the early 1950s. It had a disk shape, with domed plates giving off electrical charges. It made thrust in one direction when charged the other way.”

“Who cares about what happened in the 1950s? I guess you do since you were alive then.”

Eddied nodded. “Yeah, I care. I remember how it was with the space race. By the 1960s, the military and big companies controlled everything, just like now. They stopped smart people from building better rockets.”

Timothy wanted to tell Eddie to stop worrying about the military and classified stuff, except he was worried about them too. He remembered his dad had the same concern, which is why he hid the rocket engines so they wouldn’t be found by “spies.” Timothy said, “All I know about the space race is what I learned in history class.”

Eddie waved a hand at him. “It doesn’t matter. I’m going to keep reading through your dad’s papers. And you need to learn more about the rocket.”

“Why do I need to learn about this rocket? I can’t fly it. At least not by myself.”

“You need to start accepting responsibility for this project.”

“Why?” Timothy said scowling. “This is your project, not mine.”

“Your father sent you here for a purpose.”

Timothy rolled his eyes thinking “here we go again.” He blew out a long sigh. “You’re not my dad and I don’t have to do any of this stuff. You have the papers, so maybe I’ll just go somewhere else to live.”

Timothy turned and stomped out of the kitchen. He heard Eddie trying to catch up.

"What's wrong with you?" Eddie said reaching Timothy on the front porch. He pulled on Timothy's shirtsleeve to slow him down.

Timothy jerked around. "I don't like you telling me what to do. I don't like being responsible for launching that big rocket and I don't like that I'm an orphan with no other choices."

"Okay. You can do whatever you want. But I can't launch this rocket without you. And I need to launch this thing. Everything's ready for us to change our lives."

Timothy sighed. "My life has changed enough already. I don't need any more changes."

Eddie threw up his arms in frustration and stomped back into the house. He abruptly popped back in the doorway and faced Timothy. "I used to decide what changes happened in my life. Now things happen to me that I have no control over. I want to launch this rocket. It'll be the last thing I do in my life. If you don't want to help, then go." Eddie turned around and once again went back into the house.

Left alone on the front porch, Timothy had nowhere that he wanted to go. He knew he was being childish.

He went inside asking, "How tall is the rocket?"

"Almost sixty feet. The capsule adds another ten." Eddie headed down the hallway. Not the kitchen this time.

"How wide?" Timothy called out.

"About six feet in diameter. I'm sure your engines will easily fit inside."

"Again, they're my dad's engines." Timothy wondered if this high school janitor had any clue as to how all this rocket launching stuff would work. Timothy certainly didn't. Yeah, he thought, maybe I should stop telling myself that.

Chapter 9

Eddie led Timothy into a room that smelled like an electronic grave-yard. The older man flipped on several switches and spun a dial on the wall, breathing electrical current into the overhead lights. Dials and small lights on metal boxes lit up the room with dull surprise. The warmth from the old analog technology washed over Timothy with a slight hum.

Scattered among the electronics were faded, yellowed manuals and three-ring binders with worn edges. Timothy looked closer and read they were from the space shuttle program. Other manuals and binders came from the Apollo, Gemini, and Mercury space programs. Still, others were written in languages he figured were Russian judging from the picture of a Soyuz capsule, Chinese because of the character sketches, and French from the European Space Agency because he was taking that language and still couldn't figure it out.

"Just like the other room, it's like a museum in here. You've got stuff from around the world," Timothy said.

Eddie's head was stuck in a wooden box on the floor. He surfaced holding a binder filled with yellowed paper. "Like I said before, I've been collecting all the forgotten technology people used to get into space. I planned to have a museum one day." He glanced around the room. "But now I don't have time for a museum."

"Does any of this electronic stuff work?"

Eddie nodded. "Just like the rocket, I tested everything and it all works. I've got a series of antennas and dishes on the tower for different wavelengths and spectrums. Everything's connected to this room and the one next door in the tower which will be your launch room."

Timothy looked around some more. "How many people would it take to run all this equipment?"

Eddie put the binder down on a table and glanced around as if looking for an easy answer that was not there. "Yeah, I know. We'll need help."

Timothy let out a heavy sigh and picked up the binder. "I get that we're bordering on being illegal here, which is why you don't want people knowing about all this. Hey, I don't want too many people knowing about this either."

He looked around the cluttered room, trying to understand it all. More than anything else, he wanted his parents back. He wanted a teenager's life worrying about graduating high school rather than worrying about not blowing everything up with an old rocket.

He wished he had brothers or sisters. He could use an older one right now. Even a younger one would do. All he had was the high school janitor Eddie and a room full of cheap binders holding old papers.

Timothy flipped through the binder he had. "It says here on the first page that a rocket can produce a hundred and fifty thousand pounds of thrust with conventional fuel. The fuel we'll be using is not conventional. We don't need any of this information. We need to control the rocket using new thrust limits," said Timothy.

"Let's go over exactly what those limits are. I got what happens during launch and initial flight. But, can you explain what happens in the upper atmosphere?"

Timothy hesitated, then his dad's words came back to him as if they were being whispered in his ears. "In the upper atmosphere, the engines will use the empty mass of the rocket as an additional energy source."

"Interesting. A true single-stage-to-orbit." Eddie leaned against a table that fortunately supported his leaning.

"The engines and fuel push the rocket through the troposphere and into the stratosphere, about twelve miles up. At that level, the engines run at maximum efficiency. That's what my dad said."

Eddie grinned. "From your dad's notes, the entire skin of the rocket gets used as a means of thrust. Is that right?"

"That's right. The energy from the engines get amplified through the rocket and keeps pushing the structure into the mesosphere. At this height, the engines use another energy source. Something that lives at that altitude."

"Another form of life? There's been speculation before, but it's hard to believe."

"No, maybe not. An energy function, as my dad said." Timothy wished he had not remembered so much from his dad. If wrong, it would be Timothy's fault.

"We'll talk about that other energy source later. What happens next?"

"When the rocket reaches the thermosphere, the electrogravitic engines are at maximum efficiency feeding off negatively charged energy particles dripping down from space."

"Yeah, as I understand it, by the time the rocket reaches the last level of the atmosphere, the exosphere, the engines are feeding completely off negative energy coming from space," Eddie seemed happy that he understood this.

Timothy leaned against a wall and added, "After that, we're in space."

"Okay, so the rocket and engines work together like the high school band playing different instruments," Eddie said.

Timothy remembered with horror the last time he'd heard his high school band play. They both stared at each other, not knowing what to say. It was a bad comparison.

"I got it, now," said Eddie. "I'm going to leave you here to read up on things." Eddie suddenly looked pale. "I'm tired and I need to take a nap." He unexpectedly brushed past Timothy toward the door.

"What's wrong?"

"Nothing. Stay here and do some reading. I'll talk to you later."

Timothy thought about following him when he heard Eddie walk down the hallway and close his bedroom door. Shrugging off his odd behavior, Timothy found a comfortable enough chair and started reading. He focused on the binder Eddie pulled out of the box. The one labeled *Mercury*.

He was not sure how long he had been sleeping when he woke up with an aching neck. The binder was lying at his feet with its contents littering the floor. He came into the kitchen looking for food and found Eddie at the kitchen table sipping a cup of coffee.

"Food's in the fridge," he said.

Timothy pulled out a bowl filled with cut strawberries, tiny blueberries, chopped walnuts, raspberry jam, and crumbled potato chips all topped with mayonnaise. The salty kind of chips and the fatty kind of mayonnaise.

He gulped down two mouthfuls of the food mixture. He wasn't sure he was hungry or whether the concoction tasted that good. He eyed the old man, wondering if he could be an alien from another planet. A moment later, he decided Eddie wasn't strange enough—even if his meals were.

Timothy saw that Eddie had some contraption on the table. When he spun a dial on the side, it flipped a series of index cards in a circle. The cards had writing on them.

"What's that?" Timothy asked between bites.

"It's a Rolodex. It's like a round address book. I've been trying to contact some people I worked with at NASA."

"It looks old." Timothy wondered if Eddie also had a landline phone or, worse, a rotary which he'd read about in history class. After a few moments watching Eddie survey his card file, Timothy got up to wash his bowl. He never liked dirty dishes sitting around after seeing the cockroaches in his former home.

When he turned around, he was alone in the kitchen. Eventually, Timothy found Eddie in the tower section of the house. Timothy wished he had a friend to keep up with rather than the high school janitor.

"Are you going to use the rocket to launch something or you just want to see it fly?" Timothy came into the room trying not to fall over a box.

Eddie turned around to face the teenager. "I have a very special satellite I want the rocket to launch into orbit. It'll be magnificent."

"What kind of satellite?"

"A special satellite for a special rocket."

Eddie stood in the middle of the cluttered room looking frail. He had his hands on his hips as if he wanted to fly like Superman. "Tomorrow we're both going to school. We need to keep everything normal until we're ready to launch. Meanwhile, I'll work on getting us some help to get things organized."

Timothy didn't want to go to school. But he didn't know what else he would do.

Chapter 10

On Monday morning, Timothy stood outside the house beside a short-bed pickup built before he was born. Timothy was just glad they weren't taking the jeep.

The truck had been parked on the opposite side of the house and now sat where Eddie had left it before going back inside the house for something he forgot. Timothy leaned against the truck wondering why he was going to school at all. He woke up that morning without confidence in the launch. He thought maybe he would be better off back at his dad's place, even if it was unlivable.

He looked across the state road at an open field that was once farmland. Timothy wondered what had happened to the people who used to farm it. There seemed to be a lot of abandoned farms in the area.

Hearing a wheezing sound, he spun around and spied Eddie running from around the house. Closing in on him was a tall man wearing khakis, a black shirt, and a side holster with a large handgun hanging from it.

Timothy took off running toward the man to keep him from catching Eddie, who had stopped to hold his knees and catch his breath. Before Timothy could reach Eddie, the man streaked past both of them.

The stranger ran toward the state road and jump into a dark sedan that had just pulled up. It sped away with the strange man. Timothy ran after the car but couldn't catch sight of the license plate.

"Who was he?" Timothy asked coming back to help Eddie stand up.

"I suspect they're from some government agency."

"What government?"

"Ours. At least I think so. Did you get their license plate number?"

"No, he was too fast. What do they want?"

"I caught the guy looking in a window out back."

"What are we going to do? He had a gun." Timothy wanted to take Eddie back into the house and skip school today.

"Nothing. They don't want us. They want what we might have. My hunch is they tracked our model rocket and decided to check up on us. They'll probably stay away for a few days thinking we'd call the police."

Timothy narrowed his eyes. "Why don't we call the police?"

"They can't do anything. Nothing was taken. Besides, I don't want the police nosing around here. They might look in the silo."

"But the guy had a gun."

"Yeah, that worries me. On the good side, he didn't shoot us."

Timothy didn't find that reassuring. "Why did you go back inside the house?"

"To get my lunch. I heard something and went out back to see that guy looking in a window. I thought he was chasing me, but I guess he wanted to get away after getting caught. Could you go in and get my lunch?"

"Forget your lunch. Why don't we stay home and work on the formula?" Timothy didn't like how Eddie was sweating.

"I'm all right," Eddie said heading for the truck. "Hurry up or we'll be late for school."

Timothy got Eddie's lunch and climbed in the truck. Eddie sent the rattling vehicle down the state road in the opposite direction of the sedan. Hesitantly, Timothy turned around and looked through the back window for the car to make sure it wasn't coming after them.

Chapter 11

On the way to school, Timothy said, "What if that guy shows up again? We've gotta have a plan. You have any weapons?"

"Just the rocket."

"We can't just wait around for someone to shoot us." One of the things his dad said was never to run away from a problem. He never mentioned whether or not that problem had a gun.

Eddie waved a hand at Timothy. "I don't think they'll shoot us. Didn't this time. But I agree we need a plan. I'll try to come up with something this afternoon and you try to think of something, too."

Timothy had no idea how to come up with a plan. This was his first day back to school after his dad's death and that was all he could think about. Would anyone say anything to him? He dreaded talking to anyone about the past week.

He thought he better focus on Eddie's erratic driving. Timothy almost felt safer confronting the guy with the gun.

"Do you have a valid driver's license?" Timothy said as Eddie took a curve too fast. He didn't seem to know what side of the road he should drive on.

"It might have expired. I'm not sure. I lost it years ago." Eddie swerved to miss running into a ditch.

Timothy would have grabbed the steering wheel if he wasn't holding onto the door and dashboard. Eddie finally slowed down after Timothy screamed for him to slow down. They were driving past farm fields and the occasional empty farmhouse. Timothy wondered who was doing all the farming. Eventually, Eddie slammed on the brakes and skidded to a stop at the back of the high school near the dumpsters and without hitting them.

"I'm going to let you off here. I don't want anyone seeing me taking you to school."

"Why not?"

"People might get suspicious. They're already talking about where you're staying now that your father died. I spread the rumor that a relative moved in with you."

"I think my relatives flew away in their spaceships," Timothy said.

Eddie chuckled. "Did you see any spaceships fly away?"

"No, but why else would they leave me alone so fast?" Timothy forgot he encouraged them to leave. He was trying not to sound so desperate and lonely. Except that was how he felt. He worried about what he should be telling Eddie since the janitor had been a stranger until two days ago.

"If the school administration thinks you're homeless or living with me, they'll kick you out of school. All students must have a parent or a judge signing off on who the guardian is; otherwise, the student doesn't exist and will be expelled."

"Are you sure about that?"

Eddie nodded. "Yeah, I already checked. The school system is overcrowded and this is their way of getting rid of students."

Timothy didn't like being kicked out of school. He wanted something in his life to stay the same. He looked at Eddie drumming his fingers on the steering wheel and staring straight ahead.

"Gotta get going or you'll be late for school and I'll be late for work," Eddie said.

Timothy got out and walked around the dumpsters toward the front of the school. He kept his head down and went to his locker without talking to anyone. He kept his head in the locker as if looking for something while trying not to think of people talking about him. At his locker, Eddie came up behind and spooked him.

"I thought we were supposed to be secretive. Go clean something," said Timothy.

"Have one of your friends drop you off at that country store a mile from my place. I've gotta leave early and make some arrangements for more equipment," Eddie said.

Timothy's locker was next to the girls' bathroom. He heard some giggling going on inside. He didn't understand why the girls talked so much in the bathroom.

"I don't have any friends to ask."

"Well, make some quick and have them take you there. That girl at the end of the hallway is a good start. She's always staring at you." Eddie pointed at a girl who was yanking on a notebook lodged in her locker.

Timothy looked at his watch and saw he had two minutes to make friends with the girl, ask her for a ride this afternoon, and get to his first class. He went to argue with Eddie, but he had already disappeared into the teenage crowd like some kind of ninja.

Timothy looked back at the girl whose notebook sat torn at her feet. She stared at him as if it was his fault. Timothy turned to walk away when two girls burst out of the bathroom and swung the door into his forehead. They were giggling so much they didn't even notice.

Rubbing his forehead, Timothy turned around and the girl at the end of the hallway was standing in front of him. He wondered if he had passed out. She sure moved fast.

She was slightly taller than Timothy and stared at him with her blue eyes.

"That was pretty funny getting hit in the head. That happen to you often?"

She had a long, straight nose and her smile brought her face together like it could not be any other way. Her thick brown hair ran around on her shoulders as her long bangs pointed back to her big blue eyes.

Timothy wasn't sure what to say as he continued to rub his forehead.

"I saw you talking to the janitor. You know him?"

"He's the janitor. Everyone knows that." Timothy hated to be late for class or anything, so he took the opportunity and asked, "Can you give me a ride home from school this afternoon?" Standing this close to a girl made Timothy blurt this out with no explanation.

"I don't think you rode the bus. Who brought you to school? Did the janitor tell you to ask me for a ride?"

There were too many questions. He wasn't sure what to say and began wondering why Eddie pointed out this girl. Timothy wondered how long it would take to walk to Eddie's place.

"That's all right. I can find my way home this afternoon," Timothy said before the girl could ask more questions.

"Did the janitor drive you to school this morning and is that why you won't tell me?"

"Never mind. I'll take the bus." Timothy wondered if any bus went by Eddie's.

"You don't even know my name." She flipped her hair across her shoulders and away from her face, except her bangs still hung there covering her long forehead. "I'm Angie."

"I'm Timothy."

"Yeah, I know that from what happened to your dad. I'm sorry for your loss. Everyone's saying you're living with some relatives at your dad's place."

"No, I'm not living there. I was, but not now."

"So, you need a ride to this other place that you don't want anyone knowing about. Where is it? Is it a homeless shelter?"

"No. I'm not homeless." Timothy stopped to think about that. Was he homeless?

Angie leaned against one of the lockers. "Yeah, my parents take turns living with me. They're divorcing and won't admit it. Instead, my mom stays at our house for three weeks and then my dad lives with me for three weeks. I think it's a weird situation, but they won't talk to me about it."

"I'm sorry for whatever's going on at your home. But why are you telling me this?"

"So, you'll feel more comfortable telling me about your home situation. You're in my math class and you sigh a lot." Angie pushed away from the locker and stepped closer to Timothy. He caught a whiff of her sweet yet sour perfume.

Angie said, "I don't have a car, but I know someone who does and he'll give us a ride."

"Thanks, but why don't you just introduce us? That way you won't have to bother getting involved."

"I have to be involved. He may not like you without me there."

"Why?" Timothy wasn't sure.

"'Cause I'll tell him not to unless I can come too."

Timothy didn't understand the social situation he was getting into. Just then, the bell rang. "All right, fine. I don't care."

Timothy cared a lot. He just wasn't sure why and he needed to get to class.

Chapter 12

Throughout the day, Timothy spied Angie several times in the crowded hallway and waved, but she ignored him. She even pretended he didn't exist in math class. After the final bell, he stood at the edge of the parking lot trying to find her among the departing students.

Finally, he spotted her standing next to a faded yellow car with four doors, a long front hood, and a short back end. Like Eddie's truck, the car looked a lot older than him. Angie waved like a flag in a wild wind. Now she's waving back, thought Timothy.

Standing next to her, Timothy recognized one of the varsity football players. He was an inch taller than Angie with broad shoulders that made his head look a little too small. He had a deep brown hue about him like he was descended equally from Africa and South America. Timothy walked toward the car hesitantly not sure what to expect from a football player.

"My boyfriend is doing this as a favor for me," Angie announced.

"Hi, my name's Luke. Angie said to give you a ride." He had a slight bent to his nose and a broad smile that he used a lot. He thrust his big hand out.

"I'm Timothy." He took Luke's hand carefully, concerned about crushed bones.

Angie quickly climbed into the backseat leaving Luke and Timothy facing each other. Luke didn't hesitate and jumped in to start the engine. He got in the front passenger seat since Angie had locked the back doors.

They rode in silence except for Timothy telling Luke where to go. When they got to a two-gas-pump convenience store, Timothy told Luke to let him out there.

"This where you live?" Angie poked Timothy's shoulder. "You live in this store? It doesn't look like it sells much."

"I get gas here. I know this isn't your home," said Luke. "Just tell me where you live and I'll take you there. Angie said you're still living at your dad's place." Luke kept the car in drive and idling in the parking lot. He drummed his fingers on the steering wheel that was big enough to steer a boat. "By the way, I'm sorry about your loss. I should have said something before. It must be hard for you right now."

"I never said I lived here," Timothy blurted out to stop Luke from talking. "And, I don't want to talk about my dad."

"Sure, I get it. Then, come on. Where do you live?" Luke's big, deep voice filled the car.

"I'll get picked up here."

Angie poked Timothy's shoulder again. "Why don't you want us to see where you live? You embarrassed by your dad's place? We don't care what it looks like."

Timothy cringed at the memory of where he used to live. He wasn't sure if he ever wanted to go back there. He considered getting out of the car and calling Eddie to pick him up, but he didn't have Eddie's cell number. He wasn't even sure Eddie had a cell phone.

"Why don't you call whoever's picking you up and tell them we'll take you home?" Luke offered. "We're already in the car."

"All right, go down this road for a few miles. The house is on the right." Timothy figured they wouldn't recognize the place.

When they drove up, Luke parked in front of the house and said, "This is Eddie's house. I took him home once when his truck broke down. You're living with the janitor?"

Timothy jumped out of the car. "Yeah, I'm living with him. Thanks for the ride." Timothy got to the front steps when he heard the engine turn off.

"Luke and I don't care you're living with the janitor," Angie called out.

Timothy turned and saw the two head toward him on the porch.

"Eddie won't be home for a long time," Timothy said quickly. "And I've got homework to do."

All three turned around when they heard Eddie pull up in his pickup.

Chapter 13

"This is your lucky day, Timothy," Luke said. "I don't have football practice tonight and Eddie's here." He smiled like a joke so bad it was funny.

Before Timothy could say anything, Eddie got out of his pickup. "Good, good," he said. "Glad you found some friends to help. How about everyone grab a box or two out of the back and follow me."

Luke and Angie picked up a few boxes and followed Eddie toward the house. Timothy took too many and struggled to keep up with Luke. He dropped his load beside Luke's stack in one of the back rooms as Eddie hurried them along to get the rest. It took three loads to get everything out of the truck.

"What's in these boxes, anyway?" Luke asked after the final load.

"Some equipment for my project," said Eddie. He headed toward the kitchen.

"What project?" Luke and Angie said at the same time catching up to him.

"Don't you two have to go home?" Timothy asked, following them.

"I already texted my parents to tell them I'm with some of the football players," Luke said over his shoulder.

"I texted my mom and said I'm studying for the PSAT with some friends," said Angie. She didn't bother looking back at Timothy.

"Didn't you take that already?" Luke asked Angie as they went into the kitchen.

"Yeah, but I like taking tests a couple of times to see if I can get better," she said.

"Ah, the old competition ego," said Luke.

"Okay, so you both have excuses. But Eddie and I can take it from here. You both can go now," said Timothy. "Thanks again for the ride."

"We needed help and now we have some." Eddie said pulling some pots and pans out of the cabinets. "Since you two can stay, we'll have something to eat before we get to unpacking the boxes."

Timothy wondered if he had blacked out or something and missed a conversation with Eddie explaining why Luke and Angie were being treated like old friends. "What are you doing, Eddie?"

"Making a noodle dish." He poured already cooked pasta shells in a casserole dish along with olive oil, cut up strawberries, a slight sprinkle of cane sugar, yellow mustard, broken potato chips from a bag labeled "damaged," saltine crackers.

"You know what I mean," said Timothy.

Luke and Angie sat at the kitchen table as Eddie pulled bottles and jars out of the fridge and pantry.

"I trust them. Supper won't take long," said Eddie.

Timothy wasn't sure what to do. He didn't like Eddie making these kinds of decisions without him. He wanted to think he had some control over his life now that his dad was dead.

Timothy fled the kitchen and into the tower room. It seemed to be the least cluttered. He stood there thinking about his dad when he wasn't drunk. He tried to remember his mom when she was alive. He felt alone.

"Hey."

Timothy jumped at Angie's voice behind him. He had been there longer than he thought, but not enough to finish feeling sorry for himself.

"Come on back and let's eat."

Timothy shot her an angry look that said, Go away. She smiled and headed back to the kitchen. Timothy thought her smile came together like a party on her face. He waited a few seconds before following her. The smell of steamed pasta made his stomach growl. Angie smelled good too.

The finished dish had shredded cheddar, melted butter, previously cooked kidney beans, salt, and pepper from a grinder. At the last minute, he tossed in a bag of crushed cashews and walnuts. The iced water tasted cold as if coming from a glacier.

The food tasted good enough to limit conversation as everyone slurped up the noodles. Luke and Angie gossiped about school with Timothy keeping quiet. His bad mood got better with another helping of the pasta. Angie and Luke agreed to wash the dishes while Timothy followed Eddie into the room of boxes.

"Did I miss something? You know those two that well?" Timothy wished Eddie would slow down.

"You gotta let things happen," Eddie said, turning to face the teenager. He had his hands on his hips like Superman. "I know them well enough to trust them. I think they'll be good for our team."

"What team? When did we get a team?" Before Timothy could say anything more, Luke and Angie walked in.

"Kitchen's clean. Let's get to work," said Luke.

Timothy stood in front of the boxes and beside Eddie. "Why are you two so willing to help?"

"I knew where Eddie worked before he was a janitor," Angie said. "Plus, I'm very curious."

"I'm just following Angie," said Luke. "Besides, I like this house."

Angie gave Timothy that smile that kept leaving him confused. Luke didn't seem to care as he pulled a heavy looking piece of electronic equipment out of a box.

"What's this?" he said.

"Ask Eddie. I don't know what any of this stuff is." Timothy wondered how much electronic equipment they needed to launch the rocket. He looked around for Eddie, who had disappeared.

"He took a box and said he was going to the tower section of the house," said Angie. "He said all this stuff was for some project. What is it?"

Timothy ran off for the tower section with Luke and Angie following him. They found Eddie unloading large binders onto a long table.

Angie spoke first. "With all this equipment, this project looks complicated."

"It's a secret, special project," Timothy said.

"Okay, what's the *secret*, special project?" There was Angie again with the smile.

"It's up to Eddie to tell you. It's his project," said Timothy.

Eddie turned to Luke and Angie. "You two can't tell anyone ever."

"I'm not doing anything illegal," said Luke. "I've got my future to think about."

"Me too," said Angie.

"We're not doing anything illegal." Eddie grinned. "We'll just be breaking some rules."

"Yeah, some big rules," said Timothy.

"I'll also need to know what your parents would say if you help me with something you can't tell them about," said Eddie.

Angie and Luke looked at each other as if wondering how much they should lie to their parents.

Angie moved closer to Eddie. "How long will we be working on this project?"

"Not long. Maybe three or four months."

"I think it will be longer than that," spoke up Timothy.

Angie said, "I guess it doesn't matter. My parents might be okay as long as I tell them this has nothing to do with drugs or me getting pregnant. I can tell them it'll help me get into a college."

Timothy wished there were drugs and sex going on because that seemed more real—and less stressful—than launching a rocket.

"If I miss football practice, everyone will want to know where I am."

"We can work around football," said Eddie.

Angie waved her arm across the stacks of boxes littered around the room. "Based on the stuff we're seeing around here, you might as well tell us."

Luke held up one of the smaller boxes. "Forget about telling us. This box says 'Silo.' Let's go see what's in there."

Chapter 14

Eddie and Timothy exchanged glances and said nothing for several awkward seconds.

"We already know there's a silo at the end of the field. You can't miss it." Angie pointed in the general direction of it.

"We aren't hiding the fact that there's a silo," said Timothy.

"Except what might be in the silo," said Luke.

"In that other room where I found Timothy, I saw some of the boxes labeled with the names of old space programs," pursued Angie. "I'm more curious than ever about what's going on here with this special secret project."

Eddie turned toward Timothy and shrugged. "We might as well show them the silo and take a few of these boxes with us."

Timothy glared at Eddie. "What is it with you trusting people you barely know?"

"I trusted you when you showed up at my door Saturday morning," stated Eddie.

Timothy turned to Angie and Luke. "Both of you have got to be serious about this. You've gotta keep everything you see a secret from everyone," he pleaded.

"You don't trust us?" Angie stared at Timothy. Quickly her smile appeared again.

"I don't know. We only met today," said Timothy. He thought things were moving too fast.

"We have math class together. You see me in the hallways every day," said Angie. "And, Luke's my boyfriend so I can vouch for him."

"And, I can vouch for Angie vouching for me," said Luke.

"What does any of that have to do with trust?" Timothy wondered why he should care about the rocket. Afterall, it was Eddie's and not his. Yet, Timothy felt some responsibility since he provided his dad's rocket formula.

"I don't think you can stop me now from seeing what's in the silo," Angie said, still smiling. "Don't worry, we can keep this special project secret. Can't we, Luke?"

"Sure, Angie."

Timothy didn't feel that confident. But Eddie was already headed for the back door motioning for everyone to follow him.

Luke and Angie grabbed a few boxes marked "silo" and followed Eddie. Timothy didn't know what to do except grab a box and follow everyone. He didn't want to be alone in the house. He didn't want to be alone again.

Outside, Angie got ahead of everyone as they approached the roofless jeep. She tossed her box in the back and jumped into the front passenger seat next to Eddie. After tying down the boxes, Timothy and Luke got in the jeep as Eddie jolted it forward.

Eddie drove across the rutted field toward the tall silo, not bothering to take the longer and smoother gravel road. Whenever he hit a rut, which was often, Luke managed to hold on to his seat. Timothy kept losing his grip and ended up smacking back into his seat in his struggle to keep from being thrown out. He vowed to get a rope or something next time to tie himself down.

When Eddie stopped, everyone waited for him to slide out of his seat and lead the way to the silo. Timothy thought he looked a little unsteady on his feet. At the silo's metal door, Eddie pulled it open and led the way inside.

When Eddie flipped on the lights, Angie and Luke found themselves standing in front of a lot of white metal rising high above their heads.

Angie was the first to walk up and touch the structure. She ran her fingers gently across the smooth surface as if making sure it was real. Timothy and Eddie stood near the doorway, admiring the rocket. Timothy still had a hard time imagining this large rocket screaming out of the silo.

Luke strained his neck to see the top. "Wow. I thought you were showing us a model rocket. This is the real thing. Wow."

Speechless, Angie stood next to Luke and scanned the entire dimensions of the rocket.

"This is a *Redstone* rocket designed for a single-stage-to-orbit flight," Luke announced. "I read that only two other rockets were single-stage-to-orbit. One was used to launch the Russian unmanned space shuttle and the other was from a NASA-funded company."

"How'd you know that?" Angie still couldn't take her eyes off the rocket.

Luke looked around at other parts of the rocket. "Along with football, I like rockets. I read a lot about them. I got some model rockets at home that I fly."

Timothy looked at Eddie, surprised at what Luke knew. Timothy thought that maybe Eddie picked the right people.

Angie recovered first from seeing the rocket. "Let me get this straight. You really think you'll launch this flimsy rocket out of this old silo?"

"I'm finding this a little hard to believe, too," said Luke. "Outer space is a long way from down east North Carolina."

"We have a special fuel and engines thanks to Timothy's dad," Eddie announced. "It doesn't use toxic chemicals or need heavy equipment. Everything will be different when we launch this rocket."

This time it was Angie and Luke looking at each other trying to believe the story. The rocket loomed beside them, not to be ignored.

"I guess what you're saying is that nothing will explode like conventional rockets taking off," said Angie.

"And, you plan to control the rocket with all the equipment back at the house," Luke said.

"We'll need more equipment than that," said Eddie.

"Yeah, and a lot more people than us," said Luke. "I want to know where you got this thing. I thought the last *Redstone* was manufactured in the early sixties."

"I'm more interested to know how you got it in this silo," said Angie.

"Timothy and I will explain it all later."

"You better," Angie said as she went to her right to follow the curvature of the silo. Luke went left.

Timothy waited for the two to get out of earshot.

"What are we going to have them do?" Timothy whispered to Eddie.

"We currently have a lot of vacant positions."

"Fine, be funny. Who else do you plan on bringing on?"

"I'm still working on it," said Eddie.

"Look, I'm thinking we need to have a plan for all of this." Timothy's whispers were getting louder.

Eddie smiled. "Don't worry. It'll all come together some way."

"Nothing you're saying is reassuring." Timothy couldn't say anything more because Angie and Luke appeared from opposite sides of the rocket.

"I still can't believe you think this thing'll fly. How high will it go?" Luke kept up his look of amazement.

"It should reach at least low Earth orbit or LEO. Maybe higher," said Eddie.

"I like this. I'm in," said Luke.

"I'm in too. This is going to be great." Angie's face lit up as if a stage spotlight had found her on cue.

"Good. Now, let's move those boxes to the shed out back," said Eddie.

Timothy didn't like any of this. Even so, he helped with the boxes. When they got the last in the shed, he joined everyone at the jeep.

Angie looked straight at Eddie. "Why us?"

Eddie shrugged. "I don't know. I think you two would be good in a crisis. Launching a rocket is nothing but crises. And Luke already knows rockets."

"Who else do you plan to bring into this?" Angie glanced at Timothy for his reaction.

"I've contacted some of my retired NASA friends. I hope they'll be coming soon to help with this little project."

"Little it isn't," said Luke crossing his arms.

They climbed into the jeep. On the way back, Eddie took the gravel road, which wasn't as bumpy. He keeps true to his superstitions, Timothy thought.

Chapter 15

After Angie and Luke left, Timothy looked across the kitchen table at Eddie eating his grilled deli turkey doused in dill pickles, grape jam, and feta cheese. It was all pushed between two slices of sourdough bread.

Timothy had the same and he thought the soft, crusty bread was the best he'd ever eaten. "Where'd you buy this bread?"

"I made it. I knew a man who worked at the Edgar Cayce Health Center in Virginia Beach. He gave me part of his starter which was over fifty years old then. The starter has flavors I've never found anywhere else."

"It tastes pretty good for being that old," said Timothy taking another bite. He wanted to know who Edgar Cayce was, but was more interested in another slice of bread.

He looked up and for the first time noticed a small flat screen TV hanging on the kitchen wall near the ceiling. He didn't think someone could watch it for long without getting a neck ache.

"You watch that thing up there?" Timothy pointed at the TV.

"Not often," Eddie said taking another bite of his sandwich.

"You don't watch the news at supper?" Timothy took the last bite of his sandwich along with the rest of his cold water.

"I don't watch violence while I'm eating. The local news is all about crime and tragedy. A person should enjoy a meal in peace and quiet with conversation if there's one to be had."

"Okay, for conversation let's start with fixing things around here. The place could use some paint and I'm not sure the back porch will last much longer."

"A lot of things need a lot of things around here," Eddie grumbled. "Most of it can wait."

"Why are you in such a rush to launch this rocket?"

"Maybe I'm an impatient person." Eddie said finishing his sandwich.

"You've waited all this time. A little longer shouldn't matter."

Eddie wiped his face with his hand. "I'm not telling you everything, but I promise that I will tell you everything when the time comes. You'll have to trust me like I trusted you when you came here."

Timothy glared at Eddie. "Yeah, just like you trusted Luke and Angie. You haven't trusted me that much."

"I mostly trust you." Eddie smiled and wiped his hands on his shirt instead of the napkin Timothy gave him. After taking their dishes to the sink, Eddie reached between the table and wall and brought out a long plastic tube. Inside, he pulled out a roll of paper and unfolded it on the table.

It was a drawing of the *Redstone* with tiny writing and arrows pointing out each part of the rocket.

"This shows the inside skeleton structure of the rocket," Eddie explained. "I think some of what you need is already inside the rocket. I need to know what else you need for your engines to work."

Timothy hesitated, leaned closer to the drawings for almost two minutes. As Eddie cleaned the dishes, Timothy took a pencil from Eddie.

As if hypnotized, he drew metal canisters, some bell-shaped. He also drew lines representing tubes and wires connecting it all together. Forty minutes later he finished, realizing his dad had made him do the same sketches over and over.

Timothy stood up and stretched his back before announcing, "I still don't know why I'm here or what I'm doing or why you're not telling me everything."

"When we get home tomorrow night, we'll have a lot to do." Eddie gave Timothy a wink.

Timothy liked hearing the word "home." He also never saw anyone wink before. Timothy tried to wink back, but it felt more like he was in pain.

"When will the satellite be delivered?" Timothy asked.

"I've got some reading to do. Can you put the drawing back in the tube?" Eddie abruptly went to his bedroom.

Timothy watched him go and decided not to chase after him. After putting everything away, he turned on the kitchen TV and watched a black-and-white '60s sitcom about a talking horse. Yet, he kept thinking about the rocket.

What would it take to launch it? It was just so big, he thought. Mostly, he wondered what he would do after they launched the rocket.

After a while, Timothy checked the back door to make sure it was locked before he went to bed. At the door, he glanced through a window and outside spied a tall figure standing about ten feet away looking back at him.

Chapter 16

The man and Timothy spotted each other at the same time, except the man moved first. He took off around the side of the house as Timothy ran down the hallway, coming out onto the front porch. Just as the stranger was coming from the corner of the house.

The man headed for a dark car at the end of the driveway. All Timothy could think about was catching this man and finding out who he was. He was not thinking of the man being bigger and probably stronger than him or carrying a gun. Timothy ran down the front steps, not caring about any of this. He raced after the stranger not sure what he would do once he grabbed him.

Timothy was never going to catch him. The man was much faster and dove into the backseat of the car before Timothy could get anywhere near him. Another person drove the car away leaving Timothy standing in the driveway. But not before he spied a small light over the license plate showing "US Government" in block letters.

Timothy stood there in the darkness. Somewhere near the silo, he heard Eddie's owl give off a few hoots of criticism for not catching the guy.

Back at the house, he found Eddie asleep covered in soft blankets and looking like a small child. Timothy decided not to wake him and to go to bed himself. But not until he made sure all the doors were locked.

At dawn, Timothy found Eddie in the kitchen with a pan of scrambled eggs. On the table were two bowls of cornflakes with a dollop of ketchup in each. The table also had a glass of orange juice with green olives floating in the liquid.

Timothy took his plate and sat at the kitchen table. The eggs had rice, black eyed peas, and yellow mustard mixed in. "You missed all the excitement last night."

"What are you talking about?" Eddie sat at the table with his food.

"Right before I went to bed, I saw a man snooping out back. I chased him to the front, but he got away in a car with someone else driving. Their license plate said 'US Government.' That confirms who we're dealing with." Timothy added whole milk to his ketchup and cornflakes.

Instead of saying anything, Eddie took a bite of eggs followed by a spoonful of cornflakes. Ketchup dribbled down his chin.

After a few seconds of staring at Eddie, Timothy said, "We've got to do something about these spies."

Eddie stared back with the ketchup hanging on his chin. "I was trying to figure out what government agency they could be with. I guess launching that model rocket got the attention of someone, but not enough to arrest us or do a full-scale search of the property."

"Maybe someone's just curious," said Timothy.

Eddie nodded. "Could be. I don't think those men know what they're after, which helps us. I've got a plan."

"What is it?"

"A sort of deception. They're looking for something, so we'll give them something to find and maybe they'll leave us alone."

"Like what?"

"If they are looking for your dad's fuel, we'll make up a fake formula and leave it for them."

"We can't make it easy for them," Timothy said taking a mouthful of ketchup covered cornflakes.

"I'll bring some empty boxes home today and we'll set something up for this evening. This should be entertaining." Eddie finally wiped his chin—with his shirtsleeve.

Although Eddie didn't seem worried, Timothy definitely was. He let Eddie know it on the ride to school. Eddie didn't say much. He looked deep in thought about his plan and somehow this thinking helped him drive a little better.

At school between classes, Timothy kept looking outside for the mysterious man until lunchtime. He decided he wouldn't tell Angie and Luke about the stranger. He and Eddie would solve this problem on their own.

Chapter 17

Lunch meant Angie sitting with Luke and some of the football team players. Angie ignored them and instead watched Timothy, who stood in his usual spot leaning against the ledge of a cafeteria window. The ledge was tall and wide enough for him to use as a narrow table. He seemed very interested in what was going on outside the window.

Angie brushed her hair away from her face, thinking about getting it cut. Luke was laughing with his teammates about a joke she thought was stupid. To get away from the boyish laughter, she got up and stood behind Timothy, peering over his shoulder. He was looking out the window so intensely that he didn't notice her.

Past him, all Angie saw was a lawn of dead grass. Beyond was a sidewalk and beyond that a stand of tall, thin pine trees with a few birds darting in and out. Angie watched a small bird lay out a string of poop across the sidewalk, just missing two girls she despised. Very disappointing, she thought.

Timothy turned around and jumped. "What're you doing standing behind me? You almost made me choke."

"I was trying to see what you were looking at. Why don't you sit at a table like everyone else? Why don't you sit with Luke and me?" Angie looked around the lunchroom and realized few people were sitting in any one seat for long. Lunch was such a social minefield, she thought.

"Why are you stalking me?" Timothy asked.

"Because you're being antisocial."

"Timothy is always standing at the windowsill avoiding people," a girl said walking up to them. "Seems to be his thing."

Angie remembered Patty from physics class. This girl's hips had a lot of maturity and her hair, that she kept dyed a bluish blue, had too many little curls dancing all over her head when she talked. Like dancing ballerinas on her shoulders. Other than that, Angie wished she had her lips and long eyelashes. Maybe too her dark auburn skin tone.

"Leave us alone. We were having a private conversation," Timothy said.

Angie had no idea what Patty was doing there. Sure, they shared physics class, but they'd never talked before.

"I'm sorry to hear about your dad dying," said Patty to Timothy.

"Thanks." Timothy wondered who he was thanking. Patty's condolences or his dad's death.

"Your mom died a few years ago," continued Patty.

"Yeah, now you know my family history."

Patty pushed herself between Timothy and Angie. "Are you living alone?"

"No, I moved in with someone."

"Timothy, you don't need to answer her," said Angie. She got more confused by Patty asking these questions.

"Who did you move in with? I saw Luke give you two a ride after school. Are you living with Luke?"

"No, I'm not living with him," Timothy said. "He and Angie were just giving me a ride."

"If they give you a ride this afternoon, I want to go."

"No," Angie and Timothy said in unison.

"Yes," said Patty.

"You can't because we're working on a science project for school," Timothy said.

Angie glared at Timothy. "You don't have to explain anything to her."

Patty beamed. "Great. I need a group science project for my class. I want to join up."

"We don't need any more volunteers for our science project," said Timothy.

Patty smiled at them while holding her hands up in surrender mode. "All right, all right. Kidding over. Eddie, the janitor, told me to introduce myself to you two and Luke. He said I need to be on the 'team,' whatever that is."

A group of teenagers walking past crowded them closer together. Luke emerged from the throng.

"I'm Patty." She held out her hand to Luke.

Luke shook Patty's hand and looked at Angie. "What's going on? Lunch period is almost over."

"Eddie told her to introduce herself to us," said Angie.

"Seriously?" Luke glared at Timothy. "Does anyone even know her?"

"Hey, I'm standing right here and I'm the smartest one in physics class. That could be helpful for a science project," said Patty.

Angie moved in front of Patty. "What did Eddie tell you?"

"I don't know what you three are up to with Eddie, but I want in. I've kept my eye on Eddie for some time and I think he's up to something big. Did you know he used to work for NASA?"

"So, Eddie didn't really talk to you. Instead, you've been stalking him," Angie said.

"Yes, he did talk to me. And no, I'm not stalking him. At least not intentionally. I did this project for history class last year and the teacher told us to write about ordinary people. Everyone jumped on the Internet, but I thought the janitors here could be interesting. No one pays any attention to them. I talked to each one, and Eddie was the most interesting."

Angie didn't want to like Patty. Still, she had just broken up with a boy Angie hated. Also, Patty was really good in physics class.

Luke stared at Angie. "I can tell by that look that you're thinking about including her, aren't you?"

"Wait a minute," Timothy said a little too loudly. "First of all, this project is between Eddie and me. I never agreed on any volunteers and

I'm going to talk to Eddie before we bring in anymore from this high school."

"You talk to Eddie. Just so you know, Patty can help us a lot. She's really smart," Angie said.

Luke and Timothy stared at Angie as if she'd grown another head. Luke didn't waste any time giving up and shrugging. He had lost many other arguments with Angie.

"Don't anyone make any decisions until I talk to Eddie," said Timothy.

"All right, go talk to Eddie," Angie said. "It seems like you have some issues with him anyway."

Timothy marched off to class. He went in the wrong direction, so he had to turn around and walk past them again.

"So, what's this special project?" Patty put her right hand on hip as she stared at Luke and Angie.

"You'll find out," said Luke as he walked off.

Angie hated Patty's complexion. It didn't have the blemishes she had.

"It's a long story. We'll fill you in if Eddie says okay," said Angie.

The bell rang and they all headed in different directions. As Angie walked away from the window, she looked outside and saw a tall man dressed in black standing on the sidewalk looking at her. School security was already approaching the man, so she didn't think anything more of it.

Chapter 18

When his next class ended, Timothy followed Eddie into one of the custodian storage closets. Narrow and small, the place smelled of chemicals and wet mops. "Did you ask Patty to join us?" he said.

"Yeah, she's smart and will add a lot to our group," Eddie said while putting away his bucket of cleaning supplies.

"Why didn't you tell me about her? Am I a part of this thing or not?"

Eddie took some of the mops and brooms piled in a corner and hung them on a wall brace. "I don't like it when the other janitors just throw things in here. It only takes a few minutes to hang these things on the wall. And to answer your question, I'm not cutting you out. You can't do any recruiting because you don't know anyone because you always keep to yourself. This way you'll meet new people."

"I don't want to meet new people. And, what if I keep to myself? That doesn't mean I need to be the last one to know when you pick someone to be on this team of yours."

"It's still our team." Eddie stared at Timothy as he leaned on a broom with many bristles missing. "You're looking at this all wrong. I have the rocket and you have the formula and engines. When the time comes to launch, it'll just be you and me. The others are only to help us with the launch."

"That means I should know who you're picking to help us."

"You know them. Or you should. This is a pretty small school and you've had classes with them for years. They all know you."

"People know me because my dad died."

"They knew you before that. You've got more friends than you think."

"I don't know what you're talking about. Yeah, I've seen Angie, Luke, and Patty around school. What does this have to do with you picking people for this project without telling me first?"

Eddie continued to lean on the broom, staring at Timothy's feet as if realizing something. "I've been alone for most of my life and I've learned to do things by myself. I guess it's hard to break bad habits."

Timothy was getting sick from the ammonia and other chemical smells. "Could you just do this for me? Could you at least tell me who you're bringing on instead of me having to find out from everyone else? I don't feel like I have a say in anything."

Eddie hung up the broom. "When we launch the rocket, you'll have a whole lot to say about everything."

Timothy thought the broom should have been thrown away. He felt Eddie would say something else, but he didn't. "Who else at school are you planning to recruit for this project?"

"Patty was the last one I was thinking about. If I think someone else could help with the launch, I'll tell you first," Eddie said. He reached out and patted Timothy's left shoulder as if he wanted to confess more. "Now, get out of my way so I can get back to work and you can get to class."

Chapter 19

In physics class, Patty ignored what the teacher showed on the projector. She already understood the topic and instead doodled in her notebook. She tried to settle on what she would wear to school tomorrow. This morning she had changed clothes so much that nothing matched when she got to school.

She ended up wearing a bright-green blouse, a navy skirt, and deep-red flats that made a lot of the other girls call her weird looking. Patty decided just then that mismatched clothes were the best way to be different in her senior year and irritate those girls further.

She glanced a few desks over at Angie, who seemed just as bored with the lecture. From her angle, Patty saw Angie reading a small paperback inside her physics book. She hoped it wasn't a romance novel. She hated those.

As Mr. Greg explained topics she already knew, Patty wondered if he could be useful for Eddie's project. She always saw the teacher as different like teaching was a cover up for something else.

After class, Patty caught up to Angie. "When're going to tell me the long story?"

"We don't have time. Get it? Long story? We'll have to talk after school." Angie walked away before Patty could say anything more.

Patty thought about finding Eddie and asking him. Thinking about the team, she could not see any of them working together. They didn't seem to have anything in common. But maybe Eddie knew people more than rockets.

Patty left just before her last class ended. She wanted to make sure Luke, Angie, and Timothy didn't leave her behind. Her calculus teacher didn't say anything since Patty was acing the class. She found Luke's car and thought he could apply to the historical society for money to fix it up. While leaning against the car, she spied Angie heading her way.

"I'm ready for the long story," Patty said as Angie got closer.

Before Angie could say anything, Timothy ran up to them. "I talked to Eddie and he's going to let me know before we bring on any more people."

"He'd better tell me first," said Luke, who appeared out of nowhere. "If he keeps inviting people, I'll need a bigger car." He climbed into the driver's seat.

Timothy darted around the car and jumped into the front seat, leaving the backseat for the two girls. Patty and Angie looked at each other and shrugged as if agreeing that Timothy was being weird. How did he not know they wanted to be in the backseat so they could talk, they wondered?

As Luke maneuvered out of the parking lot, Angie blurted out, "There's a *Redstone* rocket involved."

"A real one," spoke up Luke.

"Wait. Patty, you've got to agree not to tell anyone about any of this," said Timothy in a panic.

"Hold up, everybody," said Patty raising her hands in the air. "How 'bout I talk to Eddie and he can tell me what he wants me to know. Cool?"

"Sounds good to me. I don't think I could explain this project, anyway," said Angie.

"You feel better, Timmy?" Patty smiled and winked at Angie.

"My name's Timothy." He tried to be stern.

"We're goin' to get along great, Timothy," said Patty, smiling with a wink toward Angie.

Angie did tell Patty as much as she knew while Luke drove up to an old house. Patty thought the place would look better painted a bright blue rather than the dusty brown. Eddie stood on the wide porch to greet them.

"Did they tell you about the project?" He asked as they approached.

"No, Angie and I got to talking about other things."

"All right, we'll get to it later. Luke and Angie, can you show Patty the house? Timothy and I have some stuff to put away."

Eddie led the way around the side of the house to a metal shed that seemed like the rust was holding it up.

"They're watching from the woods across the street," Eddie whispered, sliding open the metal door and producing an ear-splitting squeal of raw metal on rusty metal.

The shed shook so much that a haze of rust fell from various connections. Eddie stepped inside, but Timothy stayed outside. He thought a hard hat might be necessary.

"Come in here," Eddie beckoned.

Timothy stepped inside where wooden shelves sprouted from the dirt floor like the trees they once were. He figured they were the reason the metal shed didn't become a pile of metal debris. He noticed the chemicals from the basement was now in the shed and on the shelves.

"When did you move all these chemicals in here?"

"Yesterday. It'd be difficult launching the rocket with the house blown up," Eddie said.

He handed him a manila envelope. "You take this one and hide it somewhere outside the house. Here's a wooden box to put it in. I'll take the other folder, put it in this metal box, and hide it behind the shed."

Eddie skipped out of the shed. He was enjoying this clandestine spying too much, thought Timothy. The spying was making him way too nervous.

Timothy walked out of the shed and toward the house where he saw a thorny, crinkled bush with enough small bristly leaves at the bottom to hide the box. He then walked into the house, hoping the government men got a few cuts and scrapes when they took the box.

In the house, Eddie and Timothy found the others in the room beside the tower. Eddie explained how the tower would be the launch room and where they were would be Mission Control.

"I'm assuming you have backup power outside and antennas on the roof to capture different wavelengths," stated Patty.

"Yeah, I'm set up for at least one orbit," said Eddie.

"Orbit?" The other three spoke in unison.

"I thought this rocket went straight up and down like the original *Redstones* did," exclaimed Luke.

"With the new fuel and engines, I think we can go a little higher," said Eddie.

No one said anything for a few seconds. With a surprised look, Timothy stared at Eddie while Angie watched Timothy's reaction and Luke had a smile of excitement. Patty started rummaging in the binders lying around.

"I don't know how much of these books will help us," said Patty. "It appears we are working outside the norms for this rocket."

"This whole thing keeps getting crazy," said Luke. "I like it."

"If we're going to do this, then we need to devote a lot more time to learning how to launch a rocket," Angie said waving her hand across the electronic equipment.

"I don't know where to start with any of this," said Timothy. "You never said we're going into orbit."

"I didn't know it myself until I understood more about the fuel and engines," defended Eddie.

"I think we need to launch this thing," said Luke. "At least give it a shot."

Everyone was quiet for a few seconds until Patty spoke. "At least one thing is missing. I seem to be the only one who hasn't seen the rocket."

Eddie smiled at her and motioned with his head to follow him outside. Patty met him at the jeep and jumped in the front passenger seat.

Hearing someone running toward her, she looked back to see Timothy jumping in the backseat.

Patty relaxed in the jeep as Eddie headed across a rutted field. Ah, special treatment, she thought as she glanced back at Timothy trying desperately to hold on. When they pulled up to the silo, she looked up and saw a large barn owl on the top rim of the silo.

"He's my security system and friend," Eddie explained.

The owl stared down at Patty who stared back. After a few seconds, the owl closed his eyes as if bored with Patty.

"Apparently, my security system accepted you. Congratulations," said Eddie.

Patty went first into the silo. She walked up to the rocket, trying to steady her excitement. "This is something that doesn't belong in rural North Carolina," she said.

"I know you want to know how it got here," Timothy said, stepping up to her.

"I don't care. I only care that it's here." Patty looked back at Eddie, who was coming through the doorway. "It'll look beautiful going up. When're you going to launch?"

"Hopefully soon. I'll need your help along with the others. You in?"

"Seriously, what took you so long to invite me onto the team? My parents will be glad I have something to keep me busy."

"You've got to keep this a secret," said Timothy.

Patty narrowed her gaze. "None of this is illegal, is it?"

"No drugs, espionage, or terrorism. Just a simple launch of a single-stage-to-orbit *Redstone* rocket into Earth orbit," Eddie said.

"Yeah, that's pretty illegal. But I'm all right with it. I'm going to look around," said Patty, leaving Timothy and Eddie alone.

Their voices echoed in the silo as they argued about bringing her on. Timothy wasn't an ally. She figured she had to work on that. She came back around a few minutes later.

"I want to see the capsule on top," Patty said. "There's an elevator around the corner and a ladder in a metal housing on the outside of the silo."

"Hey, I haven't even seen the capsule yet," said Timothy.

"No one sees the capsule right now," said Eddie. "We'll do that when everyone understands the rocket better. That's the most important part."

"Also, the fuel," said Patty. "You using a solid? There's nothing here to for a liquid mixture like hydrogen and oxygen."

"We're using my rocket formula and engines," said Timothy. "They're not solid or chemical. They're bacteria."

Patty looked at Timothy as if he'd grown another nose. "All right then. Timmy, the rocket scientist."

Before he could say anything, Patty quickly stepped through the doorway and toward the jeep. Eddie followed her, leaving Timothy in frustration.

"I know you don't want to ride back with us, but it's a long walk to the house," Patty called back to Timothy.

He said nothing as he caught up to Patty and climbed into the passenger seat. She slipped into the backseat. Eddie kept to the dirt road, not the rutted field.

Patty wondered about the frail-looking janitor driving her to the old, worn house. Maybe his frailty was what made her think about death. She shook her head to get the thought out of her head.

Chapter 20

At the house, Eddie fixed a meal of bologna and cheese sandwiches, the good kind of bologna and the imported cheddar. It came with carrot sticks dipped in honey, red strawberries with salt and pepper, and a bowl of melted cheese, chocolate, and chopped up sardines. On the side were green olives and dill pickles. It all came with a stack of buttered crackers and cold Cheerwine soda.

While they ate, Angie attempted to sketch out a timeline for launch. When she was finished, her timeline would launch the rocket when they were all in college.

"You've got to cut out all that testing and learning time," said Eddie. "I can't wait around that long."

"Why?" Patty was still examining the different tastes in her mouth.

Timothy wanted to tell them about the spies, but Eddie told them first.

"Spying like cloak and dagger stuff?" Luke asked.

"No, like people coming to arrest us stuff," said Patty.

"No one's getting arrested," said Eddie. "Right now they're just curious."

"With people watching us, I guess we don't have much time. What date were you looking at?" Angie asked Eddie.

"In two months."

Luke rolled his eyes before saying, "That's doesn't leave much time. I guess it'll depend on when your NASA friends show up and how much they can help. Also, whether the football team wins and are playoff contenders."

"I don't think the football team ever had a winning season. Yet, that brings up a point. Remember, we're supposed to be going to school and keeping this project from our parents," said Angie. "We can't spend all of our time here without people getting suspicious."

"Why don't we forget about a date, learn what we can, and wait for the NASA group," said Patty.

This they agreed to. They spent the rest of the afternoon and into the evening pummeling Eddie with questions about the rocket and Timothy about the fuel and engines. For homework, they each took some documents home. Luke said the normal football practice on Wednesday had been cancelled so the coaches could go to a council meeting. They were trying to get more money for equipment. The three agreed to come back tomorrow afternoon.

After everyone left, Timothy didn't sleep much that night. He kept listening for someone trying to get into the house or roaming around outside. At daybreak, he went around to the side of the house and his box was gone. In the kitchen, he found Eddie making boiled eggs and fried canned tuna in olive oil for breakfast. Coffee was percolating.

"My box is gone too. I think we had success. Our deception should buy us several weeks as they try out the formula and it fails," said Eddie.

"Then what? Do we try another deception?"

"Let's wait and see how they react." Eddie said as he plated their food and poured two cups of coffee. "Yeah, they might come back, but we can't live our lives wondering what they or someone else might do. We need to focus on this launch."

Timothy ate thinking about all he had to do before launch. There were too many things, so he stopped thinking about them.

Going to school, Eddie's driving made Timothy so nervous he wanted to throw up. A few times he grabbed the steering wheel to keep from hitting the ditch.

"I drive better in the afternoon," said Eddie after another close mishap.

He's getting worse, thought Timothy. Fortunately, the rural roads had little traffic.

At lunchtime, Timothy joined Patty and Angie while Luke sat at another table arguing about something with his teammates.

"I'm excited about the project," said Patty.

"Don't talk so loud. People will hear you," Timothy scolded her.

"You worry too much. No one pays attention at lunch. All anyone wants is attention on themselves," Angie said as Luke came to their table.

"That reminds me. I know we're not supposed to be telling our parents, but do we want to go totally rogue and independent?" Patty chomped on a forkful of salad.

"You've already told your mother, haven't you?" Angie asked, eyeing Patty.

"I didn't tell her a lot. She's my mother, so I had to tell her something. But I didn't explain the whole thing. Ugh, stop staring at me. She would have found out anyway," Patty told the group.

"What if she tells other people? We've already got government people spying on us," said Timothy.

"Don't worry. We can trust my mother and my father won't know anything since he has another family in another state," said Patty.

"Hey, with Patty's mother we've got another team member," said Luke.

Timothy was not happy.

That afternoon after school, they had an early supper of spaghetti with Eddie's special sauce, which they all thought was the best they'd ever tasted. "A secret recipe from my Italian grandmother," was all he said when they asked about the ingredients.

"I've gotta make some calls," Eddie said, leaving the dishes for the four to clean up. "After you're done, take my jeep and check the rocket out again. There's something on top of it you should finally see."

Luke cleaned more dishes than the others like it was a contest and the prize was driving Eddie's jeep. He drove because no one else knew how to work a stick shift.

Before they left, Timothy checked in on Eddie. He was using his rotary landline with a flip phone lying on a nearby table. Eddie paused long enough to tell Timothy to go without him.

Timothy felt funny going to the silo without Eddie. He watched Eddie try to connect to people from his past. Timothy had no one to connect to except Eddie. Where were they going with all of this, Timothy thought as he left Eddie behind?

At the silo, Patty walked up to the rocket and placed her hand on the metal. She drew back as if she were a vampire touching sunlight. "I seriously can't believe this is here. In a field right in the middle of down east North Carolina."

Angie couldn't take her eyes off the tall metal object in front of her. "That's going to be a big thing to send up into the sky."

"It's going to be awesome to see this thing blast off," said Luke.

"Yeah, if we can get it out of this silo," said Timothy.

Luke said, "I can see that the dome opens and down there are hold-down bolts that'll blow away at launch. All we need is for the rocket to go straight for a couple of hundred feet out of the silo."

Pattie touched the rocket's smooth metal again. "Why the *Redstone*?"

"Eddie said in the fifties the *Redstone* was the most reliable rocket the U.S. had. It was simple in design and could be adapted for other uses like the *Mercury* launches," Timothy explained.

Luke peered underneath at the nozzle which jutted into a deep hole in the ground. "I read that *Redstones* were patterned after the German *V-2*. The *Redstone* had a simple autopilot inertial guidance system called the LEV-3. A special compartment held instrumentation and electronics like the guidance system, telemetry, and power supplies."

Patty joined the conversation. "Between the instrument compartment and capsule are ballast to improve stability in flight since it can be unstable at supersonic speeds," she said. "The extra ballast kept the rocket steady through the maximum forces or 'max Q,' as it was called."

"Wow, you two learned a lot from those documents," Angie said a little bitterly. She followed Patty who was walking around the rocket.

"If this is a true single-stage-to-orbit rocket, there'll be a lot of deadweight carried into orbit and a waste of thrust," said Luke.

"As the rocket gains in altitude, it'll use more and more of the rocket's infrastructure to help with thrust. My dad said the special engines would change the thrust-to-weight ratio," said Timothy.

"Where are the engines?"

"Eddie and I have to pick them up at my dad's place."

"I read there called electrogravitic. What is that?" Luke asked.

"They'll be eight of them around the inside with expandable tubes going out to the main nozzle. Their energy comes from counteraction with the negative energy off the Earth." Timothy was pleased that he understood this better.

"What negative energy from the Earth?" Luke said.

"My dad said the Earth uses positive energy to feed life onto the planet. It sheds negative energy from specific points across the Earth. Like the area we're in. The electrogravitic engines create an opposing force on the negative energy, like when two magnets repel each other."

"Hey, you guys," yelled Angie. "Let's go see what's at the top of this thing."

Chapter 21

Luke and Timothy found Angie and Patty examining the elevator. The narrow aluminum platform with thin metal railings represented a single seat. Cables reached to the top of the silo. It looked too self-made. The three stood aside and let Timothy avoid the elevator and step on a small platform and through the door in the silo wall.

He felt like he was crawling into a tunnel. Grabbing the wide rungs, he reached the top not too much out of breath. Timothy stepped through another door and found himself standing on an aluminum platform of solid ribbed flooring and high, thin guardrails. Like a stage, the platform spread out about five or six feet along both sides of the silo walls. The flooring narrowed toward the capsule like a silver carpet.

Nervous about being so high, Timothy waited by the door until the other three climbed up. Luke and Patty went past him toward the capsule except Angie who pushed Timothy forward.

"It's gorgeous. Looks like it belongs in a museum," said Patty.

"It's a *Mercury* space capsule and it looks new," said Luke puzzled.

"This isn't one of the original twenty that were built," Angie said. "This must be one of the later ones Eddie said was built during the Space Shuttle heyday. I read that if something happened to the Space Shuttle, this capsule was light and simple enough to be easily launched with a person or supplies."

Luke walked up to the capsule and pulled opened the hatch door. Hinges prevented it from slamming into the capsule's outer metal skin. The dark interior looked like the opening to a cavern.

"You go in first, here's a droplight," said Angie handing it to Timothy.

Timothy hooked it to the edge of the hatch and stepped inside. He wasn't sure where to put his feet while trying to avoid hitting his head. He landed with a thud in the single seat, lying on his back with his feet level with his head.

Sitting there, Timothy took a moment to accept that he was in a *Mercury* capsule on top of a *Redstone* rocket. A silver instrument panel dominated his view. Except, too many dials and switches confused him.

"I found a notebook," said Angie poking her head inside and handing it Timothy. He felt her breath flow across his face and thought she smelled like flowers.

"The retro pack at the bottom of the capsule has been removed," Angie said. "That's where the small thrusters were located to slow down the capsule for reentry. Also, the heat shield is gone. This thing isn't meant to come back to Earth in one piece."

Timothy pushed Angie back as he scrambled out of the seat. The enclosed space had already made him feel uneasy, particularly with Angie blocking the hatch. Knowing that he sat in what was a one-way trip into space didn't help.

Angie was slow moving and her hair tumbled across his face feeling like feathers. He turned his head slightly before she pulled out of the capsule making their faces inches apart.

"Here. I'll help you out." Angie held out her hand and Timothy took it, even though he didn't need it.

Standing outside the capsule and as an excuse for hurrying out, Timothy said, "That seat was uncomfortable." He hoped no one noticed the squeak in his voice.

Angie stepped inside and sat in the seat. "Some items have been removed to make extra space in this capsule. I think some of the equipment Eddie has at the house is going in here."

Timothy wondered if the extra space was for Eddie's special satellite.

"Does that notebook say anything about the dimensions of the capsule?" Patty asked.

"It's a little over six feet at the base and the outer shell is made of titanium," Angie replied. "Instruments and communication equipment sit on the pedestal that juts up from the floor. Around my feet are environmental suites and oxygen supplies. A cooling duct is on the bottom left with boxed controls on either side."

Angie climbed out and Patty went in with the notebook. Angie leaned her head inside the hatch. "The navigation controls below the instrument panel have a scope display, path indicator, and chart board," she told Patty. "Mostly the capsule was guided by a feed from ground stations to the guidance panels."

Timothy watched Luke scan the outside of the capsule as if looking for some treasure.

"This thing has jets in the cone." Luke had found a step stool to see the top better. "I think someone took out the parachute."

Timothy was torn between listening to what Luke was discovering and what Angie and Patty were saying. Mostly, Timothy stayed away from the guardrails that didn't look that sturdy to him.

"At least this capsule has a better window configuration," Patty called out. "That was one of the biggest complaints about the first *Mercury* capsules. All the astronauts had were two small side portholes. Later modules like this one had a trapezoid window that ran along the floor in front and near the pedestal. There's also an observation window at the top and a small screen at the bottom of the instrument panel connected to a periscope. Lots of opportunities to see things."

The conversations continued for several minutes until Patty crawled out and Luke went in. Being larger, he struggled to get in the seat.

"It looks in good shape to fly," he said. "But, hard to get in and out of."

Luke climbed out and suggested that Timothy try getting in again. But Timothy couldn't will himself to climb back in. He started to sweat and didn't know how anyone could live in such a tight space. He turned around and the others were leaving.

Angie told Timothy, "You can come back and study the capsule later. Let's get back to the house."

On the way back, the other three talked about the capsule while Timothy kept quiet. It seemed surreal to him. In the house, they found Eddie at the kitchen table with a cup of black coffee. He added two teaspoons of honey to it.

"Won't that coffee keep you up all night?" Luke said, rummaging through the cabinets before finding some chips.

"When I first worked for NASA, I was taking care of my parents and working a night auditor job. Over the years, I took so much caffeine in pills and drinks that I got immune."

Timothy sat at the table across from Eddie. "Why didn't you come with us to see the capsule?"

Luke sat down too and dug into the bag of chips. Angie and Patty stood nearby, leaning against the counter and whispering to each other. Timothy couldn't hear what they were saying with Luke's munching.

"I wanted the four of you to explore it without me there to answer your questions. Make some discoveries on your own," said Eddie.

"You said you had a special satellite you plan on launching into space. I guess you're putting it in that capsule. What is it?" asked Timothy.

"I plan on telling everyone before we launch."

Timothy got angry about Eddie's secret. This wasn't a good habit to get into when trying to launch a rocket into space as a team, he thought.

Chapter 22

That night after everyone left, Eddie proposed an outing for the next day. Luke had football practice and no way to get out of it; Angie had to be home when her mom and dad switched places for the weekend; and Patty had to do something with her mother to keep her happy.

In the kitchen, Eddie said, "We need to find the rocket engines that your dad wrote about in his notes."

"I don't know where they are. All I remember was him working on them in the workshop." Timothy kept silent about it being the same workshop where he found his dad.

"He must have hidden them somewhere around the place."

"Yeah, except I don't know where," Timothy said grimly. "I came home from school one day and he said they were all put away. He just never said where. He said he was afraid someone was spying on him. I didn't take him seriously, though." He paused for a moment. "Wait a minute. Do you think they were the same people who are spying on us now?"

"Maybe," said Eddie. "We can't worry about that. We need to find the engines. Let's get to bed. We have a long day tomorrow."

"You don't want the others to come?"

"I think we need to do this ourselves. They can help later to bring the engines here, after we find them."

Timothy went to bed, excited that it would be just the two of them. It made him a little less afraid about going back home.

The next day, Timothy and Eddie left school after lunch. They stopped along the way for Timothy to get a hot black coffee while Eddie had a MoonPie and a bottle of Cheerwine. Timothy needed the caffeine for courage to go back to his dad's house. Eddie shared half his MoonPie.

They passed fields of tobacco, corn, and a lot of tall pine trees. The farther east they went, the more numerous were the small streams that snaked their way under narrow concrete bridges. Timothy tried to imagine being out there when the rocket soared overhead, heading over the Atlantic and into space. At least if it crashed, he thought, there was little chance of it falling on anyone. Hardly anyone lived out this far.

He tried to think of things like that so he wouldn't be reminded of their destination—if they made it there. Eddie drove all over the road. Timothy considered taking over the driving, but he already was stressed out enough and wasn't sure he could do any better.

Less than a mile from his dad's place, Timothy considered jumping out, except he worried Eddie would run over him. Before he could do anything, Eddie drove around a slight bend and Timothy's house popped into view.

Timothy sat in the pickup sipping his coffee until Eddie jerked the passenger door open.

"I'm not going in there alone," said Eddie.

Timothy reluctantly led the way into the house where they found evidence of animals living there.

"Probably raccoons and squirrels. Could be mice and snakes. Maybe opossums, too. Watch where you put your hands and feet," said Eddie.

"I haven't been gone that long for this to happen."

"You're near the woods. They were probably lying out there waiting for you to leave."

To Timothy, his home had turned into an abandoned shack. Without electricity and with opened windows, the outside had filtered inside. Dried leaves tossed themselves around the droppings of small animals. From unknown places came the smell of larger animals that had lived in the house.

Timothy and Eddie looked around and made a lot of noise to chase away anything that could still live in the house. There was some scurrying of tiny clawed feet that lasted a few minutes.

"Do you have any hint at where the engines might be?" Eddie had come from the bedrooms empty handed.

Timothy was embarrassed that he didn't know. He got angry at his dad, maybe with his mom too, for keeping secrets from him. His mom died before telling him how to deal with his dad and his drunk dad made talking difficult.

"Maybe they're somewhere near the toolshed," said Timothy.

"Okay, let's look out there," said Eddie.

Timothy hesitated.

"You want to stay here?" Eddie asked.

"No, let's go." Timothy led the way across the lawn. Yet, at the shed door he slowed down and let Eddie take the lead to go inside the shed. Timothy stood in the open doorway, staring at the spot where he had found his father.

The beach chair he died in was still there. On it lay his blanket and a short pillow. Fragments of the liquor bottle he had smashed against the wall that morning still littered the floor. Among the broken glass, a piece of paper had fallen in the leftover alcohol.

Back when he had found his dad, Timothy didn't try to get the paper out of the broken glass and alcohol bath it was in. He didn't care about it.

He recalled touching his dad's stiff hands to get the manila folder. The last time they had touched was at a playground when his mother was still alive. When she died, there was no more touching. Timothy wondered if children and parents everywhere stop touching when someone close to them dies.

"What are you doing?" Eddie stared at Timothy, who was still standing in the doorway.

Timothy lied. "Give me a minute. I'm trying to remember the things my dad said."

His dad had to have given him a clue as to where he hid the engines, Timothy thought. But he couldn't remember. It occurred to him suddenly, did his dad not trust him? If he did, why didn't he tell his son where he hid the engines? There was nothing in his notes.

"What do you remember?" Eddie asked.

Angry at the possibility his dad didn't trust him, Timothy walked over to the beach chair. He threw the blanket and pillow off. He wasn't sure what he was looking for; maybe he just wanted to get rid of his dad's final resting place.

Timothy flipped the chair over and felt good about that. He kicked the chair toward the middle of the room with his foot to get it away from where his father had kept it. That felt better. Eddie yelled out, pointing to an envelope taped to the underside.

Timothy stood there clenching and unclenching his fists as Eddie came over and ripped the envelope off. He took it outside where there was better light. Timothy followed, avoiding the chair as if it was diseased.

"I'll wait out here if you want to finish attacking the chair or anything else inside," said Eddie.

"Give me the envelope. I'll open it."

Timothy carefully pulled out a single piece of paper. It had the layout of the house where Timothy had grown up. The same one he was now facing with Eddie.

"I see nothing unusual," said Eddie looking over Timothy's shoulder.

Timothy looked at the layout for a few seconds or so before answering. "Inside the house, the kitchen is smaller than it looks from the outside."

They both went into the house and opened all the cabinet doors. They pulled out the refrigerator and stove without finding any special door. Frustrated, Timothy kicked at the pantry door, but it won. He stumbled backward and fell against the opposite wall which collapsed around him. Timothy tumbled onto a tiled floor.

Eddie climbed in, nearly stepping on Timothy who was trying to stand up. Eddie found a light switch where one should be. A sea of naked bulbs hung from a low ceiling, bathing the room in raw light. Before them on the floor were sixteen long, narrow wooden crates. They looked like coffins to Timothy.

"This place is cleaner than the rest of the house," said Eddie. "It's sealed all around and has heating and air conditioning. There's the door to the room."

"Yeah, if I had known about this place, I would have stayed around longer." Timothy didn't tell Eddie that the door led into what used to be his bedroom closet.

Eddie went to the pickup and returned with a long screwdriver and a small hammer. A few knocks on one of the crates and Timothy pulled open the heavy lid. He reached in through packing peanuts to lift one end of a seven-foot-tall aluminum cylinder. His end had an exhaust nozzle. Eddie dug through the peanuts and found the other end that had metal fasteners to latch it onto an upper portion.

"So, two of them coupled together make eight engines," said Eddie.

Timothy placed the cylinder on top of the peanuts and stepped back. He felt a rush of energy and confidence with their progress.

"This cylinder looks like it could be made of graphene," said Eddie.

"Yeah, that's what my dad said. He told me that two-dimensional crystal graphene is the thinnest, lightest, and strongest material to use."

"Harder than diamond and steel, graphene is thick and flexible, transparent, and can conduct electricity better than copper," Eddie said as if reciting a line from a textbook. "How did he get this material?"

Eddie's question brought in a memory to Timothy. One about his parents having a rare argument. His dad had found the planks of material used in the engines that his mom had hid. They were Mom's, Timothy realized. What did she know about any of this?

Since Timothy did not answer, Eddie continued. "Graphene can extract hydrogen from the atmosphere."

Timothy finally said, "Two of these coupled together will make each engine eleven feet tall."

"Ah, a good prime number," said Eddie. "Is there more to this?"

"You think we can strap these engines to the inside of the rocket?" Timothy suddenly wasn't sure of anything.

"That's an easy thing. There are already some clamps and binding straps inside the rocket. As if it was made for these engines."

Surveying the room, they spied a smaller room tucked in the corner. The door was tight to open, but unlocked. A rubber seal kept this room cooler than the other room. Inside were eight, three-by-three-by-three-foot wooden boxes. Hanging from the ceiling was a thick three-ring binder filled with sheet protectors holding a volume of papers.

"Both rooms are climate controlled," said Eddie.

"That must be what the solar panels on the roof are for. There's a huge box on the other side of the house that is probably the heating and cooling unit."

Timothy untied the binder and the two of them stood there reading the paperwork. Timothy recognized his dad's small scrawl.

The smaller boxes hold bacteria that came from mineral sediment along the Tar-Pamlico River Basin. The ocean moves trace elements of salt up the Pamlico River that react with the mud and organic material flowing down from the forests on the Tar River. On the shoreline, we stuck electrodes with a weak electrical charge into the mud and varied the voltage while twisting the electrodes. Two versions of Shewanella and Geobacter bacteria can be enticed out of the marine mud. They feed on the electricity and excrete electricity they don't want. They are the best choice as a catalyst for fuel.

Eddie looked at Timothy. "I just realized we'll be using something alive. This makes the fuel less predictable because bacteria can introduce a level of chaos."

"Liquid chemicals will be introduced to help make the bacteria less likely to go in a different direction. Most of the chemicals are mica, sulfur, and iron dust," Timothy explained, remembering this from his dad. He wanted to know from the note who "we" were.

They both exchanged glances as they breathed in the clean air of the small room, which was getting dirty from the hole in the wall Timothy created. They shut the smaller room's door tightly and closed off the hole in the wall with shower curtains from the bathrooms and masking tape from the tool shed.

Sitting on the front porch steps with the binder, Eddie asked, "Is this really how it's going to all work?"

Timothy didn't know why his dad didn't type things into a computer. He took the binder and read:

The Earth produces and emits different types of electricity. The bacteria create heat that mixes ion charges to create exotic and mutant forms of the existing bacteria.

"Sounds like mixing spices and herbs with raw vegetables to create a different kind of plant," Eddie said, staring at Timothy as if he was wearing a tiara. "Where did your dad learn all this?"

Timothy didn't answer because he didn't know and didn't want to tell Eddie that. He wanted to keep believing his dad was an alien from another planet. How could a drunk know any of this? Did it all come from the other person helping his dad? Timothy read further from the binder.

Microbial species communicate by producing protein nanofilaments. In the soil, they're highly conductive, living on iron and other hard metals for oxygen because no oxygen exists in the seabed. The bacteria produce oxygen and energy by joining other nanofilaments. The bacteria continue this relationship from the sea, to the vials, and finally as thrust for a rocket.

"What I know about biosensing cells is that they can detect specific molecules in their immediate environment to produce an output in response," Eddie said.

"Those boxes must hold this bacteria fuel, the same stuff in the vials we used to launch the model rocket. We've got to make sure the engines are installed correctly to use this fuel."

They continued reading until Timothy realized an hour had passed. He stood up to stretch his neck and back and had to help Eddie up to do the same.

"This explains a lot," said Eddie.

Timothy didn't know what to say. He didn't know his dad knew so much. If he did, why did he drink all the time? More importantly, how did his dad know all of this? What role did his mom play in all of this?

"We've gotta be careful moving these boxes to the silo. We can do that with a better truck than mine," said Eddie. "We'll plan everything for Saturday. I'll rent a truck and the others should be able to get away."

"Will your NASA friends be here to help?" Timothy wished he knew more about Eddie's life.

"No, but when they get here they won't be surprised to see the *Redstone*."

Chapter 23

On the way back, Timothy fell asleep in the pickup from the stress of visiting his old home. At the farmhouse, he helped Eddie get things ready to store the engine crates and bacteria fuel. Supper were peanut butter and grape jam sandwiches, salty chips, and orange juice. He went to bed early, leaving Eddie to call the other three about plans for Saturday.

Timothy still hadn't fully recovered from his stress of the previous day when Eddie drove him to school. During the day, he avoided the others not wanting to answer questions about his old home. Timothy thought this might have led Eddie to make plans for him that Friday night.

After supper, Eddie didn't drive Timothy to the hardware store for supplies like he said. Instead, he stopped in front of the high school football field. A game was about to start.

"Here's some money for food and drink," he said, handing Timothy a twenty-dollar bill.

Timothy refused it. "I don't want to go to the football game."

"I know you don't, but you need some downtime after yesterday."

"Can you blame me? Animals are living where I used to live," Timothy said, remaining in the pickup. He still could not believe it had been just over a week since his dad died, leaving him not sure where his life was going.

"You sure it wasn't because you saw where your dad died? Go enjoy yourself at the game. You can sit with the girls and root Luke on."

"What would going to a football game do? Besides, I've never been to one before."

Eddie looked incredulous. "You've never gone to a football game?"

"I never had a ride." Timothy lied. He never had anyone to go with.

"At least try to enjoy yourself. Now get out. I really am going to the hardware store."

Eddie drove off, leaving Timothy to buy a ticket and walk toward the crowded bleachers. He sat near the top where there were fewer people.

Most sat close to the sidelines and this was where he spied Angie and Patty among other classmates. Before he could yell to get their attention, the band played and the teams ran onto the field amid a lot of cheering and standing.

As the game progressed, people changed seats a lot. Timothy did not think anyone was watching the game. He refound Angie and Patty several times until he finally gave up trying to get their attention.

At halftime, he jumped when Angie tapped his shoulder from behind. She had been sitting quietly behind him. For how long, he had no idea.

Angie flashed a big smile at Timothy's surprise. "Why didn't you join us?"

"I kept losing you and Patty in the crowd."

"I thought you didn't go to football games," said Patty, who was sitting next to Angie.

"I *don't* go to football games. Eddie dropped me off here. I don't know why."

"He told us you needed a break, some downtime. From what?" Patty asked, sitting next to Timothy.

"You and Eddie went to your old home to search for the rocket engines," said Angie sitting on the other side.

"Shut up," Timothy snapped. "You can't talk about that stuff out here in the open. And he shouldn't have told you about us going back there."

"We'd find out, anyway. We need to go there and get the engines tomorrow," said Patty.

Angie leaned closer to Timothy. "I know it was hard going back there, but keeping it to yourself won't help."

Timothy wanted to tell them how he wished he never had a home. He focused on Angie's brown eyes. She smiled again and Timothy looked away before he thought of her as more than a friend.

Several people crowded past them, so Angie suggested a different location to watch the rest of the game. She and Patty led Timothy to the back of the press box where Angie convinced another teenager she knew to let them in.

"He's in one of my classes. He and Luke are friends," Angie explained.

Inside, the other teenager went back to writing notes about the game for the school newsletter. Angie, Patty, and Timothy sat in the corner and away from about five people leaning over microphones while listening on headsets. Everyone focused on the field below ignoring the three teenagers.

Despite the crowd in the press box, Timothy felt like he was alone with Angie and Patty, which he enjoyed. He felt comfortable with them as they talked about who liked who in school and how the subjects were too easy. They drew him into their conversation until asking about his love life.

"No, I never asked any girl to go out," he said firmly. "I stayed home to watch my dad."

"He taught you a lot about the fuel and engines," Patty stated as the roar from the stadiums caused the women and men in the press box to talk faster into their microphones.

"When he wasn't too drunk, he told me a lot." Timothy kept talking, unable to stop himself as he explained how his dad said everything would work together – the rocket engines, the formula for the fuel, and his destiny. The last part, he wasn't sure about.

He talked about his mom and how she was always pushing him to do better in school. He never liked school and wanted to stay home with her and dad and go to the Crystal Coast for a day at the beach. When they went, his dad helped him build tall, round towers in the sand or his mom sat with him on the edge of the ocean where the waves lapped at their feet.

When he finished, Timothy let out a sigh and said, "Thanks for listening to me." He looked at the football field. People were leaving. "The game's over?"

"Yeah, once you get to talking, there's no stopping you," said Patty.

"Who won?" Timothy asked, following the two out the press box and toward the school. They soon caught up to the home team who headed to the showers.

"Hey, Timothy wants to know who won," Angie said when they found Luke.

Several of the players laughed. "Don't let them bug you," Luke told Timothy. "We don't usually win."

"You mean you won a game this year?" Angie wore a broad smile that filled her face.

One of the players proudly said, "We won two games this year."

"Yeah, but one was a forfeit 'cause the other team had an ineligible player," someone else chimed in.

Angie got up close to Luke. "Patty and I are riding together. We have to get to those places we call home. Timothy needs a ride."

"Yeah, Timothy. You're coming home with me," said Luke.

"What happened with Eddie?" Timothy tried to tone down his panic.

"Nothing. He thought we could bond." Luke let out a laugh. "Just kidding. Eddie thought you needed a break. So, relax. My mom will make us something to eat and we'll hang out. You're sleeping at my place. We probably have better beds and my mom likes making breakfast 'cause my dad and brother love to eat it."

Timothy watched Angie and Patty disappear into the night. When he turned around, Luke had gone into the locker rooms. There was nothing else to do except wait at Luke's car. Standing there, he felt very alone. He wished he was still in the press box with Angie and Patty. He wanted to feel free like that again. Maybe after they launched the rocket there would be time.

He felt the responsibility just then. A weight on him that this was serious business launching a rocket and he had to figure out how to deal with it all.

Even with the bright parking lot lights, Timothy could see Orion overhead. He stared at the waning gibbous moon and wondered if people would ever get back there. He was glad Luke came alone and wasn't giving anyone else a ride.

"How'd I do in the game? Wasn't I awesome?"

"Yeah, you were great." Timothy didn't even know what Luke's number was.

"Yeah, they didn't play me. Thanks for the empty compliment."

"Sorry."

"I'm just giving you a hard time. It's no problem. I'm pissed that the coach didn't play me since we were losing, anyway."

Timothy sighed. "I don't know anything about where you live. Can't you take me back to Eddie's?"

"Don't worry. It'll be great. My parents aren't that bad and we have an extra bedroom."

Luke talked about football during the rest of the drive, as if he were trying to convince himself he liked it. At his house, Timothy met Luke's younger brother Roger, who barely raised his head out of a gaming tablet. His parents argued with Luke about why the coach didn't play him. How was he going to get a football scholarship?

Luke's mom gave the two of them a bowl of buttered spaghetti since everyone had already eaten. In the living room, Luke's parents discussed what was on TV, agreeing that there were too many reality shows. Luke beat Timothy at several online games until they both decided Timothy had no experience with computer gaming.

Not long after, Timothy went to bed. Luke was right. The bed in the guest room was better than his bed at Eddie's.

Timothy slept with a feeling of wanting. It had been so long since he was part of a family like Luke's that he worried one day he would be the same as Eddie, someone without one. Alone, trying to achieve something that might not be achievable. Timothy dreamed about Angie in a spacesuit looking for his rocket. In the morning, he had waffles with butter, bacon, and orange juice. It became his favorite breakfast food.

Chapter 24

Saturday morning, Luke took Angie and Timothy in a rented box truck with Patty following, driving Eddie in his pickup. Timothy said nothing except where to go.

When they pulled up to the house, Angie said, "This place isn't that bad."

"It's unlivable. Let's leave it at that," Timothy said, getting out and walking to the house. He struggled with embarrassment thinking that he once lived there.

He plowed through the kitchen, tore down the makeshift door, and waited in the hidden room surrounded by the long, narrow crates. He wished there were more people so they could get the job done quicker and leave this place that used to be his home. He didn't want to come back, ever.

One by one, each person stepped into the hidden room without saying anything as if they had entered a hallowed room. Eddie was the last to enter.

"Inside each crate is half an engine. We'll load them in first," said Eddie. "In the back room are smaller boxes that we'll load last."

Luke stared at Timothy. "What's in the smaller boxes? They aren't going to blow up if I hit a bump, are they?"

"There's nothing explosive in them," Timothy answered hesitantly.

Angie crossed her arms and stepped in front of Timothy. "Then what's in the smaller boxes?"

"Bacteria," said Timothy. He couldn't help answering Angie. He could smell her sweet breath.

"Aha! That's it!" Patty approached the small room. "From what I've read, the bacteria are the secret ingredient. I've always thought bacteria controlled everything on this planet. If you think about it, every living thing has bacteria in it. Without it, living things like humans couldn't survive."

"Are the bacteria packed good inside those boxes? I don't want to get an infection." Luke said, worried and ignoring Patty's scientific enthusiasm.

"Each box contains vials secured in packaging foam," said Timothy. "My dad showed them to me once. The bacteria are floating in an amniotic fluid, keeping them in suspended animation until they're put in the engines and activated."

"What brings them alive?" Angie pointed to the small room.

"A short charge of electricity causes some of the bacteria to come alive," Timothy explained. "They build filaments and bring the rest of the bacteria alive."

"I'm with Luke on this. If these are bacteria, can we get infected?" warned Angie.

Timothy wondered what type of disease the bacteria would cause if they got out and spread. Surely his dad wouldn't be part of an epidemic. Then he remembered, "These are naturally occurring in the sand along the shoreline not far from here."

"The oceans are thought to contain an unknown number of bacteria that we never dreamed of. These could be some of the exotic ones," said Patty. "Do these bacteria need to be kept dry, cool, or what?" Patty opened the door to the small room, too curious not to.

"They can't be too hot or cold. They're safe as long as the seal on the vials is unbroken."

Luke asked, "How do we get them in the engines?"

"The vials go inside holders at the top of each engine. During ignition, they pop open and dump the bacteria through aluminum tubes to a round steel tank," Timothy said confidently.

"How are the bacteria controlled in the engines?" Angie asked while joining Patty in front of the small boxes.

"Chemicals are added as the bacteria come alive. How much bacteria are moving down depends on the voltage. The liquid chemicals are fed with the bacteria acting like a depressant to keep them calm and controlled," answered Timothy.

Angie added, "The batteries make the spark to start the engines. Like a starter in a car engine. And, the bacteria come alive with electricity like yeast put in warm water."

"I saw an experiment once where someone stuck an electrode in dirt and the bacteria ate the electricity," said Luke.

"These bacteria learned to extract bare electrons from rocks, metal, and mud out of the saltwater to survive. They can change electricity into a purer form," Timothy grew more confident in what he was supposed to know. Almost as if his dad was whispering these things in his ear.

"So, the bacteria in the vials essentially eat and excrete electricity. How does this work with negative energy coming off the Earth like I read?" Angie came back to Timothy.

"It's not just the bacteria doing the work. The shape of the engine and everything inside all work together. There's a pulling action that reverses and rides the negative energy coming off Earth." Timothy answered, enjoying that he knew the answers. "How much pull and push depends on the release of bacteria and chemicals."

"In biology, life is nothing but a flow of electrons." Patty didn't look at anyone, as if she was in her own world of scientific discovery.

"In the engines, the bacteria create a field of anti-negative electrons against the negative electrons coming from the Earth. This is how the rocket rises, by pushing a wave of anti-negative energy against the negative energy the Earth is shedding."

"Yeah, that's it," Patty said. "Biology contributes to this unknown science."

"A truly different concept," Patty continued after a pause, still being the scientist. "That there are anti-negative and anti-positive electrons that are opposite of the negative and positive. Normally you'd think anti-negative is positive and anti-positive is negative. Except these anti-energies aren't built in the standard fashion we think of."

"There should be more research in all of this," said Luke. "However, whether the bacteria are the rulers of the planet or not, I only care that they make the engines run. We're wasting time. Let's move these boxes."

Everyone got to work carrying the boxes to the truck. Timothy couldn't avoid being sad that his dad wasn't there. The place kept giving him memories he kept trying to forget.

They should have brought a bigger box truck. The engines and bacteria wouldn't have fit, except Angie had a talent for packing. When they were done, Timothy went back and stood in the hidden room.

All the crates were gone and he stood in the emptiness realizing they were one more step toward launch. It was one week ago that he knocked on Eddie's door. Luke came back looking for him.

"What are you doing? Let's go," he said jingling the keys.

"I wanted to take one more look around," said Timothy. He thought it could be the last time he would be there.

"Except the spiders, mice, and other animals want us out of here," said Angie, coming up behind Luke.

As if on cue, they all heard the skittering of tiny feet somewhere in the house. Timothy was the first to reach the box truck. He wouldn't tell anyone that it was like the ghost of his dad was pushing him away from the house toward this new adventure.

Chapter 25

At Eddie's house, everyone carefully placed the crates of bacteria inside a small room without windows. From other places in the house, they brought in a humidifier, fans, and temperature gauges to monitor the room's climate. The next stop was the silo.

The five of them cleaned out one of the metal sheds, making it more like a small house and insulated so the weather wouldn't affect the crates' contents.

"How are we getting these things inside the rocket?" Luke asked when they finished.

"We'll use the winch and lever at the top of the silo," Eddie replied. "Cables go from there to an outside, gas-run pulley system. It's next to the electric motor I use to run the elevator."

"Were the winch and lever used to put the rocket in the silo?"

"No, that was done by a large crane. The winch and lever are left over from when this was a working silo. They were used to lift a silage unloader to the top so corn silage could be blown in. Then, the unloader was set down on the silage to blow it down the chute as cow feed. The winch and lever are more than strong enough to lift the engines."

"I hope the set up still works," said Luke.

"Most of the parts have been replaced and it operates like new." Eddie surveyed the crates that were lined up in the shed. "Everything seems to be ready for when my NASA group comes next weekend. I hope we can get the engines inside the rocket then."

"This is moving pretty fast," said Luke. "Maybe we *can* launch in a few months."

Knowing that Luke could be right, Timothy's anxiety made his stomach rumble.

They opened the crates and examined how to connect the engine halves. As afternoon became evening, they studied the engines with more understanding. Timothy wondered if they were fooling themselves so they would feel like they knew what they were doing.

After carefully sealing up the engines, they went to the house where Eddie made baked beans consisting of molasses, brown sugar, cinnamon, nutmeg, apple cider vinegar, chopped walnuts, and olive oil. He poured the bean mixture over a bowl of white rice and topped it all off with cut-up red grapes, smashed blueberries, and sliced strawberries. A dollop of cream cheese and a splat of vanilla extract settled on top. He also sprinkled cane sugar and drizzled olive oil over asparagus spears and broccoli flowers that he baked in the oven until almost burning them.

"All these things were on sale this past week," Eddie said when someone asked what the dish was called. He presented soda crackers sprinkled with pepper and a dash of hot sauce to go with the meal.

At dinner, no one talked about the fuel, engines, or the rocket. They didn't talk about Timothy's former home. Instead, Angie told them about her older brother, Blake, who was in college and better at science and math than she was. She left out how her science-minded parents paid him more attention.

When Timothy asked what her parents thought about her working on the project, she said, "Like I said before, my parents are playing at divorce. For two weeks, one of them stays with me at the house. Then, they trade places. They only care that I'm going to school and getting good grades. I tell them different stories of what I'm doing when I stay here. It's like I'm living two lives. A story for each parent. I like it."

Luke brought up how some people thought he was Hispanic or Arabic. "My mother is Irish and white and my father is black from South Africa. She's a little wild and he's a little calm."

Patty talked about her mother's beauty salon and the regulars who had not changed their hairstyle since they were teenagers. She didn't say how she intended to shave her head for graduation. She ended with, "I'm an only child. My dad ran away to start another family and divorced us. He called me after a couple of months and over explained himself. Now he calls me every Tuesday night. I think we have a good relationship, far apart."

As they talked about their families, Timothy felt closer to Luke, Angie, and Patty. He remembered when his mom and dad were alive and the things they enjoyed as a family like eating supper together each evening. Happiness didn't have to be anything more than that.

The next day on Sunday, Angie's brother came home unexpectedly for a visit meaning both her parents were there, too. She complained about the obligation to spend time with them, but did it anyway "for the sake of the project." Luke had an "unofficial" football practice Sunday afternoon called by his coach who thought they had the chance to beat the number one team in a month. Patty stayed home to do more research on bacteria.

Eddie took Timothy downtown for groceries, a few things at the hardware store, and ice cream cones for the trip home. Timothy wondered if Eddie was trying to make them appear like a family. Timothy liked their outing together.

The rest of the day was a goof-off. Neither of them went to the silo or talked about the rocket or fuel. Timothy found an old Atari game set and played video games like Pac-Man and Space Invaders while Eddie read a Jules Verne novel, *From the Earth to the Moon.*

For supper, they ate a salad made of everything in the refrigerator: kale, spinach, sweet carrots, red-red tomatoes, eggs over well, cut up dill pickles, juicy strawberries, green olives, crushed walnuts, and olive oil from Italy that Eddie bought at a local market. The dressing was a combination of raspberry jam, ketchup, yellow mustard, and sour cream. They wiped the bowls with slices of warm sourdough bread.

On Monday, after school, Angie's brother was staying one more day and Patty had to help her mother at the salon. That's how Luke explained it to Timothy as he drove them to Eddie's house, who had taken a half-day off for unknown reasons.

"You have relatives anywhere?" Luke asked. They were waiting at the only light after leaving school and the only bottleneck in the county at that time of day.

"People who helped bury my mom and dad said they were my relatives, but that's the only time I've ever seen or talked to them. I think they couldn't stay because they were aliens."

"You mean aliens from another country?"

"No, from outer space."

"You kidding?" The light turned green and Luke lurched the car forward.

"Are you and Angie serious?" Timothy didn't care that he changed the subject so quickly. He remembered in elementary school when he told his classmates that he could be related to aliens. The ridicule lasted for months. Maybe Luke wouldn't ridicule him, but Timothy didn't want to chance it.

"Okay, we'll come back to the alien thing later. Yeah, despite what happened, I still like Angie."

"What happened?"

"This morning before classes started, she said we were happier away from each other. I didn't say anything back." Luke frowned. "I guess that said everything."

"You two broke up?" Timothy was shocked.

"Apparently. But don't worry about our project. Angie and I are still friends, which I think will make things easier."

"Why did she bring it up this morning?"

"I told her I was quitting the football team."

"What're you doing that for? You've played football your whole life." Timothy wanted to know how many more surprises Luke had to tell. Timothy also wished Luke would stop driving so fast. He and Eddie were at opposite ends of the age thing, yet both seemed to drive the same way.

"I just lost interest. My parents thought I would get a football scholarship. Except I'm not the best on this team and this team isn't the best in the league."

"What are you going to do?"

"I've always liked rocks. I'm thinking about being a geologist. Besides, quitting the team means I can spend more time on the rocket launch."

"What'd your parents say?" Timothy held on to the dashboard as Luke took a curve too fast.

"My mom was relieved because she never liked football. My dad was upset because he thought I'd get a scholarship. He got over it when I told him I had a way to pay for college through scholarships. Instead of spending time practicing and playing football, I could be studying and improving my grades. That got him calmed down somewhat."

"What did your coach say?"

"One thing I can say about the coach: he was the only one who told me the game wasn't going to work for me. He was the only one to tell me the truth. That's what I needed."

"You don't think this will draw attention to us, do you?" Timothy held on to his seat belt.

"No, my teammates knew I was losing interest. Besides, I want to launch this rocket. Up ahead around the next curve is a dip in the road. If someone takes it too fast, they start bouncing and end up in the ditch. I've lived here too long when a dip in a road is that familiar. Launching this rocket is going to be exciting," said Luke slowing down for the dip.

Chapter 26

After school on Tuesday and Wednesday afternoon, everyone showed up to learn and get organized. They set up and tested the electronics in the house, read more documents, and ate more of Eddie's strange food combinations.

The first evening, they had store bought baked chicken covered with spaghetti, honey, and grated cheddar cheese with a splash of cherry and vanilla extract. Eddie made a big bowl of steamed broccoli, carrots, and spinach covered with a sauce of yellow mustard and rich olive oil. A tart lemonade mixed with sweet tea came with lots of ice.

The second evening they had potatoes that Eddie baked until they were mashable and slathered with melted butter. He made sandwiches of peanut butter, mayonnaise, and tuna fish mixed with salt, raspberry jam, and store-bought pesto sauce. It went well with the store-bought pickled eggs. Snacks both days were ketchup and parmesan cheese on mixed nuts.

On Thursday after everyone left early, Eddie and Timothy sat at the kitchen table in front of papers and other documents.

"I don't know if I'm going to get all of this," Timothy said.

"You don't have to get all of it. Just know enough to do your job. Everyone has a part to play, like in a real rocket launch."

"This is a real rocket launch."

"Anyway, the important thing you need to focus on is structural stability. This includes maintaining the center of gravity as the thrust increases. Your engines can't obstruct this stability."

"I get it. The rocket and engines need to work together for stability in the launch pattern," said Timothy, confidently.

"We need the ballast and controls to be sequenced. We need to confirm the thrust factor and exactly how much push and stress the electrogravitic engines will have on the rocket's structure," said Eddie.

"Patty can help with figuring this out and exactly how much stress the engines have on the rocket." It was dusk outside and Timothy heard the frogs start their high-pitched, throaty croaks like they were singing *The Phantom of the Opera.*

"We can use the guidance system to manage the thrusts' gimbal movement as we go straight into space," said Eddie.

"Do you ever talk with the other three janitors at school?" Timothy wanted a break from all this rocket talk.

"Okay, we're on a different subject." Eddie leaned back in his chair. It creaked and Timothy worried it would fracture and come apart. It didn't as Eddie continued.

"The other three speak Spanish and I don't. It's all right because I enjoy eating my lunch alone. Neither they nor the teachers know about my previous life. Everyone passes me in the hallway and act like I'm part of the wall. Principal Halltage knows my background and I think he resents me for ending up as a high school janitor. Maybe he thinks he could end up like me one day."

"If you told people about your past, I think some of the students and teachers would look up to you. Instead, you clean toilets and say nothing." Timothy leaned across the table for emphasis, which didn't work. The table creaked badly and he sat back.

"Things are fine like they are. Everyone seems happy with the arrangement. Yeah, the principal knows, but I never liked him. I usually salute him with my dirty toilet brush. Now let's go over these documents a little more."

A half hour later, Timothy was trying to understand a thrust-to-ratio formula better when he looked up and saw Eddie had disappeared.

Timothy found him in his bedroom asleep. He thought about how he used to go into his dad's bedroom, wondering if he was still alive. He decided not to make a habit of visiting Eddie like he did with his dad in case he found Eddie like he'd found his dad.

Before leaving, Timothy saw that the closet had a lock on the door. That was odd. Then he noticed a small sign hanging on the wall. It read, ASTRONAUTS LIVE FOREVER IN SPACE, as if there was no other place to live.

Chapter 27

Eddie woke up later that night remembering when his parents became too old to take care of themselves. This happened in his second year of college and he used them as an excuse to quit school. He was failing several classes anyway after proposing to a woman.

She wanted to marry someone with a chance at being rich and she left school in that second year with a graduate student. Eddie couldn't get over the rejection and left soon after with his excuse for leaving. He told a few friends the truth and how he needed to get away from college and dating. They thought he was courageous. He thought he was more of a coward.

Eddie moved in with his parents who lived near Cape Canaveral. He took care of them during the day while taking engineering classes at night. He was excited when NASA launched the first space shuttle *Columbia*. His teachers helped Eddie find work with the shuttle program and he fell in love with rockets.

He saw every shuttle launch from the Kennedy Space Center Launch Complex 39. He tried to share the experience with his parents, but they refused to leave their small house. They complained that going into space was nonsense. They criticized their son for working at NASA. He became more determined to stay with the shuttle program and watch the launches.

After two years, his parents died a few weeks apart and Eddie became overwhelmed with the empty house. There were no good memories there. He needed a change in his life and wanted out of Florida and away from his parent's place.

He quit night school and was able to transfer to NASA's Langley Research Center in Hampton, Virginia. There he continued supporting the space shuttle during launch and flight operations. There he met Reanette.

Eddie wanted to date her, but she loved Roy who worked in another directorate at Langley. Eddie knew he shouldn't be watching everything they did. Yet, Reanette had something about her that charmed him. He became obsessed with her.

At the same time, he could not forget how fast Roy and Reanette became romantically involved. It was so fast that Eddie had no chance to interfere. Then, he didn't want to. Instead, he became captivated by their relationship as a couple. When he and fellow co-workers were invited to the wedding, Eddie decided he had enough of following them around. He went to Virginia Beach and watched the dolphins offshore until the waves got too high.

The next day, while the couple vacationed on their honeymoon, Eddie met a new project manager. They were alone in a workshop.

"People call me ET because they think I look like an extraterrestrial," was how he introduced himself. He stood six feet thin with sandy colored hair. His triangular face possessed wide blue eyes, a small mouth, and a straight nose.

Eddie was uneasy with ET. There was something different about him. After a brief talk about work, ET abruptly said, "I know you are fond of Reanette. Do you think she could be a spy?"

Eddie wasn't sure what to say. Finally, he said firmly, "No, I am sure Reanette is not a spy. Why would you ask that?"

"Good, good. I was just running down rumors. They could be an awful thing."

ET said nothing about Eddie's feelings for Reanette. Instead, the new manager congratulated Eddie on some minor accomplishments and walked quickly away. Afterward, Eddie was not sure what to think about the discussion or ET. Of course, Reanette could not be a spy, he thought. He had been watching her and Roy too much.

When Reanette and Roy got back, Eddie wanted to tell them what ET said. However, they had already made plans to move to eastern North Carolina. At the same time, ET transferred to the Kennedy Space Center in Florida. Eddie was left with too many questions.

Over the years, Reanette and Roy worked remotely supporting the shuttle and other NASA programs giving Eddie the opportunity to keep in touch with them. ET stayed with the shuttle program and worked with Eddie on flight operations.

Sometimes ET invited Eddie to watch the launches VIP style. Eddie only went when his co-workers were invited, too. Each time, Eddie was more convinced there was something odd about ET.

When Eddie learned that Reanette and Roy were having a baby boy, Eddie felt sadder that he had missed something in his life. Yet, he refused to become bitter. Working with the shuttle program become his passion.

Years later, he went to the Kennedy Space Center and watched the last space shuttle *Atlantis* land. Quickly, he and many others were retired. It was more like being laid off or fired. He felt betrayed.

For two years he worked retail and lost contact with ET, Reanette, and Roy. During this time, he used his inheritance and savings to buy rocket equipment from around the world. It gave him something to do. At the end of the two years, his loneliness made him long for Reanette.

He knew it was wrong, yet he had no one to tell him something different. He bought an old farmhouse with a silo on the other side of the county where Reanette and Roy lived.

After he moved in, Eddie felt too guilty to contact Reanette. He avoided her and Roy, not wanting to explain how he ended up as a stalker. He just kept collecting old rocket stuff since the farm was a good place to store what the space industry discarded.

One day after hurting himself on some equipment, Eddie realized he could die there and no one would know until it was time to pay the electric bill. Besides, he had grown tired of being a recluse. The high school janitor job gave him something to do.

Eddie didn't make friends at the high school. He walked the hallways doing his chores while witnessing teenagers deal with personal dramas, insignificant crises, and crazy puberty.

Now propped up on pillows and remembering all of this, Eddie pulled out a picture of the *Redstone* rocket. The teenager Timothy was different. He brought the last piece of the puzzle Eddie had always known was out there and would save him. He didn't think about failure, only success. He got up and unlocked the closet door to check on what he had stored in there.

He thought that maybe if he had told Reanette and Roy everything, things would be different now.

Chapter 28

On Friday after school, Eddie gave Timothy a new laptop with a NASA software program installed. It was like a video game simulating the launch of a *Redstone* rocket out of a silo. Luke set up the controllers and speakers, after which he announced, "Hey, everybody. This is the first Friday night that I'm not playing football."

"You're going to miss it," Patty said, smiling.

"Not as much as you think. Playing football hurts a lot."

Angie wore a terrific frown as she told Eddie, "I'd like to know where you got this software." She stood with the rest of them watching Timothy use the controllers for the first time. The simulation rocket never made it out of the silo. Timothy banged his fists on the table.

"It's modified for our launch. The people who helped with it will be here tomorrow morning," Eddie said, heading out of the tower room. Before exiting, he turned around to tell Timothy, "This is your room from now on. It'll be the launch room. The other room is for communications."

"How am I going to launch this rocket if I can't make the simulation work? I can't even get the rocket out of the silo."

"Stop whining," Angie said, leaning closer to him. "It's a simulation, meaning you can crash as many times as you need to."

"Yeah, you gotta relax," said Patty. "This is a learning tool. You need to fail most of the time."

"All right, all right. I overreacted. Now watch and tell me what I do wrong while I launch this thing again," said Timothy. "Maybe this time I can get the rocket out of the silo."

Later that night after everyone left, Eddie stole away from his reading to stand in the doorway of the tower and watch Timothy softly curse the simulation model. Timothy struggled with the wobbly rocket as it climbed into a thunderstorm. Eddie didn't know if the rocket made it or not.

He fell back against the hallway wall wracked by a fit of unexpected pain that traveled through his gut. He slid down the wall and sat on the floor.

"What're you doing on the floor? Did you fall?" Timothy stood over Eddie.

"Stop asking questions and help me get up."

Timothy got behind Eddie and easily lifted him into a standing position. "What happened? I heard a lot of banging out here." Timothy stood beside Eddie in case he fell again.

"I've been working too much. I just need to go to bed." The pain subsided, but he felt weak.

Timothy followed closely behind Eddie as he stumbled toward his bedroom. He felt the pain continue to ease up, except it made him take slow, careful steps. Reaching the doorway, he stopped and waved for Timothy to leave him alone.

"I'll be alright. I'll see you in the morning."

"You want something to drink?"

"Yeah, a glass of ice water." Eddie figured that would give him enough time to clean up his room and hide everything. It would have worked if his hand hadn't slipped off the doorknob, making him nearly fall again. Timothy was there to hoist Eddie into his bedroom and onto the edge of the bed. Balanced there, Timothy looked around.

"What's that?" Timothy pointed toward the open closet door and a clear plastic bag hanging from a ceiling hook. Inside, he saw shiny white fabric.

"A spacesuit."

Timothy looked at Eddie, the spacesuit, then Eddie. "Where'd you get it? Is it real?"

"Yeah, it's real. I got it when I worked at NASA. It was an extra suit that was never used and left sealed in a storage container until I bought it."

Timothy walked over to get a better look. "Have you tried it on?"

"Yeah, a few months ago. Everything worked great. It's the basic pressurized spacesuit. Provides oxygen, carbon dioxide removal, radiation protection, temperature control, and pressurization. I relocated the tanks from the back of the suit to the legs."

Timothy eyed the spacesuit again. "It looks old." He examined the boots, gloves, and a communications cap all hanging in bags from other hooks. "Where's the helmet?"

"In the box to your right. There's also a portable life support backpack with the oxygen tanks and carbon dioxide scrubbers and filters. The whole thing is a modified *Apollo* spacesuit with a water-cooled nylon undergarment and another layer of nylon that has fabric vents. At the bottom is a bag to collect urine."

"Yuk. I guess there's a place for the poop, too. How long does the oxygen last?"

"Up to eight hours," Eddie said. "Temperature is controlled by liquid cooling through a vented garment worn next to the skin. A suit pump circulates water through small plastic tubes woven into the fabric. In the past, one problem the astronauts had was that their hands got too cold, so I added insulation."

"Hey, wait a minute." Timothy looked at Eddie, at the spacesuit, then back at Eddie. "*You're* the special satellite. You plan to wear this suit in the capsule. I don't think I like this."

Eddie used his hands to steady himself on the edge of the bed. "You've gotta help me with this," pleaded Eddie.

"Why should I help you? I'm still not sure why I'm here helping you do any of this." Timothy started for the bedroom door.

"Wait. You want to know if your rocket formula works, don't you? You'll never find out any other way."

"I'll get one of your NASA friends to help."

"My friends won't be much help. The U.S. Air Force mostly controls NASA. All the military will do is steal your formula and engines and classify them as 'national security.' Then they'll probably throw you in jail for messing with national security. If you launch me into space, everyone will know and you'll have more people helping you."

"That logic doesn't work. What if you die? The notices on this suit are all warnings. The few instructions just explain the warnings. Whoa—stop." Timothy stared at Eddie. "Nothing in the capsule is designed to come back. You plan to stay forever in space. What's going on here?" Timothy was almost shouting.

"All right, so I'll say it. I want to stay in space."

"You're committing suicide. Why in the world do you want to do that? I'll be helping an old man kill himself and I don't want to be part of a suicide mission. I'm not helping you die." Timothy stood with his fists clenched and his jaw tense. He looked determined.

"I'm already dying."

They looked at each other. Not quite a stare. More like a look that made Timothy think he was having a nightmare and would wake up soon with his dad and mom saying he was late for school. As for Eddie, he just looked scared. A full half a minute passed. Timothy looked again at the spacesuit while Eddie tried to stay sitting up on the edge of the bed. He nearly fell on the floor.

Timothy caught Eddie's outstretched hands and helped him back onto the bed.

"Seriously, you never consider me in all of this," Timothy said.

Eddie leaned forward a bit. "Of course I considered you, Timothy. I considered everyone involved in this venture. You forget that this is my life that will end."

"What are you dying from?" he said softly.

"Cancer. It's terminal."

"Where?"

"Pancreas," Eddie said matter-of-factly. "But it's spread all over the place. A few years ago, doctors wouldn't have found the disease until the pain was already there. Now the diagnose comes sooner, except it doesn't change the ending."

"Didn't you try to get treatment?" Timothy stared at Eddie, unsure of what to say or do.

"At first I did, but it seemed to only speed up the disease."

"So, you just gave up?" Timothy asked.

Eddie shook his head. "I didn't give up. I had the choice to continue fighting the cancer with no chance of defeating it or stopping treatment and living as comfortably as possible for as long as possible. I chose to go out knowing who I am. I've got a good team of hospice people helping me do that. And, they know nothing about this rocket stuff. My deal is I go to them, which I do at lunchtime or after work."

Timothy steadied Eddie on the edge of the bed. He looked older than before. "First my mom, then my dad, now you. Why does everyone I know end up dying?"

Eddie said nothing. He just looked at Timothy, waiting for him to say more.

"I wanted you to live," Timothy said. "I wanted my dad and mom to live." He breathed heavily for a few moments.

Eddie was poised to help him if he hyperventilated.

Timothy dropped his shoulders and hung his head. "Is your cancer painful?"

Eddie shrugged. "The drugs help. I get by."

Timothy eyed Eddie, then glanced again at the spacesuit. "Why weren't you truthful with me about all of this?"

"I was going to tell you. I wanted to be further along in the launch when I did. Besides, you're not helping me to die. I'm already dying. All you're doing is moving me from one place to die to another."

Timothy kept looking at the spacesuit, maybe for hope, maybe for answers, mostly for someone else to be in his place.

"I'm dying and I want to die in space. It's my last hope and dream," Eddie went on. "Just do this for me. Promise me." He reached out and grasped Timothy's arm.

Timothy looked into Eddie's eyes for answers. "If you die in space, that's assisted suicide."

"Yeah, you'll probably get into trouble with the authorities. My NASA friends can't help if you go alone with the launch, but they may be able to help you after our launch. Some of them are pretty influential."

"How are they going to help me if I'm in jail?" Timothy leaned toward Eddie. "I'm mad that you didn't tell me about all of this before."

Eddie let out a long sigh. "If I'd told you in the beginning, you might have run off. I had to show you the rocket and get you involved first. I had to do that so you'd stay with me."

"This isn't all about you. All four of us are involved and will be held responsible when you go up into space to die."

"Yeah, I realize that," Eddie said. "But I was thinking about your future. I think that after the launch there will be truths revealed to you. Truths I can't tell you because I don't know what they are myself. All I know is that you'll learn a lot more about all of this than I ever knew."

"About all of what? You're talking in riddles." Timothy wondered if Eddie was delusional with pain. He helped him further on the bed so he wouldn't fall off.

Timothy got up and paced the room. He clenched and unclenched his fists as he did a few quick circles of the small room. Finally, he faced Eddie, who sat on the bed awkwardly.

Timothy remembered Luke talking about "truths." He thought there were a lot more truths to be revealed as he faced the old man. Timothy thought about everything that had happened to him and he wanted to walk away from everything. Yet, something made him want to stay and finish what they started.

"All right. You got me. I'm not turning back now," he said, meaning it. "So, how are we going to do all this? Like, get you in the capsule wearing that spacesuit?"

"I got it all planned out. I figured I could put the spacesuit on at the capsule and climb in. You can load in the backpack and power supply, hook me up, and put my helmet on. Once I'm in space, everything will only weigh a few pounds and I can manage."

"I don't know about this." Timothy clenched his palms together before separating them with a pop.

"There's no one or anything here for me anymore. I want to finish my life out there among the stars and planets. It's more like a sense of freedom. Like a pilgrimage into the universe. I belong out there among the cosmos."

Timothy sat on the bed next to Eddie. "I don't like any of this. But I get it. One of the last things my dad asked me to do was help him fulfill his last wish, which was to use the formula and engines. I'll help you get into outer space."

Eddie leaned against Timothy. Really, he was trying to lie down on the bed and Timothy was in the way.

Chapter 29

Early Saturday morning, the sun climbed up through the tall pine trees spraying daylight across the faces of four teenagers and Eddie. They stood on the porch watching an old sedan come up the driveway. In front of the porch, three men and one woman climbed out; all of them as old as Eddie. Timothy had hoped for someone younger. A whole generation went missing between the two groups.

Angie was first off the porch to meet the group. Patty, Luke, and Eddie followed her while Timothy stayed behind. He worried about the growing number of people involved. A few weeks ago, it was just him and Eddie, which was all right. Now, who were all these people? One of the men walked on the porch toward Timothy.

"I'm Ted." Deep tanned lines streaked across his forehead, giving him a frowning look. His friendly smile erased that look. The same height as Timothy, he had a potbelly and thin arms that made his broad shoulders look wider. He also had gray hair, short and spiked, and smooth olive skin from a land of deserts.

While shaking Ted's hand, Timothy watched the crowd in front of the sedan introduce themselves to each other. As if on cue, the new people came onto the porch.

"I'm Samantha, but you can call me Sam." She almost pushed Ted out of the way to shake Timothy's hand. She did this even though she was the shortest person. Her dark eyes made Timothy think about

Latin America and her long thick black hair, streaked with white-gray, made him feel good about her.

Next was Gene. Although slightly stooped over, he was as tall as Luke. Timothy could see reflections of the porch on his dark bald head. His ebony face made him look younger than the rest. The darkness of his skin was smooth and gentle like kindness.

Henry came last, shaking Timothy's hand in a strong grip. Slightly shorter with thick arms, he had thin gray hair that meandered around his head in no particular direction. His blue eyes stood out against his tanned face.

Ted spoke to the teenagers. "Eddie briefed us on everything going on here. *Redstone* rocket, special fuel, and strange engines. As I see it, we put it all together and launch the rocket into outer space. Sounds simple enough."

"It's not that simple," said Timothy as he faced Ted. "There's a lot to do so everything is done right. None of this has ever been done before."

"Before we get too far into the testosterone cloud, I suggest we head to the silo and show our new guests what's there," said Angie.

Sam smiled at Angie as the group filed around to the back of the house. They walked across the rutted field toward the silo—everyone except Ted who climbed into the driver's side of the jeep with Eddie as his passenger. Ted took off before Timothy could get there.

Timothy hurried after everyone else wishing there had been a planning meeting or something to decide how everything was going to happen.

With Angie in the lead, Patty dropped back with Timothy. "I don't know what's bothering you, but we've got a lot to do," Patty said, putting her hand against Timothy's back and pushing him along.

"Why do these NASA people want to help Eddie?" Timothy stumbled along, trying to keep ahead of Patty's hand.

"Eddie took care of them when they all worked together."

"When did you talk to Eddie about them?"

"Whenever. He also told us—"

"You mean Luke, Angie, and you?"

"Do you want to know why the NASA people are helping Eddie or not?" Patty said.

"Yeah."

"Eddie said his four friends were working at the Kennedy Space Center when they met some guy named ET. This guy told them that a woman they worked with was a spy and they started to believe the guy. Eddie heard about it and warned the NASA people that the woman was not the spy. Someone else was. Eddie never heard what happened, but ET suddenly left. For some reason, the NASA people thought they 'owed' Eddie."

Timothy didn't tell Patty that ET was the one who brought the rocket to the silo or that the woman was his mom Reanette. He wanted to know why ET accused his mom of being a spy. And, why did Eddie let him put this rocket here? Knowing Eddie seemed to come with a lot of mysteries.

Ted drove Eddie in the jeep along the looping, dirt road slow enough that they would reach the silo with the rest of them. Timothy thought this gave them way too much time to talk.

At the silo, the NASA group went inside while Eddie and the teen-agers hung outside waiting. Timothy fidgeted while looking at Eddie.

"Who are all these NASA people?" Timothy asked.

"Ted started as an engineer of rocket designs. He has a picture of himself shaking hands with Wernher Magnus Maximilian Freiherr von Braun." Eddie paused for dramatic effect.

"Who's that?" Timothy stopped fidgeting.

"The father of the U.S. rocket program," said Patty. "You gotta catch up on your rocket history."

Angie and Luke shrugged as if they didn't know who von Braun was either.

With a frustrated look, Eddie continued. "Anyway, on the Space Shuttle program, Ted used to be the flight dynamics officer, or FIDO, as we called him. He managed the maneuvers and monitored the flight trajectory of the shuttle."

"What about the tall guy?" Luke asked.

"Gene had several jobs on the shuttle program. He monitored the in-flight communications and instrumentation systems and also managed the onboard and vehicle navigation and guidance systems."

They all heard the NASA group talking just inside the doorway. They questioned the ability of the rocket to make it out of the silo.

"Henry was the PROP or shuttle propulsion engineer. He managed reaction control and orbital maneuvering propellants. He also was a booster engineer who monitored the main engine, solid rockets, and external tank throughout the launch."

"What about the woman?" asked Angie.

"Sam's our mathematician. On the Shuttle program, she monitored the electrical systems and was mostly responsible for the thermal controls, cabin atmosphere, and supply systems."

"We can use her in several places during the launch," said Patty as the NASA group emerged from the silo and approached the teenagers and Eddie.

Sam stared at Eddie. "Who's the capsule for?"

"A special satellite," said Timothy.

"Try that again," said Ted.

Timothy looked warily at Eddie.

Henry interrupted the sudden silence. "Right now, I'm more interested in these special engines Eddie told us about."

"Okay," said Ted. "We'll get back to the 'special satellite' later. I agree with Henry that we have to make sure we assemble the engines correctly. You have instructions on how to do this, Tim?"

The "Tim" part got Timothy fuming to the point where he couldn't say anything. After a few awkward seconds, Patty said, "Yeah, it's all in binders at the house. But Timothy knows more than what's written down."

"Before we get too far into all this, I brought breakfast. It's in the coolers in the back of the jeep," Eddie said, leading the way to the jeep.

Patty and Angie got on both sides of Timothy to lead him toward the coolers. Luke got ahead of everyone at the mention of food.

Eddie's view of breakfast didn't exactly match the standard breakfast menu. He had made separate bowls of penne pasta and doused them in crushed fried potato chips, yellow mustard, feta cheese, sour cream, and maple syrup. Everyone got a short roll of soft sourdough bread, sweet red grapes, sweeter strawberries, and another cup with sliced portabella mushrooms soaked in apple vinegar. Timothy was getting to like the ice cold water.

As they ate, Eddie got the NASA group to talk about the Shuttle days. Ted kept putting down his food and drink to use his hands when he talked; Sam wore a happy smile even when she was eating and kept calling everyone "hon;" and Gene's pockets held enough peanuts that he could share with everyone. Timothy liked Henry the most. He looked like he was dancing when he talked.

Timothy didn't say much. He kept going over in his head how to put the engines together. He hoped he could remember everything. He barely ate, worried that he might forget something simple and cause the engines to fail. He realized there was no way to test them after he loaded the fuel.

Chapter 30

By mid-morning, the group had pulled the engine halves out of the shed, opened them, and briefly inspected the halves. On the outside, they looked simple in design. No one spoke about what was inside where no one could see and existed a never before invented means of thrust. No one said anything as they looked over the engines.

Ted broke the silence. "I looked around the top of the silo. Once we open the dome, there's a lattice structure that should be strong enough to lift the capsule and lock it in place. On the inside of the silo, there's a crane we can use to lift the engines up and into the rocket." Ted sounded confident. Everyone else was not so sure.

Four sections of the dome opened using an electric motor that made a loud whirring noise. Seeing the concerned look on everyone, Eddie assured them the motor was good. Timothy was not worried about the dome closing since the weight of the sections would help pull it closed. He hoped the motor worked again when it was time to launch the rocket.

The open dome revealed the lattice structure of steel girders attached to the silo wall and rising over the rocket. On top hung cables, pulleys, and winches. Using the gas engine on the ground, it took almost three hours for everyone, either on the ground or at the top, to winch the three-thousand-pound capsule and secure it to the top. It amazed everyone that the lattice could hold that much weight.

Each person, except Eddie, went up to look inside the rocket. Narrow metal beams crisscrossed the inside, keeping the rocket from collapsing. Along the walls hung tubing and wires attached to junction boxes. Without all of this, the rocket would look like a long metal tube. They agreed it was weird how easily the engines could be attached to the inside, hanging from existing clamps and beams.

Outside the silo and off to themselves, Patty told Luke and Angie, "The inside of the *Redstone* wasn't designed like this. This was all planned. While the instrument compartment and aft unit are here, the alcohol and liquid oxygen tanks are gone. And the rocket's engine is missing. All that's left is the thrust chamber assembly where the exhaust comes out."

Angie put her hand up as though she were in class. "The person with the rocket took everything out so the engines would go in easily. If they knew about the engines, why didn't they put them in already?"

"Maybe they didn't know where the engines were or maybe they hadn't been built yet. Or they could have run out of time getting the engines here," Luke proposed.

Without more information, they could not know why. They decided to keep these thoughts to themselves as they joined the others.

Carefully, they placed the engine halves on blue tarps. The machines looked like the mysteries they were. When finished, everyone had a lot of questions for Timothy and Eddie. Mostly Timothy.

"Eddie told us about negative energy coming off the Earth. How do the engines work with this energy?" Henry asked.

"The engines produce thrust by creating a field of anti-negative energy. This reacts against negative energy flows that come out of the Earth's core electrical energy," Timothy explained. "The engines ride the negative energy until it weakens in the mesosphere, about fifty miles up. There, the negative energy is too dispersed to use and the engines funnel surrounding energy into the rocket's skin for more thrust."

Timothy remembered hearing all of this from his dad during his brief moments of sobriety. Telling his son this information was the only motivation his dad had to stop drinking, at least for a little while.

"The mesosphere is where most meteors burn up, and it's the coldest part of the atmosphere," explained Sam. She continued, "It's also where sprites exist."

"What are sprites?" asked Luke.

"Scientists believe they're created from lightning off the top of thunderstorms. Other scientists theorize sprites come from the interaction of the intense cold joining the electricity from lightning with the energy off destroyed meteors. This joined energy may remain in the mesosphere for months or years, fueled by other thunderstorms and destroyed meteors." She looked at Timothy and asked, "Are sprites the surrounding energy?"

Timothy panicked. His dad never talked about sprites. "All I know is that this surrounding energy is needed for the rocket to go higher until riding the negative energy coming from space."

"Finally, someone has made a real single-stage-to-orbit rocket," Sam exclaimed, maybe trying to save Timothy.

"What's wrong with rocket stages?" Angie asked.

"Rocket stages create risk," Gene answered. "Lots of things can go wrong when separating the stages. Single-stage-to-orbits, or SSTOs, don't need multiple parts and they have a smaller surface area, which makes them easier to glide through the atmosphere. The *Redstone* is a good example of an SSTO, although it only went to the edges of space."

"We need to get to work," Ted said, cutting off the discussion.

"I've got tools in the shed," said Eddie.

It took almost an hour to put the first engine halves together. Fortunately, the rest went easier and took less time. By late afternoon, they all stood back to survey the eight completed engines lying on blue tarps. The machines looked like robots who could rise up at any moment and take over the world.

Luke asked, "What's attaching these engines to the rocket?"

"I've got short crosshatched, carbon-based girders left over from when the rocket was put in the silo," Eddie said. "They're strong enough to mount the engines to the rocket and can be used as an energy transfer from the engines to the rocket skin. Isn't that right, Timothy?"

Timothy nodded. "Yeah, that's right." He was proud of the engines lying there completed. He wished his parents were there to see them. He didn't ask why the unique girders had been left over.

"It's getting late in the day. I say we go over how we're going to raise these engines and fasten them to the inside of the rocket. In the morning, we can get straight to work," said Ted.

After a brief discussion, they agreed that someone needed to be lowered into the rocket to fasten the engines and connect everything. They chose Henry since he was the only one going to a gym and who could fit in a harness.

The engines were carried into the shed and the blue tarps were used to cover the opened silo. Before they left, Angie made sure each person had a role. She allotted two hours to install each engine, meaning they would finish on Monday, a school day. It also meant a new set of excuses were needed for the teenagers' parents. As the NASA group finished securing everything, Eddie gave the high schoolers an option.

"So, you told Mr. Greg? How much does he know?" Angie stepped up to Eddie.

"People were getting suspicious at school. Anyway, he pretty much figured out what we were doing. He's been making up stories when people ask about any of you," Eddie said.

"I learned a lot about rocketry from Mr. Greg," said Patty.

"I have physics class with him. It's going to be weird sitting in class and knowing that he knows all of this," said Luke.

"What stories was he telling people?" asked Angie.

"Seriously, another person?" Timothy glared at Eddie.

"So, how is Mr. Greg going to help?" Patty asked.

"He'll tell people that all of you are on a field trip for a special project," said Eddie. "Tomorrow and Monday, Luke will pick up everyone early from school and come straight here."

"It could work. This is sort of like a science project and people like Mr. Greg," said Patty. Her eyes showed excitement at all this clandestine planning.

"Good. Everyone agrees," said Eddie. "Here's a list of things that need to be done before we launch next month," said Eddie handing it to Angie.

Luke asked, "What do you mean next month? Isn't that kinda soon?"

"This list is a mess," said Angie.

"Yeah, we can do all this," Patty said, looking over Angie's shoulder.

"Let's not put a deadline on this launch right now," said Angie. "Timothy is already hyperventilating. We'll get the engines in and go from there."

Timothy was glad Angie was on the team. She seemed to be the only sensible person. The NASA group joined the teenagers and Eddie near the silo door.

"Does everyone have their excuses down?" Ted asked in a joking way.

"You four have a place to stay?" replied Angie in a less joking way, suggesting they not stay with Eddie.

"No worries. We're staying at a hotel house not far from your high school," said Ted.

Looking at everyone talking about preparing for the launch, Timothy saw people who were willing to take the risk and make this thing happen. He felt like he should be as confident as they.

Chapter 31

Henry and Gene made supper of grilled salmon, seasoned well, and covered in pieces of double-fried french fries and boiled tomatoes. Over the dish they squeezed two limes and three dashes of hot sauce. The vegetables were a mix of fried, grilled, and steamed depending on what they thought fit with the texture, all done separately before mixing together. There were no leftovers.

Eddie's NASA friends stayed at the only decent hotel in the area near the high school. The teenagers went home to offer explanations to their parents, a.k.a. lies. Timothy spent the evening studying his dad's notes. Eddie went to bed early.

On Sunday, the sun had just risen when everyone showed up almost at the same time. The NASA troupe brought breakfast—muffins, bagels, and sugar donuts—which was standard stuff compared to Eddie's concoctions. Breakfast was designed to be quick. No surprise food from Eddie. Change was already happening, thought Timothy.

He saw Eddie was not eating much. Timothy led him from the kitchen, telling the others they would meet them at the silo. At the jeep, Eddie got into the passenger side leaving Timothy to climb behind the steering wheel. Eddie didn't say anything as Timothy got the jeep started, the easy part, then remembered he'd never driven before, let alone a stick transmission.

Somehow, Timothy got from first to second gear with a lot of unhealthy noise. He left the gearshift there. He didn't think third and fourth gear were that necessary on their trip. The high whining of the gears drowned out the strain the jeep endured whenever it struck one side of the road, then the other.

"Well, it's still in one piece," said Eddie, who held his hand up signaling Timothy to stop. "We're close enough that I can walk from here."

"I wanted to talk to you on the way, but that jeep is hard to drive," said Timothy.

"For you, sure," said Eddie. "What do you want to talk about?"

"You're going to have to tell the others that you're the special satellite."

Eddie kept walking toward the shed. "I'm going to wait before explaining all this. If I tell them I'm the satellite to be launched, I also have to tell them I'm dying. I need to do that when I'm ready."

Timothy looked across the field at the others starting on their way toward them. Ted was leading the group at a fast pace. There was no time to argue since Eddie walked away toward the shed and the engines.

With the blue tarps removed, they swung the crane over the silo wall. A set of pulleys and a wide boom dangled from the end. These were left over from when the rocket was lowered in, Eddie told them. With this crane system, they raised the first of the engines.

Gene and Patty had climbed up with Ted and Henry to help install the engines. Based on the rocket's blueprints Eddie brought and instructions from Timothy's dad, they installed the first engine cautiously. They checked each connection over and over while Angie kept a detailed tally of the procedure. It took almost three hours to complete the operation.

After installing the first engine, Ted urged Timothy to come up and look inside the rocket for a final check. Timothy reluctantly went up and looked down into the rocket at the wires and hoses that the other engines would connect to. The first engine had tubes jutting out of the engine's top. This would be where he poured in the bacteria and chemicals.

"All the tubes will be connected to a central junction box on the outside of the rocket here near the capsule door where you can load the fuel," said Ted. While he talked, Timothy started feeling dizzy.

"I can hook you up in the harness and lower you down to take a better look," said Ted.

Timothy froze. Ted couldn't know that he was already feeling sick from being so high up. The inside of the rocket wouldn't look good with vomit on it.

"I'm okay. Let's install the rest of the engines," Timothy said.

Timothy went back down to the loading site. He thought it would be better if he continued to inspect the engines before they were hoisted up and installed. At least, that is what he told everyone.

For the rest of that day, Ted yelled "hooray" after they completed the installation of each engine. Using Angie's notes, the whole process became routine and Timothy felt more like he was in the way.

Except for a lunch break of deli sandwiches, they worked until late afternoon. At that time, they got faster and installed five of the eight engines.

After they replaced the blue tarps across the top of the silo and walked to the house, Timothy went to the tower. It was looking more like the launch room with all its equipment and monitors. He sat there alone, avoiding everyone while reading over and over his dad's notes regarding the bacteria and engines. Timothy understood a lot more about the science of creating anti-negative energy. He stopped reading when he smelled pizza.

Delivery of the food to this out-of-the-way place surprised him. He understood when the delivery guy left with gas money and a hefty tip from Ted. Timothy went back to his launch room with a slice of pizza. Ted followed him.

"We'll have the last engine installed by early tomorrow afternoon. You think you fully understand how the engines will work?" Ted chomped down on his pizza.

"I think Timothy has a good handle on what makes the engines work," Eddie said, coming in. "Timothy, how 'bout taking a break and join the rest of us?"

Timothy wanted to say something sarcastic to Ted, but not with Eddie there. Timothy did not feel like looking at anymore rocket stuff, anyway.

He followed Eddie and Ted onto the front porch that was wide enough for everyone to gather. There, he and his classmates listened to stories from the NASA retirees about the dawn of space travel. "All the way to the Moon," said Henry. Timothy wondered about his generation and how far past the Moon people may go with the new formula and engines.

After everyone left, Timothy went back into the tower section. Instead of working with the simulator, he played a video game. Eddie's internet connection was better than Timothy expected for a rural area. When he got tired, he slipped into Eddie's bedroom to make sure he was asleep and not dead. He was still breathing.

In the kitchen, Timothy ate a slice of leftover pizza on the front porch steps where he enjoyed the quiet. Looking up at the many stars, he listened to the rustle of tree leaves in the soft wind and an occasional hoot from Eddie's owl somewhere near the silo. He went to bed and fell asleep almost immediately.

In the morning, he came into the kitchen to boiled eggs, fresh sausages, plates of fried fish, bowls of fruit, buttered toast with raspberry jam, pitchers of sweet tea, and pots of coffee. Everyone stood around the kitchen holding their plates and talking.

Eddie motioned for him to join Ted and he who stood by themselves, leaning against the sink. The more comfortable kitchen table and chairs sat empty.

"Ted wants you to look at the rocket and what they've done so far. I think it's important," said Eddie.

Ted was checking his smartphone as if Timothy didn't matter. Timothy never owned a smartphone. People just assumed everyone in high school had one and he wished he did so he didn't need to hide the fact that he didn't.

"This was all your dad's creation. Did you pay attention to what he told you about the engines?" Ted looked up from his phone at Timothy.

"Of course I did."

Ted shrugged. "Just asking. My son didn't pay attention to what I told him. Now he's grown and had to learn the hard way."

"I'm not your son," said Timothy and glad he wasn't.

"I figured you are pretty mature about things," said Ted "Okay, I'm ready to get going." He pocketed his phone.

Everyone left with Ted except Timothy, who took his time eating at the kitchen table. When he was done, he went outside and found Eddie waiting for him by the jeep. The others were already crossing the field.

"You and Ted need to get along," Eddie said, getting into the passenger side of the jeep.

"Why?" Timothy hesitated before getting in the driver's side. He didn't think he had learned much from the last time he drove.

"Yeah, you're driving. I'm not feeling well today. Also, Ted and the other men made breakfast. You should thank them."

It took Timothy two tries to get the jeep started. If another try didn't work, he was headed back to the house. The tower had become his new friend.

Except the jeep started. Timothy shifted gears, eventually got to second, and pushed the shift lever into third, except third was too fast for his driving skills. Eddie grabbed the wheel and told him to slow down. Timothy made it back to second gear before the jeep stalled or they crashed into a ditch.

If driving the jeep stressed Timothy out, how could he drive a rocket? He was afraid he would kill Eddie before he got the rocket into space. Yet, why would any of that matter? Eddie would be dead either way.

Timothy got close enough to the silo where they walked the few remaining yards. At the shed, the three remaining engines laid there ready to be installed.

"Let's go to the top and look down at the engines we've installed," Ted told Timothy walking toward the silo.

As Ted and Timothy climbed the chute ladder, Timothy said nothing. Ted talked about all the stuff they had done to install the engines. "They should be correct," he said as if any problems would be Timothy's to correct.

Henry, Gene, and Patty were already there. Timothy leaned over the rim of the rocket and peered down at the five engines already strapped and bolted to the inside of the rocket's thin skin.

"When we're done, we should test everything," said Ted.

"There's no test. The engines will work."

Timothy looked down inside of the rocket and thought how fragile the structure looked. He felt awed that something so delicate and simple could put a person into space. He leaned away before he lost his balance and fell into the rocket.

This time, Timothy stayed to watch the installation of the final engines. After a quick lunch of bologna and cheese sandwiches with salty chips and Cheerwine or sweet tea, the capsule was lowered back down. The lattice came apart easily, along with the crane. By late afternoon, the dome was closed and the rocket that much more ready to launch.

Everyone gathered outside the silo exhausted and not saying much. Some may have hoped they did everything right, others may have decided that what will be will be. A few probably wanted to check everything again. No one said much as they started for the house.

Ted drove Eddie back in the jeep, leaving Timothy to follow everyone across the field. He kept looking back at the silo, trying to imagine the rocket soaring out the top. It scared him.

At the house, Sam said they needed a celebratory dinner. She and Henry made small thin crust pizza from dough "that had aged," according to Sam. Everyone had a choice of toppings like pepperoni, cubes of cooked brisket, and slices of salmon. There were also many vegetables and cheeses to choose from. Among the many choices were anchovies that Eddie piled on his pizza. Timothy added a few, too.

They gathered on the front porch, some sitting on the steps, and some in lawn chairs Eddie got the teenagers to pull from one of the rooms. The NASA retirees talked to Eddie about when they would come back, the teenagers reconnected with their parents on their cell phones, and Timothy was glad everyone would be leaving so he could think about everything that had happened and was about to happen.

"Before we leave, we have to name the rocket," Patty announced.

"Yeah, that's a good idea," said Luke. The others agreed.

"Let's call the rocket *Betty Boop*," said Eddie.

They all stared at him. Finally, Luke asked, "What's a *Betty Boop*?"

"She was a 1930s cartoon character who had more heart than brains. Decency codes back then changed her from a flapper to a career girl, but she'd come out with her wild, jazzy side whenever she could," Sam explained. She seemed to like *Betty Boop*.

"I want the rocket named *Betty Boop* because it was my mother's idol when she was a child," said Eddie.

The teens and the NASA group exchanged glances, shrugged, and said okay. There was no arguing against the virtues of a cartoon figure from the 1930s, especially if she was Eddie's mother's idol.

Chapter 32

On Tuesday morning, Patty stood in the doorway of the tower section impatiently tapping her right foot and trying to stare Timothy out of the room. "My mom is outside ready to drive us to school. I don't know why you can't take the bus once in a while. It goes right by here. And why isn't Eddie taking you this morning?"

"I decided not to go. Now that the engines are in, I need to get better at launching this thing. I'm staying right here with this simulation until I get it right. Mr. Greg can cover me in school."

Patty heaved a sigh. "That's stupid. You need to go to school."

Eddie stepped around her. "I'm not going to school today. That means both of you have to go so things won't look suspicious."

"You don't look so good," said Patty. "Anyway, Timothy said he wasn't going to school either."

"Timothy, you're going to school," said Eddie.

"Don't tell me to go to school. My dad never told me to go to school."

"He didn't have to. You went anyway."

"According to you, we've got a schedule to keep," Timothy said. "I know what I'm doing by staying here."

Eddie crossed his arms. "You don't know anything."

Patty stepped between the two while tapping her left foot. "What's wrong with you two? Come on. Both of you, let's get to school. People are already talking and Mr. Greg can't work miracles."

Timothy's eyebrows shot up. "Talking about what? What are people saying at school?"

"If you come to school, you'll know."

Before Timothy could reply, Eddie stumbled out of the room and ran down the hallway. Patty and Timothy raced after him. He was fast for an old guy. They found him hunched over the nearest toilet with traces of green slime coming out of his mouth. Eddie held out his hand for Timothy and Patty to not come near.

"One of you get me that bottle of pills in the top cabinet there."

Eddie grabbed three of the pills from Timothy and dumped them down his throat all at once as Patty handed him a glass of water. After a few moments, both teenagers helped Eddie to a standing position.

"The pills are working," said Eddie. The color in his face was returning to a non-dead appearance.

"You need to see a doctor," said Patty. "That stuff you were spitting up looked pretty yucky."

"Could someone make me some buttered toast? I threw up my breakfast," Eddie told the two of them.

"I'll make it. You stay with him," Patty said to Timothy.

As Timothy half carried Eddie to his bedroom, he heard Patty's mother come into the house. Only Patty came to the bedroom with the toast.

"I told my mom to wait in the car. I'm going to school. You two will be alright?"

"I don't know about Timothy, but I'm doing better, thanks," said Eddie.

After Patty left, Eddie told Timothy, "You need to go to school. One day this will be all over and your life will continue."

"Continue as what? What am I going to do when you and that rocket are gone?" Timothy had thought about this way too much lately. Frustrated, he left Eddie to eat his toast and drink his water.

Timothy spent the bulk of the morning in the tower working on launching a rocket with software that was trying hard to make him fail. He kept taking breaks to check on Eddie who was asleep and snoring. And, answering text messages from his three classmates with Eddie's cell phone.

Eddie promised he'd give the phone to Timothy after he was launched. Timothy didn't think he wanted to inherit anything else. He wanted people to stop dying on him. Mostly he wanted his own smartphone.

He finally got three simulated rockets into low-Earth orbit. He would have gone higher if he could use his special fuel and engines. Timothy decided the simulation needed adjusting and he texted Luke who texted he was on his way. Timothy hoped he wasn't bringing Patty and Angie. He didn't want them seeing how often he had failed using the simulation.

A little after noon, Luke showed up in the tower launch room with Patty and Angie.

"Great, now everyone is missing school," said Timothy.

"Stop whining. We got credit since we made it through lunch period," said Angie.

"Move over and let me look at the coding," said Luke.

"I've gotta check on Eddie," said Timothy, followed by the girls.

They found him in his bedroom going over a pile of documents. Somehow the stack had grown and spilled onto the floor as if the papers were reproducing.

"What are you doing with all this stuff?" Timothy asked.

"I'm reading it."

"I can see that. What are they?"

"Documents explaining how the capsule will work, navigation systems, how we'll know when *Betty Boop* is in orbit. I'm hungry. Let's go into the kitchen."

Eddie walked past Timothy, leaving documents scattered on the floor behind him like a rocket trail. Timothy tried to talk to him, but Eddie kept walking toward the kitchen. Timothy wondered if stubbornness came with dying. The girls followed them.

Despite being ill most of the day, Eddie stopped the others from helping him. He scrambled a half dozen eggs, plated deli meats, and dropped slices of sourdough bread onto a paper plate. Condiments and jellies were already on the table. He put a healthy portion of honey on his sandwich.

Timothy got the chips and crackers and Patty put out a pitcher of ice water that looked more like ice. Angie and Luke figured out how to work the percolator and the hot coffee didn't taste that burnt. They had mixed nuts with ketchup on them for a snack.

They all crammed together around the kitchen table as Eddie explained what he was reading. "When you adjust the simulation, you should take into consideration that the rocket has a gimbaled nozzle on the end. This lets the center of gravity be adjusted easily," he said, looking at all of them with egg stuck to his chin. "Also, the rocket is controlled during flight by three gyroscopes in the nose that loop back through computers to the nozzle. This and the fins help balance the rocket during flight."

"Then what will I be controlling?" Timothy wondered if Eddie, who looked pale, was going to throw up again.

"All the thrust and the gimbaled nozzle. Too much thrust and the rocket will fly apart. Too little and it'll stall. Also, too much fluctuation in speed and the gyroscopes won't work right. That's what the simulation should be helping you with."

"You'll also have to make adjustments the higher up *Betty Boop* goes since there'll be less friction to work against," Patty told Timothy.

"Maybe we can get a steeper launch angle and reach orbit faster," said Luke.

"Except the higher G-forces could be hard on fragile components," said Patty.

Timothy thought about the G forces on Eddie's fragile body. He stared at his sandwich, which oozed mustard, ketchup, mayonnaise, and honey. He might have forgotten to add in any deli meat.

"We can increase speed through the atmosphere and keep the G forces low," suggested Angie.

Luke asked, "In space, how is the rocket controlled?"

"In the *Redstone*, there are two thrusters at the top and three at the bottom," Eddie explained. "The top thrusters are Vernier rockets that adjust for velocity and steering. The bottom three are attitude-control thrusters used for larger movements. The thrusters can be turned to slow the rocket as it approaches something, like a docking station."

"So, the top thrusters are to maneuver with and the bottom thrusters are to stop and start?" said Luke.

Eddie nodded. "Yeah, that's it. I think that's everything for now."

"Except for one thing," said Patty.

"What?" Eddie asked.

"Like when are you and Timothy going to tell us that Eddie's dying and he's the special satellite going up in the capsule?" said Angie.

Chapter 33

"How'd you guess?" Timothy exclaimed.

"We all noticed Eddie's health issues. Also, the capsule is designed for human flight," said Patty. "After I explained to the others Eddie's episode from this morning, we were almost sure of you and Eddie's plan."

"I never knew someone who was dying," said Luke interrupting everyone. He had gotten up from the table and was leaning against the kitchen counter with his arms folded in front of him.

"I don't think any of us has," said Patty.

"Except Timothy," said Angie, who stared at Timothy with sympathy. "I'm sorry."

Timothy couldn't say anything. He didn't want pity. He didn't want to talk about death. He wanted to scream at everyone that he wished they'd already launched Eddie into space and this thing was over with. Except, Eddie sat there looking at him.

"I'm glad the secret is out. I don't like secrets, anyway." Timothy avoided any sympathy from anyone. "Now let's focus on what this means. Each of you could be held responsible for Eddie's death." He got up from the table and went over to lean against the kitchen counter next to Luke.

"You seem to be all right with it," said Angie.

"There's no such thing as being all right with anything that's going on here. From Eddie dying to launching this rocket. But I'm trying to accept what's happening." Timothy took a deep breath before continuing, "I believe in last wishes. My dad never got to see the formula or engines work. At least Eddie will see them work."

"Why didn't your dad come here with the formula and engines since he told you where to go?" Angie sounded like she wanted the secrets to end.

So did Timothy. He got angry with himself. He wondered many times this same thing, but was afraid of the answer from Eddie.

"I know the answer," said Eddie looking at Timothy. The answer was coming, regardless.

"I sent your dad a letter telling him I was dying and where to find me. I wrote that ET put a rocket here. I didn't know your dad was an alcoholic." Eddie slapped his hands against his face and hid there as if trying to reverse time. "I think he tried to sober up and the withdrawal probably killed him."

Timothy couldn't say anything. He just stared at Eddie. At the person who just admitted to killing his dad. Timothy hated Eddie at that moment, more than he hated his dad for dying on him. Everyone stayed silent.

Finally, Timothy announced, "The people who came said my dad's sudden withdrawal from alcohol probably caused cardiac arrest."

"In other words, he had a heart attack. Wow, this is tough," said Luke, who paced back and forth in front of the sink. "This whole thing is getting tough."

Timothy glared at Eddie. "Why didn't you just come and see him? Why send a letter?"

Angie reached across the table and brought Eddie's hands down from his face. She kept holding them as Patty boldly went over to Timothy and gave him a hug. Luke paced faster.

Timothy pushed Patty away. He resented that her soft touch across his shoulders had relieved some of his anger at Eddie. He wanted that anger. Everyone stayed silent, still recovering from all this new information.

"Before you judge me, let me explain," Eddie said, not sure what to do with his hands. "That ET guy from NASA brought the rocket here, then died. I eventually found his notes and realized Timothy's dad had the formula and engines. I sent a letter because I was afraid the government was watching everything. The only thing they don't monitor are letters in the mail. I had no clue he was a drinker or I would have come myself."

More silence from everyone. There didn't seem to be a way to end this flood of secrets.

"At this point, I'm being selfish to ask any of you—Timothy included—to help me," said Eddie. "I never should've started this whole thing. I could be ruining your lives and you each deserve better than a selfish old man putting you at risk like this."

"I'm not leaving you here to die in this house while we have a perfectly good rocket out there to send you into space," said Luke. He had stopped pacing.

Everyone looked at Timothy wondering what he would do. After a few moments, he told Eddie, "I can't blame you for my dad's death. He did that to himself. If it's anyone's fault, I should have done more to get him to stop drinking." Timothy paused before continuing, "I don't want to talk about any of this anymore. My dad's dead, Eddie's dying, and we have a rocket to launch."

"I'm in with everything," Angie spoke up before anything else could be said.

"I'm not leaving Eddie to die on Earth," said Patty. "I'm in too."

Luke reached out with his open hand turned down. Something the football team always did before a game, he explained.

Angie got up and placed her hand on top of his. Patty came next. Timothy stood there looking at everyone and everyone looking at him.

There was more he wanted to know about Eddie, his dad, and this mysterious ET person. Timothy knew that Eddie didn't purposely kill his dad. He was sure Eddie would have preferred working with his dad than some confused teenager.

After a few moments, Timothy put his hand on top of Patty's.

They looked at Eddie who asked them to scoot closer so he wouldn't have to get up. They all shuffled over, trying not to trip over one another.

Chapter 34

"Now that we've got that all over with, let's get some work done," said Angie. "We have to start setting up the equipment in the communication room and get things linked to the silo and *Betty Boop*."

On the way to the room, Luke whispered to Patty, "I want to know more about this ET guy Eddie mentioned."

"Yeah, and I want to know why the rocket's here," replied Patty.

They had no time to finish their talk. Everyone met in the room next to the tower where they worked on setting up the electronics. Eddie told them the control room would be where the communications, guidance, navigation, and computer systems would be located. This included the life-support systems.

Around the time Eddie and the teenagers would have been home from school, the NASA troupe showed up. They didn't ask why the teenagers had been there for several hours already. Instead, they were much better at getting things set up, Timothy thought. Later that night, everyone met in the kitchen with still a lot more energy to keep going.

"We can get a lot done if we work the whole day tomorrow," said Ted. He had pushed for the teenagers to take the day off from school.

"I realize things need to get done, but I am seriously falling behind in some of my school work. No big deal, but teachers will begin to notice something's up," said Patty.

"We can't just quit school," said Angie.

"Yeah, they don't have sabbaticals in high school," said Luke. "But, taking off the afternoon shouldn't hurt as long as Mr. Greg is willing to keep helping us."

The teenagers agreed, and Eddie was quick to call Mr. Greg. He could get the four students out of afternoon classes the next day so they could work on the "special project."

With everyone gone and the clock heading toward midnight, Timothy couldn't sleep. He got up and tinkered with the simulation and got three rockets into a stable orbit. He just hoped the simulation was accurate enough with the adjustments Luke had made.

He checked on Eddie, who was snoring lightly in bed. Timothy made sure he was covered up before going onto the front porch. There, he spotted a dark green sedan at the end of the driveway. He couldn't tell how many were in the car. It didn't matter. He knew that only government people would dare drive cars that shade of green.

Timothy was tired of the spying. They both knew each other, so why didn't the government men come up and ask what he and Eddie were doing. He decided enough was enough and he waved at the car. He wanted them to come toward the house. They quickly drove away. Timothy shrugged his shoulders and went to bed.

Before falling asleep, he thought about where he used to live and memories of his dad found him.

"I'd like a BLT and a cup of coffee," Timothy's father told the waitress.

It was Timothy's sixteenth birthday and they sat in a long thin diner that smelled of thick grease the wrong way.

"What'll you have, son?"

Timothy stared at his father with sagging eyes, shallows in his cheeks, and a thin smile that broke at the edges and collapsed. The stained menu sat open on the table. The waitress, who smelled of cigarette smoke, had opened it for Timothy. He didn't dare touch it. The stains were unrecognizable. Of course, napkins made no appearance.

"Pick something, damn it," said his dad.

Timothy's birthday supper. "I'll take the cheese sandwich."

"Grill it, honey, and bring some sweet tea for the kid. Happy birthday, son."

The baggy-eyed, tired-looking waitress went behind the counter, placed the order with a man wearing an apron layered in stains, and poured herself black coffee into a stained cup. Timothy caught his dad's swiftness with a short liquor bottle upended into his coffee.

"Tomorrow's goin' to be a good day for yard work," said Timothy's dad.

Each spring, they planted a garden that the rabbits, deer, and insects ate before the weeds took over. In the fall they moved shrubbery so often that the plants were dead long before their final resting place. Timothy dreaded nice days.

Always during this yard work, his dad would eventually give up and go into the house muttering, "Reanette made the best gardens and I don't know how to make them beautiful again."

At home after his birthday dinner, Timothy watched his dad watch cooking shows on TV. The elder held an orange juice and vodka in his right hand with the changer in his left hand. At least the orange juice was healthy, Timothy thought.

While his dad flipped between several cooking shows, Timothy sat in the living room reading graphic novels. He hoped to learn something from the superheroes on how to be a person who could survive when they weren't a hero.

On the edge of sleep in Eddie's house, Timothy thought about the last days with his mom. They played board games that she let him win.

Chapter 35

The next morning, Timothy and Eddie sat on the front porch eating a toasted sandwich with scrambled eggs, shredded cheddar cheese, and sweet pickles with a little honey and a hint of hot sauce. Some saltines on it, too. And, fried tuna fish.

Timothy had convinced Eddie to get instant coffee and, with enough sugar, it wasn't too bad. When Eddie went in the house to get his keys, Timothy saw the same government spies drive slowly past the house in the same ugly green sedan.

He waved at them and they drove away. He figured they understood each other enough that there was no need for secrecy, anymore. Timothy decided not to tell Eddie since he had enough stress with finding his keys. He probably knew anyway. Timothy went into the house and found his keys on the kitchen table.

In school that morning, Timothy spent most of his time avoiding classmates who wanted to know about Mr. Greg's special project. Rumors and gossip fueled many theories. He didn't know how the other three fared. At lunchtime, Timothy was the first to Luke's car for the ride to Eddie's house.

They all told different stories to their classmates, adding to the ones already circling through the school. There were so many that no one would know that none of them were true. At the house, Eddie gathered the four teenagers around the kitchen table to go over what they were supposed to do that afternoon.

While serving lunch, Eddie announced, "The others had to leave for Langley. We're on our own this afternoon."

"Why did they leave? They mentioned nothing about going anywhere yesterday," questioned Patty. Her suspicion was evident.

"An opportunity came up to get some special equipment," said Eddie.

Patty let the issue drop. Eddie gave no indication he would offer any other information. Instead, the teenagers looked at the mismatched lunch. The food looked like it was meant to be studied rather than eaten.

Luke stared briefly at his sourdough bread sandwich, filled with crushed blueberries, and grated Parmesan before taking a big bite. There was fried deli turkey somewhere inside with chocolate chips.

Timothy held his sandwich away from his face. Between the two slices of sourdough bread were cheesy spinach with a touch of hot sauce and fried sardines. He pushed some salty potato chips in there before taking a bite. The instant coffee was hot enough that he could barely taste anything.

Angie bit into her fried deli ham and sweet pickle, sour cream, strawberry jam sandwich. Patty took a nibble from her sandwich of fried deli turkey, sour cream, a splash of hot sauce, and peanut butter with walnuts thrown in.

They watched Eddie stand by the stove making his homemade chicken noodle soup. Mostly, it was a mixture of chicken broth and cooked lima beans with extra noodles along with seasoning. Last, he mixed in crushed tomatoes and spinach leaves.

"From now on we need to focus on specific jobs," Eddie said, stirring his concoction. "Angie, you'll be on communications. Luke, you'll manage the guidance, navigation, and overall control. Patty, you'll be with the support facilities to make sure the computers and anything electrical in the structure and mechanical systems run correctly. This includes the life-support."

Angie looked concerned. "What about Timothy?"

"He'll be in charge of the fuel, meaning he'll dictate how the rocket will fly."

Angie finished her sandwich in a few quick gulps. "When are your NASA friends coming back? We could use some of their mentoring to get the computers going. We also need to build some checklists so nothing gets forgotten."

"On Friday. When they get back, everyone will be assigned one of them as a mentor in your jobs."

"I don't need anyone," said Timothy.

"Ted is mentoring you," said Eddie.

The other three teenagers eyed Timothy, waiting for his reaction.

He dropped his sandwich and held up his hands. "I don't want to have anything to do with that guy. He can do other stuff besides helping me."

"Everyone needs a mentor. Launching *Betty Boop* means paying attention to a lot of details that are only learned from experience. Also, it's important to have two people at each station as a backup to make sure nothing gets forgotten. NASA works on redundancies and that's what we're doing."

"Wait a minute," said Luke. "If they're going to be our mentors, why don't they do this themselves? Why do you need us?"

Eddie stopped stirring and stared at his soup as if looking for the answer. "I think the four of you will be better at managing any crises that come up."

"You don't trust them," Patty said slowly.

"I trust the four of you," Eddie replied carefully.

"Let me get this straight," said Luke. "They know a lot and you question their allegiance. So, you're trusting us who know little."

"Yeah, that's about it," said Eddie.

"Haven't you known them for a long time?" Patty stopped eating. Some of Eddie's concoctions were just not that good.

"That's the problem," said Angie, mostly not talking to Eddie. "This formula and engines will change everything we do in space. This will open up another industry, making at least the planets in our solar systems reachable. Eddie doesn't want them to know too much of this technology."

No one said anything for a few seconds as Eddie took his time tasting his soup with a few slurps from a spoon too big for his mouth. He finished slurping and said, "They have experience and the expertise to launch *Betty Boop*. Only the four of you will know everything."

Angie took her plate to the sink. "This raises the question I've wondered. Should Timothy patent this formula?"

"His father already did." Eddie watched Timothy, who stared back with a partially eaten sandwich hanging out of his mouth. Eddie continued. "In your father's documents is a patent naming you as co-inventor, along with himself and your mother."

Timothy dropped his sandwich again. "Why didn't you tell me this before?"

"I only found this out last night while reading some of those documents. Now you know."

"Wow, Timothy," Angie said. "One day you could be a trillionaire."

"I don't want to be a trillionaire. I don't know what I want. But it certainly isn't being super rich," said Timothy. He quickly ate the last of his sandwich.

No one said anything for a few seconds as Timothy chewed his lunch. Until Luke said, "Well, that's settled. You give me all your money and I'll buy a football team. They're great at losing money."

"I say we build our own rocket," said Patty.

"Yeah, I'd like to go see the Moon in style," said Angie.

Timothy took his plate to the sink. "Let's talk about this later and focus on getting that rocket into space." It occurred to him that everything could fail. There would be no money when that happened.

"Let's talk about Mr. Greg coming tomorrow evening," Eddie announced.

"Why is he coming here?" Patty made it almost to the sink with her bowl.

"He wanted to see the project and we owe it to him for everything he's done," Eddie replied.

The four teenagers looked at each other wondering who Mr. Greg would be mentoring.

Chapter 36

On Thursday, Mr. Greg showed up after supper. He heard about Eddie's meals and chose to eat before he arrived. Even when he wasn't in the classroom teaching, Mr. Greg didn't look like the typical high school teacher.

Like that evening when he wore a colorful, almost clownish bow tie, a loose plaid shirt, even looser fitting jeans, and penny loafers with rusty looking pennies stuck on top in small slats. He was taller than Luke and most of the football team, kept his white beard trimmed short, and let what pieces of gray hair he had go long and wild in all directions off his head. His small pot belly moved a lot when he laughed, which was mostly at his own jokes.

In class, he talked a lot about subatomic particles and quantum physics. Few students liked to hear about the fantasy lives of the charming, strange, and bottom quantum particles. Luke and Patty were two of the few.

As soon as he arrived, Mr. Greg wanted to see the rocket. Luke drove the jeep with Eddie and Patty aboard. On the drive to the silo, the teacher took the opportunity to talk about anti-negative energy.

"I agree with those scientists who think anti-negative energy exists," said Mr. Greg. "More importantly, I think it is associated in some way with dark energy. Anti-negative energy could be what dark energy emits when interacting with quantum gravitational forces."

Luke wondered why Mr. Greg didn't have a doctorate in physics. While Patty asked questions, Luke was more concerned about the physics teacher's role in this launching stuff.

They stayed at the silo for almost an hour showing Mr. Greg the rocket and bringing him up to the capsule. Many of his questions had to do with the rocket and capsule. He had no questions concerning the fuel and engines. It was as if he knew about them already.

At the house, Timothy and Angie worked in the control room getting things organized and hooked up. When they completed the first section, they tested to make sure everything connected the right way.

After twenty minutes working on the next section, a slight trickle of sweat beaded on Angie's forehead. She stopped and asked Timothy, "You ever think about me in a special way?"

"Like how?" Timothy set down a monitor next to others.

"Like a girl and not another classmate or team member."

Timothy stared at Angie as though she had become a green-skinned alien. "Yeah."

"I just want to be clear about things. Luke and I aren't together anymore and I don't want to get into another relationship. Is that okay?"

Timothy wasn't sure. "Yeah, that's okay."

Angie smiled. "All this stuff with the rocket is making me think I may want to do something other than dating. I want to be independent in college and decide on my own destiny. Then, I'll find someone or not. That makes sense?"

"Yeah, you're smart like that. You understanding what you want."

Angie gave Timothy that special smile. "Good. We'll just stay friends. Now, here take these cables. We've got a lot of connecting to do."

Timothy wished he had been prepared to answer Angie in a different way. He liked Angie and felt she could be his first girlfriend. At least they'll be friends, he thought. Thinking about it, he realized Angie was his first true friend. He was glad about that.

They were still working on getting the hardware connected, powered up, and tested by the time the others got back.

As Luke and Patty helped, Mr. Greg talked to Eddie privately in his bedroom. That's where the spacesuit was, Timothy thought. He's going to know everything. Timothy tried to focus on what he was doing, but it was hard.

After half an hour, Mr. Greg came out telling the teenagers, "I expect to see everyone in class tomorrow. I hear there might be a pop quiz."

The four looked at each other wondering if the quiz would be about the rocket. Mr. Gregg smiled on his way out. Eddie yawned as he joined everyone.

"I'm going to bed," he said.

"What did you and Mr. Greg talk about?" asked timothy. The others did not seem to care.

"You'll find out when your next story begins." Eddie smiled and patted Timothy's shoulder before heading to his bedroom.

Soon after, everyone left to join their families. With the return of the NASA group, Timothy wondered what was next. They could launch almost at any time. He went to Eddie's bedroom.

Eddie sat on his bed complaining about how crappy a day he had dealing with the other janitors not doing their jobs.

"You don't look so good," Timothy said.

"I'm an old, dying man. I'm supposed to look this way."

"Tomorrow your NASA friends come back."

"They're not my friends. I need their know-how and NASA contacts."

Timothy didn't bother asking why the contacts were important. Instead, he asked. "Don't you have any friends?"

"Right now, just you." Eddie stood up. "I've been reincarnated eleven times. One more and I might get used to it."

"Where'd that come from? How'd reincarnation come up?" Timothy wondered if this was what dying people thought about. "Besides, how do you know you've been reincarnated eleven times?"

"I've always felt it was my number. In the Bible's Book of Revelation, the Apostle John saw eleven things at the final judgment."

Timothy panicked. "Are you dying right now? Not to be mean about it, but we're pretty close to launching you into space for you to die in your bedroom."

"No, I'm not dying right now. At least I don't think so."

"Are you going crazy, then? It'll be hard launching *Betty Boop* if you're not mentally well."

Eddie smiled and waved a hand at Timothy. "No, no. Nothing like that. I've thought about this reincarnation before and I'm feeling good about the twelfth one. Anyway, I'm going to bed. We've got a lot to do starting tomorrow. I suggest you do something that isn't about *Betty Boop*. Take your mind off this launch."

"Well, I'm almost done with a Jules Verne book I borrowed from you."

"What is it?"

"*From the Earth to the Moon*. It sounded interesting."

"We had a small library when I was in high school," Eddie said. "One thing it had was all the Jules Verne books. I read them all."

Timothy nodded. "I'll see you in the morning."

"Goodnight."

Timothy went to his bedroom, worried about what would happen after this last night of calm. He planned on telling everyone that they needed to hurry and finish things up. Timothy wasn't sure how much longer Eddie had. He seemed to be getting weaker. Timothy thought they were in a race and approaching the finish line.

Chapter 37

On Friday at lunchtime, Luke drove the teenagers to Eddie's place. The NASA group was already there in the kitchen making lunch.

"They came a little while ago bringing some borrowed NASA equipment," said Eddie.

Timothy leaned toward him. "Is it borrowed or stolen?"

"If we bring it back, it's borrowed," said Ted, interrupting. He leaned over a griddle on the counter. "I'm making pancakes for lunch."

"I'm doing the eggs," said Henry, near the stove. He stirred a cast iron skillet filled with too many scrambled eggs. "I have to scramble them since I can't flip anything."

"Timothy, we need to know which flight path we're taking," said Ted. He tried flipping a pancake and half of it ended up hanging off the griddle.

"I know that," said Timothy aggravated. He did not know the flight path, but he would know as soon as he figured it out.

"Are we going to alert government agencies about this launch?" Angie asked, stopping Timothy before he said anything else. "We should give them time to clear the skies."

"We'll alert the FAA and local airports. We'll also send out a radio blast to clear any small aircraft before launch," Gene explained.

"I'm curious," said Patty. "What did all of you tell your families about coming here?"

"My ex-wives are not interested in my whereabouts," Henry said.

"How many wives did you have?" Luke asked as Sam took over from Henry who had stirred some scrambled eggs onto the stovetop.

"Two. One thought I would be rich working for NASA. Ha! The other married me only to get in bed with astronauts."

"You live alone?" asked Angie.

"I've been living with Peggy for a few years. Best relationship I've had and I'm not ruining it with marriage. She agrees. She would have come, but she's an elementary school teacher. I told her I'd give her the details when I got back. She's cool with it. She's met everyone here."

Ted managed to get a few pancakes flipped. "I was engaged once, but we split up. I got pissed about the break up and married another woman who ran off with a Latin lover who turned out to be already married. I refused to take her back."

Patty set the dishes and silverware out. "Why didn't you give her another chance?"

Ted hesitated before replying, "He was her third lover in two years. I detected a pattern with that woman. Now, I'm waiting to date again. I didn't have anyone to tell."

"What about the woman you were engaged to?" asked Angie.

Ted shrugged his shoulders. "I guess I would have told her." He went back to his pancakes.

"I couldn't have an affair on my wife. I'd be too afraid she wouldn't like it," Gene said with a wide smile. She helped Angie with the percolator. "Also, I didn't have the time. My wife and I were too busy raising the triplets we adopted as babies. They're sophomores in college now and I'm an expert at getting scholarships. My wife Linda thought it was a good idea for me to help high schoolers on a science project. I told her it was a real rocket. I guess she'll believe me when we launch it. I'm excited to see the expression on her face."

Sam handed Luke a bowl. As she scooped the eggs into it, she said, "My husband and I were married almost twenty years and ran a small farm. We decided long ago not to have kids. We have nieces and nephews to hang around with. I told my husband Donald what was going on here and to keep it quiet. He will. He said he's ready to come bail me out if we get arrested."

"Let's stop a minute," Timothy announced. "In other words, there are more people who know what's going on here." He sounded very worried.

"It's okay," said Luke. "We're almost ready to launch *Betty Boop*."

Ted got the last of the pancakes out of the pan. "Yeah, I think we're pretty close to putting Eddie into orbit."

There were a few seconds of silence from the teenagers who looked at one another, then at Eddie who shrugged.

"I told them," Eddie said, avoiding their looks.

"Good. I'm glad everyone knows. I don't enjoy keeping secrets," said Luke, stabbing and dragging some pancakes onto his plate. He put a hefty load of scrambled eggs on top of them along with a dollop or three of raspberry preserves, honey, and yellow mustard. From the pantry, he brought over a jar of green olives. Four seemed to fit on the pancakes.

The others followed Luke's lead to the food as Timothy stood in the way looking at Eddie, who sat at the table eating as if this was his last meal.

"I'm assuming all of you NASA people are all right with this assisted suicide mission?" Timothy announced.

"Yeah, we're cool with it," said Sam smiling. "Otherwise you wouldn't like us." She winked.

Timothy wanted to learn how to wink. He liked her too much to say anything back. He wondered if she was up to adopting a teenager when everything was over with.

Most found a place to lean against, except Sam and Angie who sat on clean towels on the floor near the door. The strong coffee made everyone talk a lot, except Timothy who tried to listen to what Angie and Sam were talking about.

Before they finished eating, Sam's cell phone made a loud vibration. Gene's rang like an old dial phone. Ted and Henry's went off with the same beeping sound. They all looked at their phones. Gene was the first to jump up and turn on the kitchen TV hanging over the table. All the stations were running the same news story.

"The International Space Station is in emergency mode. The Soyuz escape capsule has been damaged by a piece of space material. The crew and the international space community are determining the extent of the damage."

Chapter 38

After a few minutes, Ted got off his cell. "The ISS is in more trouble than what the news is saying. There were several debris hits to the station. NASA is readying a rocket for launch tomorrow morning."

"They're rushing that launch," said Henry. "They still had a week of prep to do."

"They never do well rushing a launch," Gene said, sounding worried.

"If that rocket doesn't work, doesn't Russia or the European Space Agency have rockets?" Patty didn't take her eyes off the TV screen, which showed the worried faces of NASA people in control rooms.

"They're not even close to a launch. They sent up some satellites two weeks ago and won't be able to launch for another three weeks," Ted said.

"What about the Chinese?" Angie was listening to Ted more than the TV reports.

"They have a rocket on their launch pad, but no one knows how close it is to launching," said Ted. "There are also the commercial rockets, but they've either just launched or configured for a shorter launch trajectory that won't reach the ISS. It's the same with the U.S. military rockets."

Eddie stared at Timothy. "We need to get ready to launch. How soon can you get *Betty Boop* fueled up?"

"Why? You can't save the ISS."

"We need to try."

Timothy felt the kitchen, TV news, and everyone disappear from his focus, leaving only Eddie's words banging around in his head.

With everyone staring at Timothy, finally he said, "It won't take long to load the fuel."

"Okay, let's get ready to launch," said Luke.

"Seriously?" Patty said. "We'll be rushing the launch just like NASA is."

"This is risky," Sam leaned toward Eddie. "You think you can help the ISS if the NASA rocket fails?"

Eddie nodded. "I think so. We can't bring anyone back in the *Mercury* capsule, but we can get supplies up there. Maybe it'll be enough until another rocket reaches them."

"If we're going to save the ISS, we have a lot of work to do. My NASA contacts said the ISS is losing power," said Ted. "They've shut down several of the modules and even that might not be enough."

Timothy searched the faces of the NASA group and his classmates. Everyone looked more than committed to saving the ISS. He did, too.

Suddenly nothing felt ready to Timothy.

Chapter 39

Sam gave assignments out to everyone and they all rushed out of the kitchen to either the communication or launch room. Except Ted who asked Eddie and Timothy to stay behind.

"I'll let my NASA contacts know we have a rocket ready to launch if theirs fails," said Ted.

"Don't put in that last part," said Eddie. "They're sensitive about expected failures."

Timothy panicked. Things were moving too fast. He interrupted loudly. "If you tell them about our rocket and theirs' makes it, they'll shut us down."

"People in NASA already know about this rocket," Ted said in a steady voice. "I let them think it was someone's hobby and probably couldn't be launched."

"That's why those spies were hanging around here," said Timothy. "They weren't looking for *Betty Boop* because they already knew it was here. They wanted to know what kind of fuel we were making to launch it."

"They weren't amused by that fake formula. They would have shut everything down, but I convinced them not to. I still have some pull there," said Ted.

"You only convinced them so you could figure out what the formula was yourself," Timothy said accusingly.

"I had no interest in the formula because I didn't think was real. If it was, I didn't think it would work. I'm more of a believer now, though. It doesn't matter since I found out about Eddie's condition. Now I'm all in."

Ted and Timothy faced each other with mistrust in their eyes.

"I hate secrets." Timothy stood in the center of the kitchen, his hands by his side, fists clenched.

"I promise you, Timothy, there are no more secrets," said Ted. "At least not from me."

Henry came into the kitchen. "I got a call from one of my NASA friends. They're sending a team here."

Timothy turned to him. "What team?"

"NASA people who want to help us launch this rocket," he said.

"You lied, you already told them," Timothy hissed at Ted.

"Whoa, Timothy," said Henry. "Turns out they had some spies hanging around outside and told NASA."

Before Timothy could apologize to Ted, they heard Eddie try to get up from the table. They watched him lose his balance and plop back down in his chair.

"I'm alright," Eddie said waving off their help to stand up. "We don't have time for these arguments. We have a rocket to launch."

Eddie had a look of confidence. He also looked like he was going to throw up.

Timothy asked, "Should we call your hospice people?"

"I'm already loaded up on drugs from my hospice nurse who stopped by earlier. I'll never know I'm hurting for at least twenty-four hours." He grabbed Timothy's shirtsleeve and said, "You need these NASA people. Don't worry; everything will work out."

Timothy stared at Eddie wondering how things will work out. Finally, he said, "We'd better get things ready to send you into space then," Timothy was boosted by Eddie's look of determination.

"Follow me," Henry told Timothy. "We need you in the launch room."

Timothy followed Henry, wondering what his parents would have thought of him trying to send a dying old man into outer space to save the International Space Station.

Chapter 40

Angie met Henry and Timothy in the hallway. "We have to get the bacteria near the capsule so it can be loaded into the engines when it's time." She had stopped them outside the climate controlled room where the vials were stored.

"Why?" asked Timothy.

"It'll save time when we get ready to launch the rocket," answered Angie.

"I get it," said Henry. "If the NASA rocket is successful, we're still launching Eddie. But we'll have to make it fast with a lot of outsiders in the way. I'll get the others."

"The temperature of the bacteria has to be kept within a certain range," Timothy said as Henry walked off.

"We've got it covered." Angie held up a cooler she was carrying. "The NASA people brought several of these this morning. They're high-end coolers and can maintain the bacteria's temperature for days."

Before Timothy could ask more questions, the others showed up. Soon the boxes of vials were inside the coolers and in the back of Eddie's jeep along with the spacesuit and its accessories. The jeep was crowded, but Timothy managed to wedge himself in with the coolers.

Henry drove while everyone else, including Eddie, stayed at the house. With the coolers snuggled up beside him, Timothy thought about how the bacteria were his dad's and would soon be gone. Just like his dad. He wished both his parents were with him through all of this.

He missed them both. But there was no time to think about that too much. Henry was driving and said he forgot his glasses.

They made it without running off the road or hitting the silo. Inside, Henry and Timothy used the elevator to bring the coolers up and stack them beside the capsule. They also brought up the spacesuit and carefully placed it and the accessories between the capsule and coolers.

When done, Timothy examined the side of the rocket. Just below the capsule sat a plastic panel with two tubes for each engine sticking out, ready to be filled with the fuel. They would make loading the fuel into the engines easy and fast, Timothy thought. Finished with the fuel, he could swiftly take away the panel and zip up the metal skin with no trace of the opening.

Henry looked at the tubes. "How long can the fuel be in the engines before they go bad?"

"We have three hours," Timothy replied.

"Tight window. There can't be any delay once we're fueled up." Henry turned his attention to the spacesuit. "I always wanted to wear one of those in space. Except they look too uncomfortable."

He led Timothy toward the ladder. "I'll take the elevator down. That way it'll be in place for our special cargo."

Back at the house, everyone worked for hours on the communication and launch room getting the equipment to talk to each other. They took a break before supper to gather in the kitchen and watch the latest news on the false-color TV. After a short while, they heard a noise outside.

Walking onto the front porch and turning on the lights, they saw two dark green SUVs in the driveway.

"At least they knew the way here," said Eddie joining Timothy on the porch.

Chapter 41

Next to one of the SUVs stood a short woman with pale skin and black hair pulled into a knot on top of her head. She wore a dark gray pantsuit and white blouse that made her slightly heavy body seem heavier. Behind her stood two tall, men. One was bald and had spent too much time in the sun. The other had an olive skin tone with short curly, black hair. Both looked relaxed in their open-collared shirts and ready to fight to the death, if necessary.

Out of the other SUV stepped a tall, husky woman with a short burgundy ponytail and wearing a dark pantsuit that looked more like a uniform. Three tanned men stood behind her, looking like they would topple over with their thick, muscular shoulders and heavy necks. They wore suits and ties that looked more like weapons than business clothes.

Ted and Sam joined Eddie and Timothy on the porch, but it was Sam who went to greet the knot haired woman.

"I'm Samantha. You must be from NASA." She extended her hand.

"I'm Cathy Wright, director of NASA's Human Exploration and Operations Division." She grasped Sam's hand.

"And those other people?" Sam pointed to the other SUV.

"They're from the Department of Defense," she said, poking her thumb over her shoulder at them. "I'm told you have a rocket that could reach the International Space Station using some special fuel."

"Hi, Cathy," said Ted coming down and standing next to Samantha.

She ignored him and looked toward the house where the others had gathered on the porch. "Who are those people?"

"A few retired NASA friends and some teenagers from the high school to help," Ted replied.

Cathy eyed everyone as if she could wish them away and replace them with NASA people that she knew.

She turned to Ted. "We have a serious situation with the ISS and I'm not interested in playing games with a carnival of outsiders or you."

"Apparently you two know each other," said Sam.

Cathy ignored Sam's statement. "Before we go any further, I want to know the whole story here." She walked up the porch to meet Eddie.

"We don't have much time, so I'll get to the point," said Cathy. "I want to know what the fuel is made of and I want to see the rocket and launch systems. If I see that you're serious, we'll need to cooperate with each other. That means no secrets. Or else those Defense Department people will introduce themselves."

"The fuel isn't toxic or radioactive or anything. You'll have to trust us on that," Timothy said, determined to make Cathy pay attention to him.

Cathy ignored him and told Eddie, "Are you going to show me everything or shall I invite those others to take over?"

"We'll show you some things now and everything after we launch," Eddie proposed.

"I'm not negotiating."

Eddie took a step closer to Cathy before saying, "There's no negotiation. In the end, we'll be completely transparent. To minimize interference and not jeopardize our mission, we need to keep some things to ourselves. At least for now."

Eddie and Cathy stood in each other's personal space, less than a foot apart.

"I don't like secrets," Cathy said between clenched teeth.

Timothy thought Cathy was in trouble if she listened to Eddie, the king of secrets.

"I'm keeping secrets only to protect the mission, which is to save the ISS," Eddie responded.

"You're assuming we might fail with the rescue rocket."

"You made that assumption when you came here," said Eddie.

They stared at each like gunfighters, only they were too close to each other to shoot.

Finally, Cathy said slowly, "NASA will succeed. I came here only out of caution and somebody's influence."

"We'll tell you everything if your rocket succeeds," said Eddie. "I promise."

After a few seconds, Cathy said, "I need to make a phone call."

She walked back to her SUV, leaving the two men at the bottom of the stairs. Except everyone else went back into the house muttering that they had things to do. Timothy ended up alone with the two NASA men, who were more interested in watching the Defense Department people as if daring them to approach.

Thinking he didn't want to be involved in a confrontation between two U.S. federal departments, Timothy went into the house to find Eddie. He was at the kitchen table, sipping on a glass of ice water. Everyone else had gone to the communication and launch rooms.

"Why do you always drink ice water?" Timothy wanted to talk about something other than what was going on around them.

"Everything else messes with the drugs I'm taking."

Timothy wasn't sure what to say. Instead, he asked, "If you weren't taking the drugs, what would you like to drink?"

"Before the drugs, I liked a cold, dark beer. One for when I got up in the morning and one when I went to bed."

"Didn't a beer at night make you pee later?"

Eddie chuckled. "Yeah, but I never had trouble going back to sleep."

Cathy rushed into the kitchen alone and approached Eddie. "Many people in the government want to know what's going on here and you haven't provided enough answers." She held her right palm up before Eddie could argue. "However, there are enough people at NASA who argued not to interfere with what you have. Yet, I'm here and they're not. I want to know what's going on. I want to see the rocket and the fuel."

"I also want to see what you have in that silo," said the ponytail woman, who had barged into the kitchen.

She proclaimed she had a doctorate in aerospace engineering. No name, just a doctorate, as if that was the only identification they needed to know.

Cathy rolled her eyes before asking Eddie to lead the way.

"Okay, follow me," he said.

Timothy was shocked at how fast Eddie could move. The drugs must have been working overtime as the women scrambled after him with Timothy trailing behind. The doctorate's ponytail bounced up and down in front of him, making him dizzy.

They got to the jeep where Eddie pointed for Cathy to drive. No one talked along the way and, at the silo, Eddie was the first out of the jeep.

Timothy hoped the doctorate would fall and maybe sprain her ankle so she couldn't walk to the silo. Instead, she hopped out faster than Timothy. At the silo, Eddie swung the door opened for the women to enter.

"Okay, so you have a rocket," Cathy said calmly as if it was normal to have a *Redstone* rocket in a backyard silo.

"Where the hell did you get this?" The doctorate's voice echoed against the rocket. She sounded less awed and more pissed off.

"Now that you two have seen the rocket, let's go upstairs to see the rest," Eddie said.

The doctorate stood looking up at the *Redstone* as if she couldn't believe it was there. Or maybe she was trying to wish it away. Timothy figured Defense Department people didn't like to be surprised at finding a rocket off the East Coast of the United States. One that was three hundred miles from the capital.

The doctorate turned around and realized Eddie and Cathy had already left to go to the top. She stomped past Timothy as he jumped back to keep from being stomped on.

Eddie took the elevator while the doctorate followed Cathy up the chute ladder. Timothy was right behind them, anxious that the two women might ask too many questions about the capsule. Worried that they might ask even more questions about the fuel.

Before he got to the top, he panicked. Both women would see the spacesuit. He lunged up and through the doorway to see a canvas covering the suit and accessories. Only the coolers were in the open. Eddie had gotten there first and covered everything up.

"Sorry about the door. Sometimes it sticks," Eddie explained to the two women with a secret wink to Timothy.

"Just leave the door open next time," complained Cathy. She didn't appear to believe that doors stick.

Ignoring her, Eddie explained the basics of the *Mercury* capsule. The two women barely paid attention to him as they approached the coolers.

"This is what you were trying to hide with your 'stuck' door," said the doctorate. She pulled out a compact Geiger counter from her oversized pocketbook and waved the short wand close to each cooler. The machine stayed silent. She looked disappointed.

When the doctorate went to open one of the coolers, Timothy jumped in front of her. He was ready to fight her, if it came to that.

"The bacteria inside must be kept at a constant temperature. We can't risk anything at this point." Timothy put his hands on his hips, determined not to move. The doctorate looked just as determined to push him out of the way.

"Inside the coolers is a stable mixture of bacteria that's combustible only when certain elements come together inside the special engines," Eddie explained. "Whether or not we launch, you'll have access to everything. Isn't that right, Timothy?"

"You can't open the coolers," was all Timothy would say.

Cathy stepped between the two and faced Timothy.

"I don't have the time to discuss this anymore. Everything becomes the property of the government whether or not you launch," she said.

"You have a lot to hide," the doctorate said, gritting her teeth. She stared at Timothy with a firm look.

"Let's deal with the current situation first," said Cathy. "If this *Mercury* capsule gets to the ISS, how will you open the hatch?"

The question startled Timothy, who looked at Eddie for an answer.

"The original hatches had seventy bolts that exploded for a quick opening," Eddie explained.

"Yeah, I know all that. Get to the point," said Cathy.

"This capsule has no exploding bolts. Instead, it has a two-foot lever on the inside that operates a series of latching mechanisms. The hatch can be opened from the outside by shoving a long screwdriver or long rod in a hole near the door handle."

"What's powering the capsule?" the doctorate asked Eddie.

"A bank of lithium cobalt, ion rechargeable batteries under the seating area. Nothing exotic."

"Where did you get the batteries?" asked the doctorate.

"A foreign source."

The doctorate looked even less happy. Although, she hadn't looked happy since they'd met, thought Timothy.

The doctorate told Eddie, "I don't like any of this. Whatever's in this rocket better not be nuclear."

"Where would we get nuclear material?" Frustrated, Timothy threw his arms in the air.

They faced one another for a few more seconds, waiting for someone else to talk. They all knew this strategy. Cathy pulled out her cell phone and tapped the screen as if popping balloons. They heard at least her side of the conversation.

She briefly confirmed the rocket and the mystery regarding the fuel to someone else. She didn't seem to care that the three heard her. After a few more "all rights," she turned to face Eddie with her back to the doctorate and Timothy.

"We're taking a chance on you. This will only happen if we have no other choice. If we succeed in reaching the ISS without your help, there'll be a lot more people here wanting to know what's going on and you won't be able to keep your secrets."

The doctorate nodded. "Yes, people will demand to know how you got a *Redstone* rocket in this silo, a rocket that's launchable using some unknown secret fuel."

Timothy looked at Cathy's eyes and saw she trusted him. At that moment, he wanted to tell her everything. To not hold back on the formula, to tell her how he thought his dad was an alien and not a drunk, and to say he just wanted to graduate high school without all this stress. He couldn't tell her about Eddie, and because of that, he said nothing. Particularly with a Defense Department person here whom he didn't trust.

"There's got to be some coordination with the European space agency and Russia's Roscosmos space agency to launch. We need their tracking stations. In other words, a lot of other people have to make the case to use this rocket. In the meantime, more people are coming to help you launch. Not to interfere or try to find out anything about your setup, but to save the ISS." Cathy leaned toward Eddie like a snake. "Just in case we need your rocket."

She spun around and headed down the chute ladder with the doctorate reluctantly following.

Right after they disappeared down the ladder, Eddie told Timothy, "We need to launch whether or not the NASA rocket works." He jumped into the elevator to go down.

Timothy stood there for a few more seconds, feeling scared and even more stressed out. He was mostly relieved that no one had asked what was under the canvas.

Chapter 42

No one said anything on the way back. At the house, Eddie and Timothy met Ted in the kitchen to wait until Cathy checked things out in the communication room. The doctorate stayed outside and Timothy worried that she could be inviting more doctorates.

Eddie turned on the TV in the kitchen and started watching an old sitcom, *Get Smart*. Timothy wondered if any of the actors were still alive. He liked the "cone of silence" part because it fit with all the secrets everybody was keeping.

Soon, Cathy came into the kitchen and leaned against the counter. Ted leaned against the opposite wall and they looked like they were facing off from each other. Timothy and Eddie sat at the table, out of harm's way from any confrontation. Timothy turned off the TV so he wouldn't be distracted.

Elsewhere in the house, he heard different people come in greeted by Sam, Gene, and Henry. More NASA people bringing in more equipment. In a lot of ways, Timothy was glad. He had been nervous about the mix-matched equipment they had to launch the rocket.

Timothy wished his classmates and the NASA group were together for what Cathy would say. The separation made him feel disconnected from everything and everyone and alone.

"NASA will launch a rescue rocket to the ISS at eight in the morning and I have confidence in its success," Cathy looked at Eddie. "However, in case things don't go as expected, you'll have until noon to launch your rocket and still reach the ISS in time. You and your crew need to be ready."

"We'll be ready," Timothy blurted out.

Ted shook his head as if telling Timothy to shut up.

Cathy stayed focused on Eddie. "In the meantime, some people from the NASA Langley Research Center in Hampton, Virginia, are bringing supplies that the space station will need. They're also bringing more people with better equipment to help you launch. Don't worry; they won't interfere with what you have here. They're here to guide the rocket to the space station, if that's necessary."

Cathy walked over to Eddie. Timothy thought she was going to kiss him.

"I want to make this clear. You're keeping a lot of secrets that have upset many people. But there are just enough people taking a chance on you and your crew. None of that matters to me. We have people on the ISS whose lives are at risk and that is my priority."

"You can trust us," Eddie said.

"Talk about trust with Ted." Cathy walked out of the kitchen without looking at anyone.

"What did she mean by that?" Timothy was angry. Now here's another secret to deal with when they had lots to do and even that might not be enough.

Ted said, "Not that it's anybody's business, but since she brought it up—Cathy and I once worked together at NASA Headquarters. We dated and were going to be married until she got a job in management. I thought the job became too important to her. She disagreed. Eventually, I got laid off and she didn't. She owed me."

Ted left the kitchen so fast that he said most of this on his way out.

Timothy looked at Eddie, unsure what Ted was talking about. Eddie smiled. Then he laughed. One loud bellow.

"So, that's why Cathy is going along helping us. Ted got her on our side with a little guilt trip. And, I bet it's working because those two are still in love with each other." Eddie got up and went to the communications room, where most of the people had gathered.

Alone in the kitchen, Timothy didn't understand how Ted and Cathy could be in love. They sounded angry with each other. Maybe it had something to do with them trusting each other that this was the right thing to do. Timothy decided it was too much to think about.

He got back to worrying how unready he felt. He headed to the launch room, ignoring the new faces he passed in the hallway. He became more focused than he'd ever been. He had to get as much training on the simulation as he could.

Ted came about midnight, telling the teenagers to get some sleep. They were all in the launch room watching Timothy on the simulation. Timothy felt he could launch the rocket in his sleep, which he might have already done several times.

Angie, Patty, and Luke had already talked to their parents.

Mr. Greg told them about the rocket and how NASA might use it to send supplies to the International Space Station. Their children were only there to observe the launch. Mr. Greg left out a lot.

Patty's mom confirmed that the rocket was the science project, but she knew nothing else. For some reason, the parents trusted Greg. *Maybe not after they find out the truth,* Timothy thought. The parents promised they would be at Eddie's in the morning to help their children "observe" and nothing else.

Before bed, Timothy stepped onto the porch lit up by floodlights. Tents had popped up across the front lawn and in the field on the other side of the road. Vans, trucks, and SUVs littered the driveway and lawn. No vehicles were in the field leading to the silo, as if it was sacred ground. He wondered how many of the new people were doctorates.

A few figures roamed around dressed in dark clothing, obviously guards. Timothy jumped when Angie touched his shoulder.

"You scared me."

She laughed a little before entering into a soft smile. "There's nothing on the news about us. I'm guessing the media were told to keep silent for a few more hours. We should enjoy this quiet. Did you talk to Eddie? This might be the last few hours he spends on Earth."

Timothy looked at Angie in horror. "Oh, no. I forgot. I need to talk to him."

Eddie was already in bed when Timothy came in and pulled over a chair to sit beside him. He wondered if this was how it felt to give last rites.

"Everything's going to be alright. You got this," Eddie said, lying on his back and staring at the ceiling.

"What else can we do to be ready?" A nearby lamp didn't give enough light for Timothy to see Eddie's face clearly.

"We're ready, at least as much as we can."

"In less than twelve hours, you're going to be in space."

"That's the plan." Eddie rolled over onto his side to face Timothy.

Footsteps echoed elsewhere in the house before everything went quiet again. In the semi-darkness of the room, Eddie said, "It doesn't matter where a person dies. It matters that people missed them."

"Yeah, I'll miss you." Timothy's voice shook a little. He didn't want to feel too emotional and get teary eyed. He wanted to show Eddie he was strong and, yeah, everything *would* be all right, even if everything *might* go wrong.

"You're doing the right thing." Eddie winked at Timothy. He didn't know how to wink back. When he tried, he looked like he was in pain.

Eddie was not looking. He said, "Now get some sleep. I certainly need it."

"One more thing," Timothy said. "I hid the formula and the rocket engine design in case the military or someone else tries to steal it."

"That's good. When the time comes, you'll know what to do with the new technology," said Eddie.

Timothy didn't know what else to do except leave. In his room, he wanted to stay awake thinking about everything going on in his life. Except, he fell asleep.

Chapter 43

Timothy woke up to Luke yelling for everyone to wake up.

It was six in the morning. Someone had scattered fast food across the kitchen counter and table, along with canned drinks. Food that Timothy was sure Eddie wouldn't have allowed.

Eddie, the teenagers, and the NASA group gathered in the kitchen in front of a new, larger flat-screen TV. Elsewhere in the house, a small army of people left them alone.

"More vehicles arrived last night," said Luke. "Fleets of sedans, vans, SUVs, and a few hybrids."

"And, everyone is armed with smartphones, tablets, or laptops," said Angie.

"You'll notice, our smartphones are on some 5G network. Probably from those vans," said Patty. "If the kids in school saw this, it would blow their minds."

"I could get into some serious gaming with this network," said Luke. "A lot of places around here can't even get a signal."

Sitting at the table, Eddie had a short coughing spasm. He held his hand up to say he would be okay and he was after Sam brought him some iced cold water. Timothy turned on the TV. Overwhelmed with determination, he wished they could launch Eddie right then and not wait for the NASA rocket.

Angie and Patty sat at the table with Eddie while the others leaned against something to help soothe their nervous energy. On the wall above their heads, the flat-screen showed an unmanned *Delta IV* rocket hanging off a launch tower waiting for liftoff. Clouds of white smoke from the fueling circled the rocket as if hiding flaws.

To Timothy, it seemed right for all of them to be there together and not watching the launch on some portable device. He gripped his hands in front of him, hoping to ease his stress. If the *Delta* rocket launched successfully, he wasn't sure they could get a launch off with these government people outnumbering them. They would have to hurry.

Timothy panicked. Their plan was to run for the rocket. He looked at Angie and asked, "Do we have another plan if the NASA rocket works?"

"Yeah, we run faster," she said.

The others nodded their heads. Timothy didn't like the plan, but he could not think of anything else.

Time eroded as the NASA countdown continued logically and routinely. Everyone in the kitchen stood still as a deep male voice from the TV counted off the last ten seconds.

In the last five seconds, heavy plumes of smoke rose around the launch tower and drifted into the early morning air. At T-Minus zero, the rocket hesitated slightly before rising above the launch pad into a pale blue sky.

Timothy imagined himself one day riding a rocket into space. Sailing in a widening arc beyond Earth. He definitely wanted to make that trip one day.

As the *Delta* rocket continued skyward, the TV voice gave out routine status reports. The tension in the kitchen increased as everyone braced for the mad dash to the rocket.

They waited impatiently for Eddie to give the word to run as the *Delta* rocket gradually continue upward. Yet, he sat patiently at the table not saying anything. Minutes into the launch, everyone jumped at the image of an exploding rocket.

The *Delta* rocket disappeared in a ball of black and white smoke framed against the cloudless, blue sky. The man's voice droned on reciting altitude and azimuth without realizing there was nothing to meet those high places. The droning voice stopped abruptly. A few seconds later, a woman's voice announced the loss of a signal.

The cameras stayed on the widening fireball of smoke, which sailed in the wind somewhere off the Florida coast. Announcements from the Mission Control center in Houston became more frantic and less methodical. Falling debris from the plume looked like shooting stars as the woman's voice announced "catastrophic failure" amid shouted demands to shut down.

Timothy's stomach tightened as he realized their rocket was next in the launch queue. At least they won't have to run.

Chapter 44

Cathy stormed into the kitchen, stopping in front of everyone. She faced Eddie, "I don't know if you can do this or not, but we have no choice and I don't like that. You—we launch at noon."

She spun around and left so fast Timothy wondered if she was ever there. Moments later, the house erupted in movement. People ran in with thick black cables, pulling them down the hallway toward the communication and launch rooms.

Amid the mounting chaos, Eddie led the teenagers and his retired NASA friends through the crowded hallway and into his bedroom where he closed the door. His bedroom was just big enough for everyone not to bump into one another. Timothy stood next to Angie, wishing Eddie's bedroom was a little smaller.

Luke guarded the door. "There's a lot of activity going on outside."

"They're linking up communications so this place can talk to Houston and other radar stations around the world," Gene explained.

"They're also making sure the rocket can be tracked accurately," said Henry.

"We don't have much time," Ted said. "We need to get Eddie and the ISS equipment to the rocket with no one else involved."

Henry spoke up. "I know the two guys driving the van with the equipment. I've already talked to them about helping. They're rooting for us."

Timothy wondered why anyone would root for this mess. "How much do they know?"

"I told them we had special cargo to load with the equipment and suggested they didn't know anything more. They're too close to retirement. They were okay with that."

Sam said, "Good. We'll go with the plan we talked about." She paused before continuing. "This is the plan: I'll take Eddie in the jeep. Timothy, Ted, and Angie can meet us there with Henry and his friends. The others can help the NASA people by keeping them very busy and away from us."

Everyone nodded in agreement.

"This is it," Patty announced breaking the brief silence. She pushed her way to Eddie and gave him a long hug. "I'll miss you. I'll never stop thinking about you."

Luke was next to hug Eddie. "Just so you know, I'm not really a hugger," he said, pulling away.

"I like this thing you got going," said Gene. "Dying in space. I might try it when it's my turn." He gave Eddie an awkward hug.

Eddie wanted to say something, but he couldn't get the words out. No one said anything for a few moments. Finally, Sam took Eddie's hand in hers and led him out the back of the house and to the jeep.

Timothy followed Angie and Ted out the back and across the field at a run. Henry headed for a brown van while the others went to the communication and launch room.

Running across the field, Timothy looked up to see an almost cloudless blue sky. The air felt cool and there was a slight wind. He was thankful for the good weather. At least there won't be any stress there, he thought.

Just before the silo, he turned around and saw the doctorate standing on the back porch watching them. She directed two men to go across the field and toward the silo. Timothy yelled at the others to hurry.

At the silo, Timothy's mind was racing. He watched Sam help Eddie into the silo followed by Angie and Ted, who ran faster than

Timothy. Overhead, Timothy heard Eddie's owl screech and he looked up to see it soar toward the men running across the field.

The owl swooped low, making the two men stop and duck. One of them fell on the ground to avoid the bird. The other almost started back to the house until he saw the doctorate standing on the back porch. He got the other man up and they continued to the silo while doing their best to avoid the owl. They both fell twice.

Meanwhile, Henry and the two men drove the van to the silo. Timothy got there in time to help them move four vinyl bags of equipment onto the elevator and up to the capsule. Everyone was already at the capsule as Henry and his friends stayed behind to confront the two men sent by the doctorate.

When Timothy got to the top, he saw Sam and Angie helping Eddie into the spacesuit. Ted was stowing the vinyl bags inside the capsule near the hatchway. Quickly, Timothy went to the coolers and took a deep breath to calm himself down. He relaxed as if his dad's ghost was there to help. Maybe he was.

Timothy pulled the first of the coolers to the edge of the rocket and knelt beside the panel. He peeled off the rubber cap of a vial and did not hesitate emptying the contents into a tube. The fluid emptied easily. For the same engine, he repeated the procedure with the liquid chemicals.

Ted carried the other coolers over, although Timothy didn't notice. He blocked out everything going on around him and held his breath each time he emptied bacteria and chemicals into the tubes, careful not to spill anything. Everything seemed to have fascinating clarity. Everything had to be exact.

Timothy did not know how long it took him to finish. He let Ted seal the rocket's panel. Standing up, Timothy heard angry voices downstairs. One of the doctorate's men had started up the chute ladder.

Angie pushed Timothy toward the capsule hatch. Inside, Eddie sat in his seat strapped in with his spacesuit and helmet on. Through his visor, he gave Timothy a strong smile.

Timothy reached out and held Eddie's gloved hand. For a few seconds, they gently squeezed a goodbye until Eddie turned his helmet away. An urgency had accumulated around them.

Ted grabbed Timothy's shoulder and pulled him out of the capsule. "Take the elevator. We'll tell them you went down with Eddie."

Timothy didn't want to leave. He wanted to spend more time with Eddie. He wanted to say that maybe he loved him. Timothy was scared about his feelings. He wanted people to stop dying on him. Timothy realized that his greatest fear was leaving Eddie.

Angie grabbed Timothy's face in her hands as if she would kiss him. She said, "Eddie told me to tell you that he loved you. Now, get out of here."

That was all Timothy needed. He understood the bond he shared with Eddie. It was more than *Betty Boop*. It was a destiny his dad was trying to tell him about.

Angie let go of his face and shoved Timothy toward the elevator. He overcame his fear of heights and that Eddie had built the elevator. As he descended, he glimpsed Sam closing the capsule door. It made him shudder, like watching a casket being closed. At the same time, Timothy heard Ted argue with an unwanted man who tried to enter the platform from the chute's door.

At the bottom, Henry and his friends had parked the van sideways across the silo entrance to keep anyone else from coming inside. Timothy jumped into the van through the side door. Outside, he heard the doctorate yelling for Henry to move the van and Henry yelled back that they were loading the equipment. There were other voices, but Timothy didn't care.

Henry drove the van away fast enough that the cloud of dust behind would make anyone following them cough a lot.

On the ride to the house, Timothy thought about his mother's death, which his dad shielded him from. He thought about his dad's death, which he didn't accept. He tried not to think about Eddie's death, except he couldn't stop. Everything had become about mortality.

By the time they reached the house, Timothy had accepted his mortality. People had destiny. Fate existed in the mortal world and Timothy had a meeting with his destiny.

He trusted Eddie's NASA friends and his classmates to make sure everything worked as they should. He jumped out of the van and ran through the back door, reciting the launch sequence of fuels and thrust.

Except Cathy Wright confronted him in the doorway of the launch room.

"That doctorate told me the equipment needed for the ISS is in the capsule." She tensed her jaw and clenched her teeth in frustration. Her crossed arms ended in fists. "Why did it have to be put in under secrecy?"

"We were in a hurry and couldn't wait. Besides, the doctorate lady and her military people were interfering with the mission."

Cathy stepped closer to Timothy. "Don't talk to me about 'mission.' This is an unmanned launch with supplies for the ISS. Where's Eddie?"

Timothy tried not to panic. He did not know what to say and wanted to escape into the launch room. Before he could come up with an excuse, Cathy's cell phone emitted a loud buzz. She whipped it out and punched a button, almost driving her finger through the device.

It came alive with the doctorate's shrill voice. She shouted that Eddie and Timothy had left in the van. She wanted to know where they went.

"I don't like what's going on here." Cathy didn't care if the doctorate overheard through the cell phone. "We're out of time and the lives of people on the ISS are at stake."

Her phone buzzed again and she hung up on the doctorate to take another call. Timothy heard Ted's voice. The call was short.

Pocketing the smartphone, Cathy's face was red with frustration. "All right, you win this one. But I'm liking this less and less."

Timothy didn't hesitate to say, "Everyone needs to clear the silo for the launch."

Cathy stepped closer to Timothy. "After the launch, whether or not it's successful, you're going to answer all of my questions."

Timothy felt her breath on his face. She was chewing on a peppermint. Timothy didn't like peppermint. Spearmint was better, he thought.

Cathy put her hands on her hips and looked at Timothy as though she wanted him to disappear. Two women and a man approached from behind with clipboards. Timothy didn't know they still made clipboards. Cathy called the doctorate and said, "I'm ordering you and everyone else away from the silo—now. We are preparing to launch." To the people surrounding her, she said, "Prepare for launch."

She twisted around and stomped down the hallway toward another group of people headed her way. One of women stayed and asked, "How far from the silo should everyone be?"

"The exhaust will be less than from a chemical or hydrogen/oxygen engine. What comes out can be handled by the pipes leading out the back of the silo. Everyone should be safe if they stay in the field on the other side of the road."

She wanted to ask more questions, but Timothy ducked into the launch room finding it empty. Everything had already been checked out, turned on, and lit up for him. He was glad the decision had been made for him to be alone for the launch. He could concentrate without distractions.

Timothy remembered the first time he'd seen *Betty Boop* and smelled her metal. He remembered feeling the rocket's skin. He remembered Eddie's smile through the visor. He hurried these thoughts out of his head while grabbing the controllers. The room was alive with the soft buzz of electronics.

He felt comfortable sitting at his console. Like visiting an old friend. There was nothing else to do but launch *Betty Boop* and hurl Eddie into space.

Chapter 45

One of the monitors showed a live video feed of the silo as it sat framed against tall pine trees in the background. The dome was folded back revealing the top of the *Mercury* capsule where Eddie sat waiting. Timothy remembered the exploding *Delta* rocket with a shudder. He put on his headset, trying not to think of anything but what was on the monitor before him.

In his headset, he heard strangers going through a test of the communication equipment and link up with Houston's Mission Control Center. They were talking mostly in acronyms that made Timothy glad Gene was there among the voices.

Patty barged in. "Eddie's readings are good."

Luke came in next and said over Patty's head, "I can't believe it. We're going to do this."

Patty stepped over to Timothy. "It won't be that hard. Just like the simulation."

Outside, they heard the jeep stop short, throwing gravel. Less than a minute later, Ted burst into the launch room. "I got a call from some friends at NASA HQ. The White House contacted several companies who can launch rockets. They're looking for other options instead of us, but I don't think they have any."

"What happened after I left the rocket?" Timothy asked.

Sam stepped in front of Ted. "We told the one goon who came up the chute ladder that we had the order to launch and made him go back down. We disconnected the elevator and platform and went down the chute ladder where we used cranks to retract everything against the silo wall. We kept both men outside the silo until we got the real order to launch."

Behind the crowd, Angie called out, "What is everyone doing in here? Get out and to your stations. We need to get *Betty Boop* in the air."

Chapter 46

Angie made sure everyone was out before walking onto the front porch. She watched as State Police officers took positions close to the house while sheriffs and deputies from different counties tried to organize a growing crowd of people walking down the road. It looked like a pilgrimage.

Angie spied a short man in military camouflage slip out of a black SUV. Behind him were two taller men in camouflage fatigues. The short man swaggered toward Angie, who stood with hands on her hips, blocking his way.

He approached Angie looking as though she were a gnat buzzing in his face. "I'm here in the name of national security. Who are you?"

"I'm here to make sure no one interferes with our rescue mission."

"I'm Air Force Colonel Mark Chass and I have authority over Ms. Wright and you—whoever you are, little girl. This rocket isn't launching until I'm satisfied the mission can be accomplished successfully." He tried to stand a little taller since Angie had an inch in height on him.

She had little patience with his arrogance, a trait she resented. This was not a battle to be won, she wanted to tell him. "We have a team that has everything loaded in the rocket. And, NASA has given us permission to launch. Your interference can only stop this rescue mission."

Scowling at her, Colonel Chass said, "I don't know why I'm listening to you. You're just a kid."

Angie heard Ted's voice in the distance. She glanced around to see him losing his argument with some State Police officers. They were pointing at the colonel and his men, maybe planning to side with the military.

Another military like black SUV came skidding onto the gravel driveway in front of the house. Before it stopped, a tall, broad-shoulder man hopped out and stomped his way toward Angie and the colonel. His military uniform looked so starched that Angie wondered how he could move.

"Give me an assessment of the situation, Colonel."

"Who are you?" Angie saw one silver star on each shoulder.

"This is Brigadier General Crawford. This girl thinks she's in charge." Colonel Chass said shoving his thumb toward Angie.

"Why are you listening to her?" the brigadier general faced the colonel, ignoring Angie.

Cathy came from behind Angie and jumped between everyone. She faced General Crawford. "You're not the contact I was working with."

"That woman was a civilian and has been ordered to leave," the general said. "This is a military operation now. I have my orders to secure this area in the name of national security."

"I'm Cathy Wright, the NASA director in charge. As military on U.S. soil, you must obey civilian authority. In other words, my orders are clear. Yours are not."

"My orders come from the White House," said the general.

"We could say all of our orders come from the White House. This is my decision: as the civilian authority, you aren't allowed in the house or near the silo unless you can come up with more authority than your word. The equipment needed for the ISS is loaded in the rocket and we're ready for launch. Are you going to be the one who makes this mission fail and put lives at risk?"

Crawford took a few moments to stare at Cathy, maybe for intimidation. Except, Cathy was better at it. He abruptly spun around and stomped back to his dark SUV, followed by his colonel and a few other military men.

When they were alone, Cathy turned toward Angie. "That doctorate woman from the Defense Department is telling people the fuel won't work."

"They don't know anything about the fuel," Angie said. "I trust Timothy. I know we can get those supplies to the ISS."

The two women stared at each other. Finally, Cathy said, "I don't know how successful the doctorate will be, but I want you to know that all of us at NASA are taking a huge risk with this launch. You and the others have a little more than an hour. If you fail, the people on the ISS will die."

Before Angie could respond, Cathy marched to the NASA vehicles parked beside the house, demanding to know their progress.

Several vans pulled up with men and women carrying cameras and microphones. Word of the rocket was certainly out. Behind the media came two fire trucks struggling to move past the crowds and vehicles. The trucks stopped a hundred feet before the driveway, unable to go further.

The sheriff and deputies continued to move the growing crowd across the road to the open field. No one seemed to question whether that was far enough to safely watch the launch of a *Redstone* rocket into outer space.

As the media people headed toward Angie, she escaped into the house and rushed into the communication room announcing, "Things are getting messy outside. That stuck-up doctorate woman and some military thugs are trying to shut things down. How soon can we be ready to launch?"

"We were told to launch at noon. I think we can be ready by then," said Gene.

"The other NASA people came in telling us what's going on outside with the military," said Luke. "I made a call to some people. The football team is already on their way to help."

"I got the cheerleaders to come," said Patty. Everyone looked at her. "Yeah, I know the cheerleaders."

They all smiled. Angie was just glad they had more help coming. She hoped it was enough.

Chapter 47

Timothy jerked off his headphones and spun around when he spied Angie enter the room.

"How are things outside?" Timothy wanted to run over and hug Angie. He needed her now and liked everything about her, except the serious look on her face.

Before she could say anything, Luke barged into the room. "I peeked outside. The football team, all the coaches, the cheerleaders, teachers, and other kids from school got here faster than I thought. I think they were already on their way when we called. They've got the military men surrounded. I gotta get back to the communication room."

"That's how things are outside," said Angie after Luke dashed away.

"Can you hang out with me for a little bit?" Timothy asked.

Angie pulled up a chair next to him.

Timothy showed Angie his monitor. "Some of the NASA people fine-tuned the sensors and communications going to the rocket. I can monitor the conditions of the fuel pretty good now. How's Eddie doing?"

"Sam and Patty are monitoring his condition. He's probably bored sitting in the capsule not being able to talk to anyone," said Angie.

"What'll you think will happen afterwards?"

"Let's make sure this part works first." Angie nodded toward the monitor showing the silo. "I've gotta get back. Gene's been standing in for me on communications and I've got to catch up."

"With everything going on about Eddie, I've been thinking a lot about mortality," Timothy said.

"Listen to me." Angie leaned closer to him. "You have to think about this launch and nothing else. I think this is what we're meant to do at this moment in time. Everything will work out as it should. Things have worked out so far, haven't they?"

She leaned over and gave Timothy a quick kiss on his cheek. He created a weak smile amid the blushing and turned his head toward her, probably expecting a better kiss. Except, Angie was already up and out the door.

She ran into Cathy in the hallway.

"We're all ready to launch," Angie told her.

"The military are still trying to interfere. But I think with all those high school kids we can keep them away until after the launch," said Cathy.

"The military should know that if we don't launch, there's no one else who can reach the ISS."

Cathy said clearly, not caring who heard. "They're afraid that if the rocket launches, they'll lose the technology. They believe it's worth the risk not to launch. Even if the ISS crew die. They want to capture the technology now."

Angie stood there, horrified that someone would do that. Risk all those lives on the ISS just to steal the technology. She didn't know what to say.

"We have a backup plan with the Chinese, who've been left out of the ISS program because of stupid politics," said Cathy. "We told them what supplies the ISS needs, but they haven't said whether or not they'll launch their rocket."

"Why doesn't the President just ask them?"

"Like most politicians, he's too egotistical and owned by big business and lobbyists to ask for help. Even if it means losing the ISS or counting on what you people have to save it."

Angie tried to understand how people could sacrifice lives just so they could be right. She was still troubled by the military willing to sacrifice the ISS so they could steal the technology. Cathy spun away, barking orders at NASA technicians down the hallway.

Approaching the communication room, Angie heard a technician shout, "Thirty minutes to launch."

Chapter 48

Timothy concentrated so much on the readings and monitors that he didn't think he'd notice if an elephant came into the room. In his headset, Patty said everything was working in the capsule, meaning Eddie was ready. Timothy wondered what he was thinking about sitting there.

He wished he could talk to Eddie one last time, but he knew that couldn't happen. He glanced at the monitor showing the silo standing alone in the field. He looked back at his controls when, through his headset, a NASA communicator said, "Twenty minutes to launch."

Timothy wanted to remember something important while he waited for the launch. If he remembered Angie, he'd lose his concentration. He let his mind wander back to after the football game, the night he slept at Luke's house.

"The important thing is the structural stability of the rocket. That includes the center of gravity and center of thrust. Your engines can't obstruct this stability," Luke had said that night.

"I get it. The rocket and engines need to work together for stability," Timothy said.

"Yeah, we need to make sure the ballast and controls are sequenced up. I've been reading up on this stuff with Patty's help. She's like a real scientist. I think I'm going to catch up with her after all this is over."

Timothy didn't catch Luke's last remark. "I need to figure out the thrust factor," he said, "and exactly how much push and stress the electrogravitic engines will put on the rocket's structure."

"I think you already got that figured out with the simulation. It's all in the timing. When the rocket clears the silo, the fins will pop out, lock in place, and off we'll go."

Timothy had gone to bed that night worrying about what would happen if the fins came out too soon or not at all. He decided that was enough of that memory.

He focused on the monitors before him. Watching the readings coming from *Betty Boop*, he reassured himself that the fuel and engines were in a good state of readiness. Yes, the readings fluctuated some, but not beyond the norms he and Eddie set. He just hoped the sensors had enough sensitivity to register correctly, what with the unusual fuel mixture and engine design. After all, they were made to monitor rocket engines using solid or liquid fuels, not bacteria.

Timothy clenched his eyes shut, trying to rid himself of the thought of failure. He opened his eyes thinking about Eddie in that capsule. Was he worried too? Fifteen minutes left to launch.

He went through what he would do if the rocket leaned in one direction or another. Yeah, I got that, Timothy thought. But what if there wasn't enough lift from the engines for the rocket to even clear the silo? He went over how he could adjust the fuel mixture and add thrust.

"Ten minutes to launch," the communicator said in Timothy's headset.

"Everything on my end checks out. Internal engine pressure and fuel stability are a go," Timothy radioed to the others in the room next door.

"Patty here. Sam and I checked the computer data link, electrical systems, and power units in the rocket and capsule. All are go for launch."

"Luke here with Henry. Guidance, navigation, and controls are go for launch."

"This is Angie. Gene and I have a good link with Mission Control Center in Houston. All communication channels are open and go for launch."

Timothy understood that this meant the *Redstone* rocket and *Mercury* capsule were using the bank of batteries underneath Eddie's seat to keep things energized and powered up. The rocket had become untied to Earth and free to fly. Outside the house, Timothy heard Ted and Mr. Greg shout directions at people.

The kids from school were blocking the apparent arrival of more military officers. Picturing a fleet of teenagers facing off against the military made Timothy feel confident.

"Timothy, this is Angie. Someone from Mission Control center wants to talk to you."

A deep male voice replaced the mild tone of the previous communicator. "We'll launch when the ISS is thirty minutes away from prime intercept orbit. That gives you time to follow the Earth's curvature and make orbit somewhere over Russia. Then you'll intercept the ISS as it passes over the US. On the mark, you can launch in eight minutes."

Breathing slowly, Timothy watched another gauge show pressure on the capsule bounce up and down slightly. Maybe it was Eddie moving around. There was more yelling outside the house. The deep voice came back through Timothy's headset.

"Hold on, everyone. We have confirmation of a storm developing off the coast. We'll postpone launch for ninety minutes until the ISS gets back around in position. We still have time for intercept before the ISS goes to critical."

Sweat dripped down Timothy's back. Why didn't anyone detect this storm before? He worried about Eddie being in the capsule that long. He worried about the yelling outside and the fuel mixture lasting another ninety minutes. Timothy said clearly, "Houston, continue with the countdown. We will launch on schedule."

"Based on the trajectory, the storm could disrupt the communications and radar," said deep voice.

He wondered if the communicator was making up a reason to delay the launch. Were the Chinese launching? Was the military winning? A lot of crazy assumptions hit his head. He mentally shoved down his panic.

"This is Henry. Luke and I agree we can navigate a steeper trajectory and avoid the storm by flying over it. Timothy, you'll have to adjust the fuel slightly using the controls at your console."

That meant more G's, or gravitational forces, on Eddie. They planned on no more than three G's, but maybe an extra G wouldn't hurt Eddie, Timothy hoped.

"This is Mission Control Center. That's impossible. You don't have the thrust capability. You need the curvature of the Earth to reach orbit." The deep voice sounded demanding and angry, as though his authority was absolute. "Wait for the ISS to orbit around again," he insisted.

"Mission Control, we can meet the new trajectory. We have the thrust," said Timothy. "We're launching as scheduled."

The airwaves were vacant of voices for about fifteen seconds.

"Timothy, we're giving you approval for an approach to the ISS with the new trajectory." The deep voice sounded very unhappy.

"Launch in five minutes," said Luke. "Mission Control, please give me a link for an intercept to the ISS at the new trajectory."

Someone sent Timothy a link showing the new trajectory allowing them to "likely" miss the storm. "I got it. New trajectory locked in."

Chapter 49

In front of him, Timothy surveyed the keyboard and two game controllers configured for his use. Luke and Patty had put labels on everything to help him remember what was what. He knew he wouldn't have time to read them during launch. Even so, he was glad the labels were there, like a security blanket.

He glanced at another monitor showing the launch site and saw Eddie's owl sitting on top of the silo, looking back at the house. It was almost as if the owl was staring at Timothy and saying, "Don't screw this up or I'll peck your nose off."

Timothy mouthed, "I won't." He needed his nose.

The owl spread its wings, leapt from the silo, and flew in the opposite direction of everything that was happening. Timothy hoped he saw that owl again one day.

With two minutes to launch, the NASA communicator's deep voice came back on and declared, "We're set for launch. All systems are go at our end." He sounded disappointed.

Outside, he heard Ted and Mr. Greg shout at people that the launch was happening and to get across the road and into the field. Some military men yelled back in resistance until the police announced their civilian authority.

In his headset, Angie's voice sounded strong and confident, but a little tense. "One minute to launch. Communications are go."

"Patty here. All systems go for sequence launch."

"Luke here, all go for launch."

Timothy flipped two switches. On top of the rocket engines, he visualized the jelly-like contents slowly trickling down narrow tubes. The bacteria and chemicals were entering separate and final stations, prepared to merge and unleash their energy, sending *Betty Boop* upward.

"Everything is go for engine start." Timothy was surprised his voice was so steady. He flipped off the cap to a large, plastic blue button. Then he flipped two of three switches in sequence. As Eddie predicted, these felt better than pushing buttons.

Angie continued the countdown until reaching the final seconds. "Nine seconds."

Timothy wrapped his right hand around one of the controllers. "Eight seconds."

He watched the dials fluctuate and quietly move back into position, meaning the bacteria were anxious, maybe sensing the nearby chemicals.

"Seven seconds."

A drop of sweat pulled itself down his cheek.

"Six seconds."

"Five seconds."

He flipped the final switch.

"Four seconds."

"Three seconds."

"Two seconds."

Timothy pushed the blue button. A soft roar began to emanate from across the field.

"One second."

"Hold down bolts blown. Stabilizers released," came Luke's easy voice.

"Zero."

A scream roared across the field as a family of vibrations shook the house. Not caused by millions of pounds of thrust, but by millions of bacteria, excited by simple chemical compounds searched for negative energy as relief.

Timothy hoped the pipes under the rocket were enough to keep the silo from crashing down.

"I have confirmation of liftoff," said Luke, barely audible over the roaring scream and the shaking house.

The dials registered *Betty Boop*'s gradual rise. Timothy had no idea it would be this loud. It was as if the bacteria were screaming in excitement at being free. He focused on his monitor, watching the thrust ratio. At T-plus five seconds, he glanced at a monitor and saw *Betty Boop*'s manifold pressure go viral.

"Pressures remain strong. All systems nominal," Luke said a few seconds later.

Timothy barely heard him as he watched the readings show all in the norms that he and Eddie had set. The required thrust-to-lift ratio kept steady, pushing the rocket to gradually exceed gravity's hold. The ground slowly stopped shaking.

Timothy watched the dials register *Betty Boop* climbing into the sky—fast.

Chapter 50

Timothy focused on the single monitor in front of him showing a cross of two white lines. Using the left controller, he kept a yellow ball from wavering too far off the crossing point. With the right controller, he steadily increased the fuel mixture to add more thrust.

The world could have ended and he wouldn't have noticed. He glanced in the upper right corner of his monitor and saw the G forces increase inside the capsule. NASA would see it too. Yet, they would be more concerned with the payload.

At seven thousand feet, almost at the end of the first atmospheric layer or troposphere, Mission Control took over the rocket's guidance system. They sent it on a higher trajectory toward the ISS. All Timothy had to do was keep providing enough thrust. He worried how high he should let the G's go.

What could he do if they went too high for Eddie? How high was too high? They hadn't discussed any of this. Through the stratosphere, *Betty Boop* was at three G's and rising to four. Timothy felt trapped because he couldn't reduce thrust or *Betty Boop* would fail to make orbit.

"Ten seconds to supersonic speed," came Angie's firm voice.

"All support systems holding steady," said Patty. This meant life-support systems in the capsule were good.

"Trajectory is on target," said Luke. He then called out the altitude, azimuth, and rate of climb.

The NASA folks had provided launch limits and azimuth angles for a spacecraft to reach a durable orbit. Timothy couldn't remember any of them and was glad Luke had. *Betty Boop* accelerated quickly through the first supersonic speed toward the second as it ran to escape Earth's gravity.

"Inside capsule pressure holding steady. Spiking to six Gs," Patty announced. "All support systems still go."

Panic hit Timothy. But he kept applying thrust. Eddie might be uncomfortable, but he was still alive.

At forty seconds, Patty called out a drop to two G's. Timothy hoped the high Gs were over fast enough that they hadn't affected Eddie too much.

"Altitude fifty-five miles," came Luke's voice.

Betty Boop left the second level of the atmosphere and entered the mesosphere. At this height, Timothy had to change how he applied thrust. He had warned Eddie that *Betty Boop* would shake at this point.

"Conversion of the engines to phase two completed," Timothy said, trying to imagine tiny electric sprites being attracted to jump on board *Betty Boop* and help accelerate the rocket out of their mesospheric domain.

"We're receiving vibration readings from the rocket. Intercept to orbit is stable and on track." This was the worried voice of someone at Mission Control.

The rocket's skin became something like a jet's afterburner reaching for the next atmospheric level or thermosphere. There the engines would use the negative energy falling from space. Timothy worried that the electric sprites could rip the rocket apart for invading their level of atmosphere. He breathed slowly, trying to ease his tension.

"Vibrations receding," said the Mission Control voice, less worried.

"Phase three initiated," said Luke.

Betty Boop had started to use negative energy descending from outer space. Timothy again adjusted how he controlled the thrust.

"This is Blanche at Mission Control. I'll guide you for final approach to the ISS." She read out course trajectory numbers for an intercept to the International Space Station. She sounded young.

"We estimate rendezvous in fifty-seven minutes," Blanche concluded. Her calm tone was a welcome relief from the stress Timothy felt from the other communicators.

Timothy remembered his dad talking about the effect of Earth's negative energy on the rocket. From space it could be all the more exotic and unpredictable. Timothy worried about unknowns. At least at this height, the air was thin enough that there would be no more worry about gravitational forces.

The G's fell quickly below one. Two more minutes passed.

"I've got an altitude warning," said Luke. "We're at T-plus eight minutes. Velocity twenty two thousand feet per second and approaching maximum speed of seventeen thousand five hundred miles an hour."

"Timothy, you need to throttle back to maintain acceleration. You have to account for the lack of atmosphere," Blanche ordered softly.

He reduced the bacteria entering the engines and cut back on the chemicals. They both continued to produce thrust, but at a slower rate as the rocket's speed decreased.

"Prepare for orbit insertion," Blanche said.

Betty Boop was in space and so was Eddie.

Chapter 51

"Prepare for orbit rendezvous with the ISS in forty-eight minutes," Blanche said. Then, just for Timothy she added, "Normally intercept would take longer. I understand you have special fuel allowing a faster approach. Let's be careful and make sure you can decelerate as the rocket approaches the ISS."

Timothy panicked. They never talked about decelerating to rendezvous with something. The *Redstone* was always meant to keep accelerating.

Henry's voice came through Timothy's headset. "Turn off the engines. We'll use the top thrusters to spin *Betty Boop* around one eighty degrees. Then, we will pulse the engines to slow the rocket. We'll use the bottom attitude control thrusters to turn the rocket back around for final rendezvous capsule first. NASA will direct the turn-arounds and final rendezvous."

Timothy immediately shut off the bacteria and chemicals going through the engines. A minute and a half later, the engines had fully shut down. It felt like forever to Timothy.

"Engine shutdown," he said in a weak voice.

It took almost ten minutes to turn *Betty Boop* around. Henry told Timothy, "Pulse the engines by dropping short doses into them. Let each dose burn off. Then drop another until the rocket has slowed to a manageable speed. It's easy and we have time. Final adjustments on approach can be made by the thrusters."

Less than twenty minutes before intercept, *Betty Boop* was turned back around with the capsule facing the ISS. NASA monitored the approach slowly in meters.

The world listened as *Betty Boop* drifted toward the ISS from a lower orbit. Going higher increased orbit speed and it would overshoot the station.

"Patty, how are the support systems?" Timothy wanted to know if Eddie was okay.

"I have a good reading on all support systems."

Although he desperately wanted to, Timothy didn't dare open a channel and expose Eddie. Instead, he hung on every meter of approach as *Betty Boop* neared the space station.

"Intercept on track. Timothy, you did a great job," Blanche said patiently.

Timothy thought about the thrusters firing to control the *Redstone*'s pitch, yaw, and roll. Some astronauts described the firings as sounding like howitzers going off. Timothy wasn't sure what a howitzer sounded like maybe Eddie would.

"The *Redstone* is in stable proximity to the International Space Station. We have Commander Dominika tethered outside the ISS on EVA, or extravehicular activity, ready for capture. All systems on standby as the Commander obtains visual." Blanche sounded passionately calm.

A monitor to Timothy's left showed the image of a large, bright irregular object against the blackness of space. He spotted Angie coming into the room and took off his headset.

"That's the space station," Angie said. "There's a camera on the nose of the *Mercury* capsule. Something Ted installed. That way NASA and the ISS can control the rocket's approach."

She sat down beside Timothy and plugged in another headset next to his. She pointed for him to look at the monitor instead of her and to listen. He put his headset back on.

"Commander Dominika, do you have visual on the space station?" Blanche asked.

"This is Commander Dominika. We have a clear visual of the approaching spaceship. Intercept is in two minutes. Ready to receive."

"Approach to the ISS is fifty meters. Rescue spaceship in stable orbit," said Blanche.

"We'll be glad to get that equipment," said the Commander.

Outside the house, Angie and Timothy heard a lot of shouting for people to link arms, as if they were making a human chain. They both made out Mr. Greg's voice shouting against other men barking military orders to push through the chain. That was when Cathy burst into the room.

Angie and Timothy pulled off their headsets.

"NASA identified a rocket launch from China. Destination and purpose unknown," she said.

Timothy held the headset up so Cathy could hear.

"This is Commander Dominika. The hatch on the *Mercury* capsule just opened. We aren't alone up here."

Chapter 52

Cathy shot Timothy and Angie a look like she wished she had never met them. She stomped out of the room, slamming the door hard behind her.

Although he felt very much relieved to hear Eddie was alive, Timothy hated that he had deceived Cathy. Angie's worried eyes said the same thing.

She picked up a spare headset and sat next to Timothy who put his headset back on. They listened as Mission Control continued to steer *Betty Boop* on approach to the International Space Station 250 miles over their heads.

"Mission Control and Commander Dominika, this is Eddie Pantrelly in the *Mercury* capsule. Please proceed with intercept and capture. I have the payload ready for transfer."

A tense silence hung in the airways for several seconds. The deception had been revealed and no one was happy.

"Payload capture in ninety seconds," said Commander Dominika, refocusing everyone on the mission. Her life and others depended on success. "Mission Control, Mr. Pantrelly is partially out of the capsule to assist in payload transfer. Everything is go. I just hope we have no more surprises."

Someone switched images on the video monitor. Now the view came from the space station.

It showed a smallish *Mercury* capsule and a long *Redstone* rocket hovering above the curvature of Earth. The upper part of Eddie's body stuck out of the capsule door as he held one of the equipment bags for delivery. He looked like a small boy with a bag of candy.

The Commander floated toward Eddie, trailing her tethered cord. Behind her came a second person in a similar spacesuit on EVA and carrying a long pole with a net at the end. Their cabled tethers to the ISS seemed fragile, floating at odd angles in the vacuum of space. They maneuvered by shooting jets of steam out of small ports from towers high enough to avoid their helmets.

Timothy watched intently as the ISS Commander reached back and caught the pole and net in her thick glove. With careful motion, she extended the net toward Eddie, who shoved each bag into the net. The net kept getting bigger and bigger. Timothy worried that everything might not fit. Eddie shoved the last bag in and clamped the net shut. Another bag would not have fit.

Timothy lost all track of time as this was happening. When the Commander finished, he looked around and saw Angie had gone back to the communication room.

"Commander Dominika here. We have the equipment. Transferring to the ISS."

Timothy watched the commander hand the pole and net of equipment to the other person hanging in space. After she was done, she turned to Eddie.

The Commander held out her hand. "We're ready for your transfer on the ISS. Just shove off toward me. I won't let you go."

They were meters apart, enough to almost touch if they reached out to each other. Except there would be no touching or reaching.

From the space station viewpoint, Eddie waved her off. "I'm staying with my *Betty Boop.*"

"Eddie, come with us," pleaded Commander Dominika. "We can accommodate you on the ISS."

"I'm not going back to Earth." He waved his arms across the many stars filling his view. "Outer space is now my home."

After a few seconds, they all heard, "This is Mission Control. Commander Dominika, return to ISS. That is the priority."

The Commander hesitated once before abruptly turning around and propelling herself toward the ISS. Her fellow excursionist had already returned. She didn't acknowledge Eddie and seemed to act as though he had ceased to exist.

The ISS camera showed *Betty Boop* hanging in silhouette against the blueness of Earth and the blackness of space. Eddie's upper body hung out of the capsule as if he were in a convertible with the top down—except he was ready to ride into deep space rather than take a drive down a sunny road.

It took fifteen minutes for the Commander to radio, "Mission Control, airlock secured."

"This is Mission Control. China announced their unmanned rocket can rendezvous with the ISS in approximately ninety minutes. The U.S. Defense Department asks you not communicate with the Chinese yet."

"Mission Control, we will welcome and accept China's help when they arrive."

"Copy. We'll let the politicians decide."

"Not a good decision, Mission Control. Politicians are not good decision makers." Commander Dominika hesitated before saying, "Eddie Pantrelly, I request you hold your position. There's a launch from China. Will you accept their help?"

"Thank you. I do not need help. Timothy, you copy?" Eddie's voice was stern.

"I'm here, Eddie."

"Let's go."

Timothy pushed a special gray button overriding Mission Control's ability to control *Betty Boop*. Everyone in the communication room guided him as he used the thrusters to back *Betty Boop* away from the ISS. From their camera, it wasn't a pretty maneuver, but good enough.

Betty Boop twisted in the vacuum of orbit with the *Mercury* capsule pointed away from the ISS and Earth. Without a specific direction except somewhere in space, Timothy pushed a blue and yellow striped button. The rocket moved soundlessly toward the stars.

After a minute, Timothy shoved a lever to its farthest position, giving full power to the rocket. All the bacteria emptied into the engines as they joined the chemicals already there. *Betty Boop* accelerated away from the ISS camera. Through his headset, Timothy heard an alarm go off.

A light flashed on another monitor. Eddie's oxygen supply had just entered critical red. They had miscalculated his oxygen supply.

Chapter 53

"Eddie, I have the engines on full thrust. You'll be leaving Earth orbit somewhere around twenty-five thousand miles an hour. There might be some pressure from gravity drag. After that, you'll be on a trajectory out of the solar system. Just like we planned." Timothy was amazed he managed to say this with such a clear voice.

"Yes, I'm feeling some pressure from the acceleration, but it's not bothering me."

The sound of the oxygen alarm had stopped, probably by someone turning it off. On the monitor in front of him, Timothy saw the many stars Eddie was headed for. The special imaging came from the camera on *Betty Boop*'s nose.

Timothy didn't want to see the stars. They were too many of them and they reminded him that Eddie was going away forever among those stars. Timothy turned away from the monitor to stare at the far wall, which needed painting. That was better than looking at what Eddie was viewing.

Outside the house, he heard Luke's booming voice direct the football team to stand their ground. He heard Angie and Patty in the middle of whatever was going on shout commands at the cheerleaders and teachers. Mr. Greg was yelling too. Timothy had never heard him raise his voice before.

No one was needed in the communication room. The mission was over—except for hearing Eddie's last words, which the whole world could hear on the open channel they used.

"Timothy, I saw the sunrise when I was chasing the ISS. There was all this blackness. About a minute before the sun rose, I saw a thin arc of deep purple. It was the deepest purple I've ever seen."

Timothy remembered from his science classes how the atmosphere bent and split the Sun's rays like a prism. Indigo was the first color to be seen. "What was it like to see the Sun come up?" he asked.

"Shades of blue came first, followed by vivid orange and red. Gradually a wide arc along the horizon showed so many colors I couldn't see them all. When the sun broke the horizon, it drowned away all the color and the blue Earth burst into view. It was the most beautiful sunrise I've ever seen. And as old as I am, I've seen a lot of sunrises."

Timothy felt a wave of sadness thinking this was the last sunrise Eddie would ever see.

Eddie continued, "I know I won't see any more sunrises. I'm glad I got to see that one. I can imagine the sunrises on the other stars I'm seeing right now. Those stars are all so gorgeous. The universe is such a peaceful place. You've gotta come up here someday and see all of this. Promise me you'll do that."

"I promise." Timothy imagined millions of people saying the same thing as they listened.

"All around me, stars are shining with blues, whites, reds, and yellows like tight, tiny beams of light." Eddie paused before adding, "I feel like I'm becoming part of the universe. I know what you're thinking. That all this might be from the lack of oxygen. Yeah, I know the oxygen is running low. It's not that. I've got enough oxygen to see and feel all this wonder. It's almost too much to take in."

Timothy tried to control his squeaky voice. "I'm glad you got up there to see it all." He was very glad...and sad.

"I couldn't have done this without all of you. I know I was selfish and put everyone in a tight spot."

"We'll be alright." Timothy wished he sounded more confident.

Eddie's voice shook a little. "I know all you kids will go on and achieve great things when this is over. I just know it. Especially you. I hope to be there to help. In spirit, of course."

"Hey, no offense," Timothy said, "but I don't want you haunting me."

Eddie chuckled. "I'm not going to haunt you. I'll come when you need me. If I can, that is. After all, I might be busy."

"Yeah, living on the other side of life. You're going to miss us." Timothy struggled to be as upbeat as Eddie.

"I definitely will miss everyone. I'll miss you most." He paused as if trying to control his squeaky voice.

Timothy couldn't say anything, either for a few moments. But they both knew their time was limited. Eddie talked first.

"Being up here makes life on Earth seem so small. If aliens from another planet find me one day, they'll wonder what I'm smiling at."

"If they know what a smile is."

"I think they will. It's the universal sign of happiness."

Timothy pictured Eddie still sticking out of the capsule and spreading his arms wide as if he could capture all those stars in his hands. He wondered how they had miscalculated the oxygen supply so much. He was thankful they hadn't made a mistake with the fuel. The engines would burn long after Eddie's oxygen was gone.

"I'll miss your crazy meals," said Timothy.

"I'm a good cook, aren't I?"

"A better word is 'creative.'" Timothy noticed the delay in transmission was taking a few seconds longer.

"Hey, I'm looking behind me and I can see all of the Earth. It looks like a blue balloon floating out there in space. It's hard to believe something so fragile can hold so much life."

Timothy wondered how fast *Betty Boop* was going. He couldn't ask anyone in the communication room since they all seemed to be outside yelling. Anyway, he was sure NASA was recording everything. He hoped.

Eddie said, "Speaking of life, does my death scare you?" He sounded like he wasn't sure himself.

"I'm not scared of you dying," Timothy lied. He thought he should be used to death by now after losing his parents and now Eddie.

"I've got a confession. I lowered my oxygen supply on purpose. Don't be angry. I didn't want a long goodbye."

Timothy didn't hesitate. "I'm not angry. I probably would have done the same thing." Timothy thought that, really, he probably would have.

"I'm glad I didn't choose to stay alive with drugs and medical operations. People should accept the end and go out happy that they had a life. That's what's great about hospice."

"Just tell me one thing," Timothy said. "Are you committing suicide or is this euthanasia? Someone will probably need to know for your death certificate." Timothy wanted to keep the talk lighthearted, but it was getting harder. By the sound of things outside, the military seemed to be winning. Timothy wondered where the police were.

"Can anyone commit suicide when they're as happy as I am? No, this isn't suicide. I feel alive in my death. Besides, I would've been dead in a few months, anyway. I'm just ahead of the game."

Eddie's voice sounded like an echo. "Gee, I want to take off my helmet and shout to everything I'm seeing. To feel space close to me."

"Stop! You won't last long if you take off your helmet. You won't explode or anything, but there's the cold and you won't be able to breathe. We also won't be able to talk anymore." Timothy glanced toward the monitor. In the bottom corner, he watched the oxygen readings drift toward zero. What's the difference? He thought that there wasn't much time left, anyway.

"Don't worry. I'll keep my helmet on. There's a lot out here to see and talk about."

"I'm going to miss you." Timothy wished he hadn't said that. It made him want to cry and he wanted to not turn into a wreck of emotions. There would be time for that later.

"For reasons I don't understand, I've been brought among people like you to help me do this. I think I was meant to be here. Before I go, I want you to know you were the first true friend I ever had. I had a great time hanging out with you on this project. I wish it could have been longer."

"I had a great time too, Eddie. A really great time. I won't ever forget it." Timothy did a bad job of keeping his voice from quivering.

"Don't be mad, but I've got to tell you one last secret," Eddie said.

"Another one? You should have made a list." Timothy didn't care. Eddie's life was falling away.

"I promise this is the last one. It's about that person ET. He worked at NASA under a disguise."

"Go ahead, I'm listening."

"ET was an extraterrestrial from the planet Tyche and he was the one who brought *Betty Boop* to the silo. Like everyone from his planet, he said he had lived on Earth too long and needed to get home. He was sure the engine and fuel were nearby, but he died before finding them. I only found out your dad was involved when I matched the alien's notes with what I knew about your parents."

"What did you know about my parents?" Timothy had a feeling he might already know.

"Only that they were working on a special rocket formula and engines when they left Langley. I felt they had to have some connection to aliens like ET."

Timothy could almost imagine the conspiracy theories erupting at that moment. Would anyone think Eddie was delusional from the lack of oxygen?

"My dad mentioned Tyche several times."

"ET said his planet was in the Oort Cloud and created its own temperate heat. The sun was so far away it looked like any other bright star."

"Commander Dominika here. Apologies for interrupting. Just want you to know the equipment works. We're back online and our oxygen levels are returning. Also, we've got a link with the approaching Chinese capsule and they'll be here soon with supplies to make a more permanent fix. I and the ISS crew want to thank you, Eddie, and your team for saving our lives."

Timothy heard a soft bell dinging in Eddie's suit telling him his air had been used up. It was a chime that seemed to play a Tchaikovsky tune.

"I'm happy I and my friends could help. Ya'll have a good trip back down to Earth when you go. Now, Timothy, my time has arrived."

"I don't want you to go." Timothy heard yelling in the hallway outside his door.

"I'll be alright and so will you. Come up here one day and find the planet Tyche. I think you'll be surprised at what you discover."

Timothy was too overcome with emotion to say anything more.

"I know I keep saying it, but Timothy it is truly all so beautiful out here in space. I can see so many stars I can't see them all."

Timothy heard Eddie's breathing grow shallow. After a few seconds, Timothy asked, "Eddie, can you hear me? Are you still there?"

The silence came back at him and he refused to call out to Eddie again. The silence was enough.

Chapter 54

Timothy kept listening for Eddie's voice. He wanted to hear anything, even Eddie's breathing. After several minutes, he slipped off his headset and let it fall to the floor.

Sitting there alone, he thought about how he had lost his mom and dad and now Eddie. Who'll be next? he wondered. Tears welled in his eyes as he heard shouting in the hallway. He didn't care.

A minute later, the door flew open and Cathy Wright burst into the room followed by the county sheriff.

"General Crawford and his men are trying to use their military authority to take you away. You need to go with the sheriff," Cathy said.

"Am I under arrest?"

"Not now. But the district attorney's office is considering charging you with the murder of Eddie Pantrelly," said the sheriff.

Timothy blurted out, "I didn't murder Eddie."

The sheriff approached Timothy. "I'm Sheriff Hank. Just come with me until I get things sorted out. We need to get going."

"Go with him," said Cathy. "You owe me for not telling me Eddie was in the capsule."

Timothy followed the sheriff toward the front door, leaving Cathy to deal with the military.

Timothy slipped into the front seat of a patrol car as a deputy drove slowly between the crowd and other vehicles. When he reached the open road, the deputy turned on the blue lights and siren and sped off.

At the sheriff's office building, other deputies led Timothy inside and into a small windowless room. He felt like a pull toy with too many strings to pull. At least there were no bars, he thought. When they left him alone, he tried the door and it was unlocked.

Alone and feeling helpless, Timothy worried about what was happening to the others back at the house. He wished he could be there to help.

Pacing the small room, Timothy struggled to get his head straight about everything that had happened leading to Eddie's death. He questioned what he did or could have done. So many confusing emotions filled his head that he ended up thinking about school. How would all this affect his grades since he would probably miss too many classes?

Timothy looked around the room at four gray chairs and a vinyl-topped table, all pushed against one wall. He scooted on top of the table and rested his back against the wall to wait, but not for long.

Sheriff Hank slipped into the room and closed the door behind him. The equipment on his chest and hips seemed to weigh more than he did. He sat in a chair and leaned back.

"I want you to know that not all military people are like that back at the house. Most of the military are good guys defending our nation. Yet, sometimes you find people with too much ambition. They give the military a bad name."

Timothy said, "I guess there're people like him everywhere."

"From my experience, I would guess the general in charge, Crawford, is with some defense intelligence agency. They act like that. Always claiming to be protecting 'national security' when they are only protecting their own ego and narcissistic self-worth."

"Isn't that true for a lot of government and military people?"

"Yeah, at all levels. They may be in the minority, but they surface when our supposed leaders do not say 'no' to these people."

"Is there anyone to say no to me being charged with murder?"

"There's always hope." Sheriff Hank stood. "Anyway, you're safe here. Outside, there's a crowd growing and I'm not sure what Crawford is planning. I'll be back as soon as I can."

As he closed the door behind him, Timothy wondered where Eddie was in space at that moment. The engines would continue to burn for at least another hour, further accelerating *Betty Boop* and propelling Eddie eventually out of the solar system. If extraterrestrials found Eddie, will they know what death is? Timothy wondered.

Half an hour later, he heard people walking toward the door. He stood up, hoping it was not General Crawford and his men forcing their way in. The footsteps marched closer until the door flew open.

Luke, Angie, and Patty almost ran into the room.

Luke hung back as the other two hugged Timothy at the same time.

"What'd the police say to you?" Angie sat on the table where Timothy joined her.

"The sheriff said the district attorney is considering charging me with murder."

"You didn't murder anyone," said Luke, sitting in one of the chairs.

"We all agree on that point," said Angie.

"The police were going to interrogate us," said Patty, sitting on the table on the other side of Timothy. "But our parents and Mr. Greg stopped them. I saw Cathy talking to Ted and the other NASA people. I'm not sure what'll happen to them."

Timothy thought, without parents to speak up for him, he could be going to jail.

"The military and NASA didn't find anything they wanted at the house and silo. They're not happy, so none of us are in the clear," said Luke.

"I hope you didn't hide the formula and engine designs at your dad's house," said Patty. "They're looking there too."

"I hid them in my locker at school," Timothy said.

"Why did you hide them there?" Luke looked like he wanted to run out to Timothy's locker to make sure everything was still there.

"It's such an obvious place, no one will ever look there," said Timothy. "Besides, hardly anyone uses lockers anymore. I use the textbooks reserved in the classrooms."

"Yeah, you could be right. I carry what I need with me all the time," said Luke.

"Patty and I use online textbooks," Angie added.

Somewhere outside the building, people chanted Timothy's name.

"That's all the people wanting you released," said Patty. "There's a lot of them out there and more are coming."

"So, what are you going to do with the formula and the engine design?" Sitting shoulder to shoulder, Angie nudged Timothy for an answer.

"I'm not giving anything to the military. That's for sure," said Timothy.

Timothy jumped off the table and faced the others. "Maybe I could be a trillionaire if I started my own company. But I don't want that. I want to give the formula away so everyone can have the chance to go into outer space."

They were all quiet for a few moments before Patty said, "That's an odd thing for you to do. Very unselfish. What makes you want to do that?"

"My dad told me that once the formula was used, I had to give it out to anyone who wanted it. He said it was a promise he made to my mom and I can't break a promise like that."

"I see a bigger destiny in store for you." They all looked at one another, spooked by what Patty said.

"We can sort all this out later," said Angie. "We have to hope the sheriff can convince the DA not to press charges against Timothy, us, or the NASA four."

They all nodded while saying they wished the off-key chanting outside would stop. "Couldn't someone hire a hip-hop or an R&B band?" Luke asked.

Soon, there was a rap on the door and two deputies brought bologna and cheese sandwiches, half of them with yellow mustard and half with mayonnaise. The food came with bottles of Cheerwine.

Luke grabbed a sandwich, tore off the wax paper, and took a bite. "Wow, this is the good kind of bologna and real cheese."

"I got these made at the Piggly Wiggly," one of the deputies said proudly.

Timothy took a sandwich. There was also a bag of chips and a Moon Pie for each of them.

"Outside, a very big crowd is getting bigger," said the other deputy. "I grew up here and I've never seen this many people in one place before. Not even for the fireworks show. You're better off here. We'll come back and check on everyone later."

"Our lives are going to be very different from now on," Angie said after the deputies had left. She surveyed her partially eaten sandwich as if it could give her the answers to her future.

"Yeah, we get to meet aliens one day," Luke said, smiling.

Chapter 55

After two hours, Sheriff Hank stepped in followed by a short man in a tight black suit. The man's flaming-red tie looked like a smear of blood.

"I'm with the District Attorney's office. We've reviewed your case and conferred with federal prosecutors." The man sounded frustrated and aggravated as if he wanted a different decision. "We determined that Eddie Pantrelly committed suicide after refusing Commander Dominika's assistance. Your case will not be brought before a grand jury."

He thrust a manila envelope into Timothy's hands. "These papers clear you and anyone involved with any wrongdoing regarding the death of Eddie Pantrelly."

Timothy looked at the folder realizing this was basically Eddie's death certificate.

"Take the papers, go outside, and tell the crowd you won't be charged with anything. You and your friends are free to go," Hank said. "I'd like to get all these people off my lawn and out of the parking lot."

Angie faced him. "What about General Crawford?"

"He's being called back to the Pentagon."

"I don't care about him. I'm ready to get out of here," said Timothy taking the manila folder.

As he walked out of the room, he wasn't sure what to expect. He led the way down the short hallway and through the front doors. There, he hesitated.

It was night and he stood before a flood of lights on a concrete porch a few steps above the crowd. Through the glare, he saw more people than he'd ever seen. Everyone let out a loud cheer and clapped before going quiet, waiting for Timothy to speak. He looked at the crowd and realized he'd never made a speech before. He felt like throwing up.

"Show them the envelope," Angie whispered from behind, pushing at his elbow.

Timothy thrust the manila envelope into the air. "I'm free!"

Cheers exploded as two deputies led him around the crowd. Timothy saw a lot of people holding signs supporting his release. He waved to everyone, wondering when they had time to make signs.

The deputies tugged Timothy along as other deputies kept the people back. Timothy landed in the front passenger seat of Luke's car. Patty and Angie jumped in the back. Luke drove out of the parking lot and onto the State road in the opposite direction of Eddie's house.

"Where are we going?" Timothy looked back at the crowd waving to him.

"Outta here," said Luke.

He drove fast, not worried about traffic tickets. Timothy thought he should worry about crashing. They quickly left the throng of people behind and sped down a two-lane road where the tall pine trees were less plentiful. Looking up through the windshield, Timothy saw stars and wondered which one Eddie would visit one day.

"I can't take you back to Eddie's place because the military quarantined the place. You're going to stay at Mr. Greg's house for the time being," Luke said.

Timothy was glad. Mr. Greg's wife made a pretty good cherry pie, which she sometimes brought to school functions. Timothy wondered how the pie would taste with ketchup and mayonnaise on it.

Twenty minutes later, Luke stopped in front of a small brick house. Mr. Greg sat in a lawn chair, waving to them from the screened in front porch. His wife stood in the doorway of the house wearing an apron that hosted the remnants of what she had been cooking.

Stepping out of the car, Timothy smelled fresh, sweet aromas wafting out of the house. He was going to like living at the Greg's.

Chapter 56

The Greg's two sons were out of college and living on the West Coast. Timothy felt like he had become the Gregs' third son. He was glad to be living with them. He felt like he belonged to a family again.

There was no going back to his dad's house, which was unlivable when he left and probably had gotten worse. He could not go back to Eddie's place. NASA planned to turn it into a museum. Timothy was happy. It would be like a memorial to Eddie.

No one in the U.S. military or other government agency found anything significant in either place. And, they stopped asking Timothy questions after he mailed copies of the formula and engine designs to people in the U.S. and around the world. The Government had been waiting for Timothy to post the technology to his social media accounts, and Timothy knew his accounts would have been shut down if he did. The U.S. Post Office is not monitored that well.

After Timothy sent the new technology to everyone, the media left him alone. Instead, they ran after stories of the scientists and engineers making improvements to the technology. A new age in rocketry and space exploration had begun, along with a new fuel source other than oil and coal.

Everybody talked about the planet Tyche, but only Eddie knew about this and he probably said all that he knew. The astrophysicists who first theorized the planet existed were on every TV talk show.

Alien theories made the news everywhere. The rush to find Tyche was on.

It wasn't until the middle of October that Timothy, Angie, Patty, and Luke went back to school. The media attention had died down by then. It wasn't easy with people treating them as celebrities. Things got better for the four of them in late October when their high school football team beat a team that hadn't lost in two seasons.

It was like their team had won the State championship. The football players became the new celebrities, despite losing the rest of their games. That one win was enough to headline the yearbook. By November, with the celebrity status dying down, Timothy had one more thing to do.

He convinced NASA to hire Sam, Ted, Gene, and Henry as consultants to help him put together a lecture explaining the formula and engine design. Although the new technology was getting to be widely known, people had questions about the details. Timothy, Mr. Greg, and the others agreed to a one-day event.

On December 1, Mr. Greg drove Timothy to Raleigh, which had a large auditorium.

Selected scientists, engineers, and other prominent people from around the world attended. It was the first time Timothy had ever been west of the interstate and away from eastern North Carolina.

Behind him on stage sat the NASA four, his three classmates, and Mr. Greg. Timothy stood looking out at people from around the world, all waiting for him to talk. A massive screen overhead displayed the details of what he would explain. He should have been nervous, and he was, but he knew he had to give this lecture. He relaxed enough not to have a squeaky voice.

It took most of the day to present all the information and data and answer questions. Strangely, talking about the technology made more sense to Timothy than he thought it would. It seemed simple to explain, as long as he stayed away from the math. Giving the talk, he felt he was learning who he really was.

Having everyone onstage with him helped a lot. When it was over, Timothy was sure he had done the right thing. While Sam, Ted, Gene, and Henry talked with some of the scientists and engineers who they knew; Luke, Patty, and Angie hung back with Timothy. Mr. Greg strangely wandered off as if expecting what was coming next.

"This bacteria energy will replace fossil fuels," said Patty.

Angie nodded. "The planet will certainly be better off."

"And if Earth isn't better off, at least we can get off a lot easier," said Luke.

They were alone, heading toward the back of the stage when they met a slim woman taller than all of them. She had green eyes and light blue hair cascading around her rich ebony face and shoulders. Her hair looked as though it was talking to her body. She waved hello with both her hands. As she came closer, Timothy thought she smelled of life.

"Beautiful talk," she told Timothy. Her voice sounded wispy like leaves rustling in a soft, summer rain.

"Thanks, Mom."

The three teenagers couldn't say anything. Angie stared at Timothy, Patty stared at the woman, and Luke finally leaned over to Timothy and whispered, "You said she was dead. Is she a ghost?"

"No, she's alive," said Timothy. "It's a long story. We met this morning before the lecture and I'm still working on getting over the shock myself."

"Like my son said, it's a long story." She touched Timothy's hand. "Let's finish that story."

The three teenagers stood gaping at mom and son as they stepped into a back room filled with costumes and displays. A Christmas play was scheduled later that week. His mom found a seat between a Santa Claus suit and elf hats adorned with tiny green bells. Timothy sat across from her beside a four-foot-tall lamb with fluffy pink fur.

"We didn't get a chance to talk much before your lecture. I thought now would be the best time. I was surprised you recognized me so quickly this morning. Before when I lived on Earth, I made myself look human and a lot different than I look now."

"When I saw you, I had no doubt you were my mom and the extraterrestrial in our family. Everything just became clear to me."

Timothy paused, remembering how they met in a corner of the over-sized hotel lobby. If anyone looked up from their coffee and bagels, they would have just seen two people talking quietly. Timothy surprised himself at being so calm when he met his mom. As if he expected to meet her.

"This morning, you said a rescue ship took you away," Timothy said. "You said Earth's negative energy fields were eroding your body. How long are you staying this time?" Timothy wanted his mom to stay a long time.

"I never fully recovered from my previous stay on this planet. My body is already eroding and I have to leave soon. I took a risk seeing you, but I had to. I have things to say."

"Like how I'm half alien." Timothy now knew this for certain. He stared at his mom, realizing she didn't have pointy ears like Spock. She looked like any other human, just a little different.

"When you left, why you didn't take Dad and me with you?" Timothy didn't mean for this to come out so resentful.

"Neither of you would have survived the conditions on the ship. Our propulsion system is toxic to humans. Before I left, I explained the formula to him and helped him build some of the engines so he could do the rest himself. Our plan was for him to get a rocket from NASA and the both of you come to Tyche. I couldn't contact NASA myself without exposing who I was. I would have become imprisoned as a research topic and you and your dad would have been in danger too."

Reanette let out a sigh and scanned the ceiling as if looking for strength to continue.

"After I left, your dad couldn't go to NASA for a rocket. The military was too involved and he didn't want to take a chance on them taking the technology away. He hoped I would come back. Then, he started believing I was gone forever."

"Why didn't you tell Dad about Eddie's rocket?"

"I knew nothing about it. Another Tychian, the one Eddie called ET, got that rocket without me knowing about it. At Langley, he convinced humans to work for him. He wanted to conquer this planet."

Timothy's mom took a deep breath and looked at her son warmly before continuing.

"We are a selfless, peaceful society without a desire to dominate or conquer. However, we learned that humans can contaminate us with their aggression. This is what happened with the Tychian called ET. He became overwhelmed by human insecurities which turned him into what humanity feared the most. Someone who would conquer Earth like the Conquistadors conquered Native Americans."

Timothy didn't fully understand. "But why wouldn't it go the other way with humanity learning to be peaceful?"

"In our home world, there is no hunter and hunted. We evolved into a balance between the strong and weak, where diversity is promoted, and no one is exploited for benefit or advantage. Humans haven't evolved to that stage. Killing is too relaxing and enjoyable. Too justified without reason. Aggression dominates from the political structure to what children are taught. War and battles continue to define periods of history. Aggression silences the peace until only anger is left."

Timothy studied his mother's soft face, which had experienced more laughter than hate. She picked up a small, plastic Frosty the Snowman. "Roy liked to build snowmen when we lived in Virginia." She put the plastic object down.

"When did you and Dad meet?"

"On a two-lane road west of Richmond, Virginia, where my spaceship crashed. I was researching environmental changes in the atmosphere. I escaped just before the military took my ship away. Your father saved me."

She paused as if remembering the first time she met Roy. Timothy felt her smile fill the room with caring.

"Others from Tyche were already here and got me a job with your dad at NASA's Langley Research Center."

"What were the other Tychians doing there?"

"They're in space programs all over the world, helping to discover a new energy source through rocketry. But that's another long story."

"You loved Dad, right?"

"We fell in love like we were old souls who had just found each other again. When you were born, we celebrated, rejoiced, and rose to a new level of love. But, everything changed when I learned about ET's plans. He wanted to stop me before I could stop him, so he convinced the Defense Department I could be a spy. Maybe they thought I was an alien, but being a spy was more believable to them."

"Is that when you and Dad moved to eastern North Carolina?"

"Yes. After leaving Langley, I had no communication with that other Tychian ET. If I had, he might have put you and your dad in danger with other humans. When I went back to Tyche, that corrupted Tychian produced false suspicion about me to hide his actions. It's not like being arrested, but close. I had to prove my innocence and I couldn't get word back to your dad. The people on Tyche couldn't understand our love or that ET could be corrupted."

"I should have believed dad when he said you hadn't died. I thought it was the liquor," Timothy said, picking up a six-inch plastic wise man that strangely looked like his dad. "He drank so much after you left."

Reanette's eyes glistened with tears; she seemed at a loss for words. She paused for a long moment before continuing. "When I was cleared, the corrupt Tychian ET brought the rocket to Eddie's place hoping to find the formula and engines so he could escape from being captured. Except, his human accomplices at Langley abandoned him."

"How did you prove your innocence?"

"By finally explaining the love your dad had for me."

"Don't you have love on your planet?"

"Yes, but it's on a different level and in a different way. We have a strong love for everyone almost equally. I showed the Tychians the love your dad had for me individually."

Timothy didn't understand how love could be different like that, but he didn't understand love that much, anyway. He wished he would meet someone one day and feel the way his dad had felt about his mom.

"I wish Eddie had contacted you. He followed you to North Carolina, but didn't want to interfere with you and Dad," said Timothy.

"I knew about Eddie's affection for me at Langley, but I thought he had gone to Florida."

"After ET died, Eddie sent a letter to Dad explaining everything. He thought Dad's heart gave out when he tried to sober up so fast."

A pained expression enveloped Reanette's face. It seemed to radiate throughout her body. "I didn't know your dad would suffer so much from my absence. Eddie's letter might not have made him suddenly give up drinking. That was the time I contacted your dad to tell him I was coming home."

Timothy did not know what to do. He was torn. Either Eddie, his mom, or both caused his dad's death. He quickly recovered and decided they didn't cause anything. Dad did this all to himself, he concluded. All out of love. He dropped the plastic wise man on top of the other decorations.

Timothy's mom reached out and held her son's hands in hers. "I'm glad we were able to save him."

Timothy jerked his hands away. At first, he couldn't say anything. The shock of what his mom said seemed to shake him with tiny shivers.

Reanette looked frightened. "I'm sorry. I thought you knew he was taken away to be cured. We got there just in time. In his near-death state, we could transport him on our ship. Are you all right?"

Timothy gulped air a few times, let out a loud burp, and realized that explaining things like this was probably different on Tyche. "I thought he was dead. What happened to him? Where is he now?" Timothy stopped talking, not sure what to say.

"We took him to the Martian moon Deimos, which is really a special satellite we built. He's healing in a way that lets him live on Tyche, but not on Earth. It's his choice. His sacrifice. I am growing to depend on his deep love. I now know I would do the same for him if given a chance."

"I want to see Dad."

"He wants to see you too. It'll be soon. We discovered that being half alien allows you to ride in our spaceships with some adjustments. We have a lot to talk about together as a family."

The door flew open. Luke, Patty, Angie, Sam, Ted, Henry, and Gene flooded into the small room.

They all seemed to shout at once, "There's a flying saucer outside."

About the Author

I grew up on a dairy farm in Spotsylvania, Virginia and ended up living across the Rappahannock River in south Stafford County. From there, I commuted by train to the Pentagon to work on defense budgets. To keep my sanity, I wrote short stories. More than two dozen magazines published them.

I eventually escaped the long commute and politics to move to New Bern, North Carolina. A place my wife and I had never been to before. Here, I belong to several writing groups and I volunteer at a few non-profits that include writing grants for them.

I wrote this novel because I always had an interest in rocketry, extra-terrestrials, and outer space. I hope you enjoyed *High School Rocket Science (For Extraterrestrial Use Only)*.

My blog is www.stanleybtrice.com

www.ingramcontent.com/pod-product-compliance
Lightning Source LLC
Chambersburg PA
CBHW061031120726
47910CB00006B/2199